# FRIGHTFULLY FORTUNE

## A Miss Fortune Mystery

*REST WHEN YOU'RE DEAD?*

NEW YORK TIMES BESTSELLING AUTHOR
# JANA DELEON

# MISS FORTUNE SERIES INFORMATION

If you've never read a Miss Fortune mystery, you can start with LOUISIANA LONGSHOT, the first book in the series. If you prefer to start with this book, here are a few things you need to know.

Fortune Redding – a CIA assassin with a price on her head from one of the world's most deadly arms dealers. Because her boss suspects that a leak at the CIA blew her cover, he sends her to hide out in Sinful, Louisiana, posing as his niece, a librarian and ex–beauty queen named Sandy-Sue Morrow. The situation was resolved in Change of Fortune and Fortune is now a full-time resident of Sinful and has opened her own detective agency.

Ida Belle and Gertie – served in the military in Vietnam as spies, but no one in the town is aware of that fact except Fortune and Deputy LeBlanc.

Sinful Ladies Society – local group founded by Ida Belle, Gertie, and deceased member Marge. In order to gain membership, women must never have married or if widowed, their husband must have been deceased for at least ten years.

Sinful Ladies Cough Syrup – sold as an herbal medicine in Sinful, which is dry, but it's actually moonshine manufactured by the Sinful Ladies Society.

# CHAPTER ONE

THE THEME SONG FROM *JAWS* ECHOED THROUGH MY HOUSE and I couldn't help but grin. It was Halloween time in Sinful, and I had to admit that I'd been looking forward to it ever since that first cold front blew through in late September and dropped the temperature to a very tolerable eighty degrees. Now it was actually even better—in the low seventies—which was a definite plus when you were covered in costumes, masks, and makeup.

Every year, Sinful had a weeklong Halloween celebration, starting seven days before and culminating on October 31. It had a horror maze made from hay bales, with scary scenes set up with adults in costumes all the way through it, movie night, games, and tons of food. There was a different main activity every night, even on weeknights. And as teachers weren't permitted to give homework during the festivities, the kids could stay out later, load up on candy, and not have to worry about missing schoolwork the next day.

Years ago, Gertie and Ida Belle had steamrollered the highly religious then-mayor into doing the event by pitching it as an alternative festival for warding off evil rather than a celebration of it. It was so popular that it became a regular event, much to the dismay of Ida Belle and Gertie's archrival, Celia Arceneaux, who had protested it from the start. Celia dressed up as Rose Kennedy every year, thinking that inserting a famous Catholic in the mix somehow gave it decorum. I'd bet no one under the age of forty even knew who Rose Kennedy was.

Gertie had arrived before Ida Belle and now stood in my kitchen staring at her best friend as she entered the room. Clearly, she was not impressed.

"That is *not* a costume," Gertie said. "It's what you usually wear except it's a god-awful dress sort of thing instead of pants."

"This is definitely a costume," Ida Belle said. "It's a pinfold dress and green sweatshirt."

I had never heard of a pinfold dress, and one look at Ida Belle and I knew why. It was sort of like overalls but with a skirt. The drab brown dress thingy combined with the forest-green sweatshirt might have rivaled Celia in some of the ugliest clothes I'd ever seen. Not that I was about to mention it. The dress had suspiciously big pockets, and Ida Belle could still draw like Doc Holliday.

"What kind of costume is it then?" Gertie persisted.

Ida Belle grinned. "I'm Annie Wilkes."

I frowned. "Is that the crazy woman who battered that author's ankles in *Misery*?"

She held up a sledgehammer. "The one and only."

"Okay," Gertie said. "I'll grant you that it's a costume now that you've shown the hammer, but why in the world would you pick that? The last time you wore a dress was your wedding. The time before that was when you were three and hadn't learned to shoot yet, so you couldn't draw on your mother for putting you in it."

2

"Well, since we're not working scenes in the maze this year, my usual chain-saw killer idea is being used by someone else," Ida Belle said. "And Walter's been making noise lately about writing a book, so I figured I'd mess with him."

Gertie shook her head. "Why that man waited around his whole life for you, I have no idea."

"Me either," Ida Belle agreed. "And while we're critiquing costumes, Gertie, what are you trying to accomplish?"

"She's opting for a go-straight-to-hell card," I said. "Do not pass purgatory. Just walk on in."

Gertie was dressed as a nun, but not a regular nun—an evil, demonic nun from the movie by the same name. I had to admit, the makeup that made her look like a partially decaying corpse combined with the bright yellow contacts was pretty creepy.

"I'm trying to make Celia as mad as possible," Gertie said. "That witch got Francis banned from the park."

"Francis got loose and snagged french fries and a hot dog, and made off with an ice cream cone before you managed to catch him," Ida Belle said. "The sound of preschoolers crying was probably heard all the way in Canada."

"He's a bird," Gertie said. "A hawk could swoop down and do the same thing."

"But a hawk wouldn't do that because they are afraid of people," Ida Belle said.

Gertie waved a hand in dismissal. "Let's talk about what's really important, and that's Fortune's costume."

I grinned and put on my relatively expensive, very detailed, Freddy Krueger mask.

"That is awesome," Gertie said. "And with your slim build, you can totally pull off horizontal stripes, just like me."

Ida Belle snorted.

"This is my favorite part," I said and pulled on the razor-

3

fingered glove. "This is so incredibly cool."

Ida Belle took a step closer to inspect. "That's a really good piece of work. What costume company did you find that at? Is that real metal?"

"I didn't find it at a company," I said. "Scooter made it for me. He does good work, right?"

Ida Belle shook her head as she ran a finger down one of the blades. "I knew the boy could fix about anything with an engine, but I didn't know he could fabricate like this."

"I know," I said. "I was in the store a couple months ago, and Walter asked me about my Halloween costume. I told him that since you guys were eliminating the *Nightmare on Elm Street* display from the maze this year, I wanted to be Freddy Krueger, but I'd already ordered and returned three different razor-blade hands. They were so incredibly cheap-looking."

"And yet the idiot playing Krueger last year still managed to cut off his own pinkie with a cheap one," Ida Belle said.

I grinned. "He must be really talented. Anyway, Scooter overheard us and said he could make me something better than anything I could buy, so I told him to go for it."

"Well, it looks great," Ida Belle said. "You're going to scare the heck out of the kids."

"What's the agenda, anyway?" I said. "We're not working the maze at all, right?"

Gertie shook her head. "After last year, we figured we'd take a break from maze work."

"After last year," Ida Belle said, "we were *asked* to take a break from maze work."

"It wasn't our fault that someone cut off a dead guy's head and propped him up in my scene," I said. "In fact, we caught the person who did it."

"Gertie also threw the head at Celia," Ida Belle said.

"She threw it at me first," Gertie said. "And it's not like we killed the guy."

"Guilt by association," Ida Belle said. "Anyway, it's good to take a break. At least we can show up and enjoy the festivities without being on the clock or trying to fix the two thousand things that inevitably go wrong at the last minute."

"But you still organized everything, right?" I asked.

"Of course," Ida Belle said. "Trust me, we've put in the hours. How many did you work setting up the maze?"

I shrugged. "Most of the day, but I considered it a good workout. Those hay bales are heavy. Itchy, but heavy."

"Smart," Gertie said. "You were burning off the calories you're going to consume. I should have thought of that. Instead, I baked a thousand cookies for the food booths and tasted at least two from every batch."

"Yeah, I'm really glad I can't offer anything on the food end of things," I said. "My self-control when it comes to good Southern cooking is seriously lacking."

Gertie grinned. "And funnel cake."

I groaned. My addiction to funnel cake was a well-known problem.

"Please tell me there's not going to be a funnel cake booth," I said. "There's not enough hay bales in Sinful for me to work off what I would eat."

"Your flat stomach is safe," Ida Belle said. "At least for now."

"Well, it's good and dark outside, so let's get this show on the road," I said. "What's on the agenda for tonight? I'm sorta confused about the scheduling since Halloween falls on a Friday this year."

"It does work better when it falls on a Saturday," Gertie agreed. "But the basic format is the same with just a little tweaking. The maze opens tonight instead of Saturday and will be open tomorrow night as well. Nothing on Sunday as we'd all go to hell. Then Monday resumes normal evening activities, minus the maze, and the big culmination is next Friday night on Halloween, when the maze will reopen as soon as it gets dark."

Ida Belle nodded. "Mostly tonight is the maze and the food stands and people walking around in costume."

"Where's Walter?" I asked.

"He and Scooter are on maintenance duty," Ida Belle said. "There's a lot of extension cords over there. Tons of lights and generators, and there's always a problem with something."

"Is he wearing a costume?" I asked.

"Not in this lifetime," Ida Belle said. "This is one of those rare occasions where I'm more whimsical than he is."

"I wouldn't call a pinfold dress 'whimsical,'" Gertie said. "I'm surprised he didn't file for divorce when he saw you in it."

"He was afraid of the sledgehammer," Ida Bell said.

We headed out to Ida Belle's SUV and hopped inside.

"I assume Carter is doing foot patrol?" Gertie asked.

"Of course," I said. "The whole department is out there, except dispatch. Carter made me promise not to find a dead person this year. A real one, anyway."

Gertie shook her head. "He acts like you *want* to find dead bodies."

"Weellll..." I said.

They both laughed.

"Okay, so maybe you don't mind it all that much," Gertie said. "But it's not like you kill them personally or put them in your path. You just seem to be there when things happen."

"I'm a death magnet," I said. "It doesn't sound nice, but I'm okay with it. Everyone has their special talent, right?"

Ida Belle grinned. "You should have *I Find Dead People* printed on T-shirts."

We parked a couple blocks away and started walking. The

streets near the park were closed for the event to make room for the food trailers and game booths. We could hear fun screams from the crowd before we arrived. The food booths were doing a steady business, which put money into next year's festival and charity coffers, and everyone appeared to be having a good time.

I didn't see a single dead person. Not a real one, anyway.

"Look at the Pennywise costume," Gertie said. "They didn't get that one off the rack."

"No," I agreed. "It's definitely custom. And check out the zombie near the scarecrow. He has that limp perfected."

Gertie nodded. "Could be an extra on *The Walking Dead*. That scarecrow is horrible, in a good way, I mean."

"It would definitely keep birds out of the corn," Ida Belle said. "It looks like people went all out this year. I'm glad everyone's so invested. I was a little worried after that stuff last year."

"I'm just glad I don't have to be a mummy again," Gertie said. "Do you have any idea how hot that costume was? And good Lord, it took an act of Congress to take a pee."

"We know," Ida Belle said. "We're the ones who rewrapped you afterward, remember? I'm just glad I won't be seeing your underwear this year. And do not take that as an opportunity to tell us about them."

"There's a good chance of seeing Celia's," Gertie said. "You know she'll have on a Rose Kennedy dress and since she seems to have more trouble remaining upright than I do, it's always on the itinerary."

"Sinful should pass a law requiring Celia to wear shorts under everything," I said. "Maybe you could talk to Marie about it. So what do you want to hit first?"

"Let's grab a corn dog," Gertie said. "I need some protein. All those cookies have made me slightly sick."

"A corn dog is more carbs than protein," Ida Belle said.

"Then I'll get Frito pie to go with it," Gertie said. "It's got beef and cheese."

Ida Belle sighed.

We headed for the corn dog booth and we all grabbed a dog. Carter, who was standing near the maze, spotted us and waved. We made our way over and he grinned when he took in Gertie's costume.

"Taking a run at Celia, huh?" he asked.

"You know it," Gertie said.

He gave her a high five.

"Anything going on tonight?" I asked.

"Nothing that isn't on the agenda," he said. "A few scuffles between high school students—we confiscated the beer—but nothing out of the ordinary. It's been really quiet, but now that you've arrived..."

"I'm off the clock," I said.

"You've been off the clock every time trouble started," Carter said. "Didn't stop it from landing in your lap."

"Yeah, well, I'm a changed woman."

"Since when?" he asked.

"Since tonight," I said.

"Hey, we can hope, right?" he said.

"Come on, Carter," Gertie said. "What are the odds of someone turning up murdered at the Halloween festival two years in a row?"

We all stared.

"Never mind," Gertie said. "This corn dog didn't do it. Let's go hit the candied apples. Fruit is good for you, right?"

Carter was still laughing as we headed off. We acquired our candy apples and were considering a ring-toss game when Celia spotted us. As expected, she had on a hideous dress and hat and was wearing a cross larger than a vampire hunter's.

"Are you going to pray with that thing?" Gertie asked, pointing to the cross. "Or have a sword fight?"

"I would expect crude comments about religious icons from you," Celia said. "The way you are dressed is wholly inappropriate and I'll be filing a complaint with the city."

"A complaint about what?" Gertie asked.

"Religious discrimination," Celia said.

"This is the opposite of discrimination," Gertie said. "This is inclusion. Nuns can be evil, too."

"Nicely played," I said.

"You are *not* going to mock the most devout of my religion and get away with it," Celia said.

"Why the heck not?" Gertie asked. "Your existence mocks the best of the female species and we're still tolerating you."

"Keep talking," Celia said. "Marie won't be mayor forever."

"Probably not, but you won't be mayor either," Ida Belle said. "Now, can you take your negativity somewhere else? This is a festival. You know, fun? I know the concept is somewhat foreign to you, but you can at least try to fake some normal human emotion from time to time."

Celia flushed and I could tell she was gearing up for a tirade that no one had the time for, so I sliced a hunk off my candied apple with one of my razor fingers then held it out to her.

"Want a bite?" I asked.

Her jaw dropped as she stared at the apple dangling from my hand, then she whirled around and stalked off.

"I think you scared her," Ida Belle said.

I nodded. "I might wear this thing everywhere."

"It's fine unless your butt itches and you scratch with the wrong hand," Gertie said.

"I don't think I've been in the South long enough to go around scratching my butt in public," I said.

"Give it time," Ida Belle said.

We all laughed, and I couldn't help but think how different my life was now than when I was working for the CIA. When I was living in DC, I didn't have friends. I didn't go to events. I certainly didn't dress up like horror movie villains to eat fattening food. Heck, I didn't even eat fattening food at all. Sugar and carbs that used to be the enemy now curled up with me like a warm blanket on a cold night.

"You know what?" I said. "I really enjoy this stuff."

"You say that like you're just realizing it," Gertie said.

"Maybe she is," Ida Belle said. "She had a totally different kind of life for a long time."

"I think I knew it, inherently, a while back," I said. "But I guess I just figured it was a good time to say it out loud. All this town's festivals, celebrations, quirky laws, church wars, banana pudding races, and people who should headline their own sitcom are a lot of fun. And they continue to surprise me, so that element of my life hasn't disappeared."

"Except most of them aren't trying to kill you," Gertie said.

"True, but I have seen a lot more naked body parts in Sinful than I ever did with the CIA," I said.

"Uh-oh," Gertie said. "Don't look now, but I think Celia is trying to get you arrested."

She pointed to Celia, standing next to Deputy Breaux, waving her hands, and pointing at me. Deputy Breaux glanced over at us and sighed. He came our way, Celia right on his heels.

"See!" Celia said and pointed to my hand. "She has a weapon."

"Ninety percent of the people in this park are carrying a weapon," Ida Belle said. "And the other ten percent are in kindergarten."

"I suppose it could be considered a knife," I said. "But if

you kick everyone out of the park who's carrying a knife, your festival is going to be pretty grim."

"Not to mention that Ida Belle has a sledgehammer," Gertie said. "And I see at least three swords from where I stand, and I happen to know they're all real. You really need to stop wasting law enforcement time."

Deputy Breaux nodded. "There's nothing illegal about having a knife in the park."

Celia put her hands on her hips and glared at him. "Well, if you won't do your job, I'll find someone who will."

"I hear a horse coming," Ida Belle said. "Maybe you can take it up with Sheriff Lee."

We turned and looked across the park in the direction of the approaching horse, but it wasn't Sheriff Lee's old steed. This one was young, muscled, solid black, and running like a demon. The black-cloaked rider seemed to be holding on for dear life as he swayed in the saddle, but I had to give him props. The Headless Horseman costume was perfect—if he had been missing his head.

We watched as the horse approached then realized that he was about to run into the crowd and hadn't slowed. I glanced over at Ida Belle, whose eyes had widened. Okay, this wasn't part of the show.

"Move!" I yelled, and the crowd began to scramble like the Israelites leaving Egypt as the horse ran through the middle of them.

Complete chaos ensued, with people scrambling and screaming as the horse ran straight for us. I was just about to shove the others and do a dive behind a tree when the horse slid to a stop about twenty feet in front of us.

And the head flew off the horseman.

# CHAPTER TWO

THE SPEED AND THE HEIGHT OF THE HEAD WHEN IT launched resulted in a good amount of travel. It flew straight at Gertie, who involuntarily stuck her arms up and caught it, then immediately tossed it in the air, where it landed squarely in Celia's arms. Celia screamed and started running, still clutching the head, then realized what she was doing and dropped it...right in her own path.

Her foot hit the head and she flew backward, legs over her body, and landed in a butt-flashing heap on the ground. I didn't want to look but couldn't help myself. Right in the middle of the big span of white cotton was the Virgin Mary.

"And she called *me* sacrilegious," Gertie said.

"People in this town really lose their heads over Halloween," I said.

Ida Belle sighed.

"Too soon?" I asked.

Carter came running and drew up short at the scene. I wasn't sure if Celia's Virgin Mary underwear or the severed head was causing him the most distress, but I had a guess.

"I need everyone to clear the scene," he yelled at the

crowd. "Deputy Breaux, get these people out of the way. And call Sheriff Lee. We need to secure that horse as a crime scene."

After his mad dash and sliding stop, the horse had meandered around and started munching on grass. He looked completely nonplussed about the entire thing even though the body that had been carefully strapped into the saddle was starting to lean off to one side. On the last grab of grass, he'd taken in some of his rider's hair and now the head was dangling from his mouth.

You just couldn't make this stuff up.

I pulled out my phone and snapped a couple pictures of the head and the horse, careful to avoid Celia's butt, before Deputy Breaux waved us away. The paramedics hurried up and stopped short at the head before Carter directed them to attend to Celia. They stuck some smelling salts under her nose, and she bolted upright, arms waving wildly.

"She needs a checkup," Carter said.

The paramedics looked as if they'd just been issued a death sentence, but they hauled her toward the ambulance, probably wishing they hadn't used the smelling salts, as her mouth was on full speed complaining.

We headed off after the crowd, and I pulled up the pictures and showed the head to Ida Belle and Gertie.

"Do you recognize him?" I asked.

They both took a turn at a close-up look. Ida Belle shook her head, but Gertie pulled her glasses out of the nun costume and studied it a bit more.

"I think it might be Gilbert Forrest," Gertie said.

"Really?" Ida Belle took the phone and enlarged the face a bit more. "Hmmm. You might be right. Well, that's interesting."

"A man just rode a horse through the park and his head fell off, but the man's *identity* is the interesting part?" I asked.

"Well, yes," Ida Belle said. "You see, Gilbert Forrest was killed four days ago in a carjacking in New Orleans."

"That explains the lack of blood," I said. "I was going to go whimsical and say it was a vampire thing or maybe a chupacabra, but embalming is probably the logical explanation."

I flipped to a picture of the horse and pointed. "Look. See how the body is tied to two-by-fours that are strapped to the saddle?"

"So that's how he was upright and didn't fall out," Ida Belle said.

"Doesn't explain the head," Gertie said. "It didn't fall off by itself."

"Or why a dead man, who should be at the funeral home, is riding a horse through the festival," Ida Belle said.

Gertie grabbed our arms and pulled us forward. "We need to get moving. Carter is giving us the stink eye."

I nodded. "My house for debriefing and snacks?"

Ida Belle grinned. "I thought you'd never ask."

———

I GOT US ALL A COLD BEER WHILE GERTIE GRABBED A container of cookies that Ally had left, and Ida Belle snagged crackers and peered into my refrigerator for something to dip them in. She looked over at me, her expression almost reverent.

"Is that a container of Molly's cream cheese candied jalapeño dip?" she asked.

I grinned. "She dropped it off this afternoon."

"You've been holding out on us," Gertie said.

"Only for a couple hours," I said. "I haven't even had any myself, so it's not like you missed out."

Molly was a local caterer and her dip was legendary. I liked it almost as much as funnel cake. Ida Belle removed the medium-size container, opened the lid, and smelled the spicy and sweet goodness.

"This isn't a lot," she said, rather wistfully.

"There's four more containers in the freezer," I said. "Molly said to defrost them in the refrigerator a day before I want to eat them."

"Then you might want to put another in now," Ida Belle said. "Because I don't think this one is going to make it past tonight."

We all sat and munched on crackers and dip for a bit, then I grabbed my laptop to make some notes.

"Okay," I said. "Give me the details."

"Lord, where to start," Gertie said. "Gilbert was a bit of a personality."

"That's putting it mildly," Ida Belle said. "Think Ronald but pushier and less fashion-forward."

"So I take it you both knew him well?" I asked.

They both nodded.

"Gilbert was born and raised here," Ida Belle said. "His mother, Josephine, was one of those salt-of-the-earth sorts and loved her Jesus. She passed about eight years ago or so. His father was a geologist and got killed on a rig back some twenty years ago. Between insurance and a settlement from the oil company, Josephine was pretty well set. She never had to take a job, which suited her introverted personality."

Gertie nodded. "On the other hand, Gilbert—or Gil as he insisted he be called—was the exact opposite of both his intro-verted parents. He took extrovert to the extreme level."

"Was he a car salesman?" I asked.

"Worse," Ida Belle said. "He was an actor."

"An actor living in Sinful?" I asked. "Is there really a lot of call for that?"

"Sinful has a small acting troupe," Gertie said. "But they lost a lot of members over the years and haven't put on a production in ages."

"So Gil was a member of this acting troupe?" I asked.

"For a bit," Ida Belle said. "Until he found a bigger troupe in New Orleans back maybe three years ago. They traveled to perform, and he got bigger roles and audiences, so he was thrilled to be in the spotlight again."

"Again?" I asked. Surely Sinful wasn't considered the spotlight.

"When Gil graduated from high school, he hightailed it to Hollywood," Gertie said. "His parents couldn't have been less impressed. His father was a highly educated man and held a respectable position in a tough field. He wanted his son to follow in his footsteps."

"And Josephine thought everyone in Hollywood was the devil," Ida Belle said. "She called it Gomorrah."

"I take it he never got his big break?" I asked.

"He had a few small roles," Gertie said. "But nothing of merit. The biggest career move he made was getting Harper James to marry him."

"Who is that?" I asked.

"I forget you weren't much of a movie watcher until I got hold of you," Gertie said. "Harper James was an actress and a fairly famous one. I think she could have gone on to be an A-lister."

"But...?" I asked.

"Drug overdose," Gertie said. "Her relationship and marriage to Gil was a whirlwind sort of thing and since their son, Liam, was born eight months after the wedding, we all had an idea why it happened so quickly."

"That's rather an old sentiment, isn't it?" I asked. "Especially for Hollywood. I thought they were more progressive about such things. I mean, it's not like it was the 1950s."

"Who knows?" Gertie said. "I mean, the press photos showed two people who were clearly into each other. Maybe it was infatuation and it burned off as quickly as it started. Maybe the harsh reality of parenting tempered all their relationship joy."

"Or maybe he couldn't handle her success when he could barely book a commercial," Ida Belle said.

Gertie nodded. "Probably a combination of a lot of things. But regardless of the why, the reality is they hung in there for a couple years, although Harper spent most of it filming in other countries. That's probably the only reason it lasted a couple years. Anyway, they split and Gil got primary custody. Based on what I heard back then from Josephine, Harper wasn't all that interested in being a mother."

"And Gil needed the child support money since his acting career hadn't taken off," Ida Belle said drily. "LA isn't the cheapest place to live."

"So when did Harper die?" I asked.

"When Liam was five," Gertie said. "She was on location somewhere...Africa maybe. There had already been press about her partying habit and apparently it caught up with her."

"So what happened with Gil and Liam?" I asked.

"There was an insurance policy that Gil was still the beneficiary on, but she didn't have much else except furniture and personal items," Gertie said. "Apparently, her lifestyle was running about par with income. And since Gil didn't have a career to speak of there and was going to have to find a way to make money now that the big child support checks were gone, he came home to Sinful so that his mother could help him with Liam."

"And became Sinful's famous resident actor?" I asked.

"And an insurance salesman," Gertie said.

"Ha!" I said. "I was close with that car salesman guess. But why haven't I met the guy? Usually insurance salesmen hit up someone new in town before they've even unpacked."

"He bowed out of the business for the last few years for the most part," Ida Belle said. "I assume he draws a percentage off of existing policy renewals, but he stopped actively seeking new clients himself a while back. Rumor has it he inherited a good amount when his mother died, so he probably doesn't need to work anymore."

"He was a good salesman, though," Gertie said. "He was always a looker and had that smooth personality. That and his acting ability had most people trusting and liking him, and so he did a good business."

Ida Belle frowned. "If only he'd been a better parent."

"I take it his acting ability didn't extend to being Mr. Mom?" I asked.

Ida Belle shook her head. "He mostly left Liam to his mother to raise. Even when he purchased his own house, I think Liam still spent more nights at Josephine's than he did with Gil."

"And then there was the Tiffany disaster," Gertie said.

"Who's Tiffany?" I asked.

"Tiffany is from Mudbug originally and was Liam's girl-friend," Gertie said. "Until she married Gil."

"Wow!" I said. "I did *not* see that one coming. Definitely not parent of the year."

"Not even of the afternoon," Ida Belle said. "As far as I know, Gil and Liam haven't had much to do with each other since then."

"I can't imagine they would," I said. "So how did Gil die?"

"I just heard about it yesterday, so I don't really know much," Ida Belle said. "Apparently, Gil had finished up rehearsal in New Orleans Monday night and was in the parking lot about to leave when he was held up. He was shot once in the chest and the guy made off with his Mercedes. Far as I know, the police haven't found the car or the shooter."

"That car is probably on a container ship ready to go overseas," Gertie said.

Ida Belle nodded. "That is one of the criminal benefits of boosting cars where there's a port."

I slouched back in my chair, my mind trying to process everything I'd learned. When I finally sat back up, I stared at Ida Belle and Gertie.

"But why was he strapped headless to a horse?" I asked.

Gertie shook her head. "*That* is the $64,000 question."

———

I WOKE UP THE NEXT MORNING FEELING INVIGORATED, which left me at somewhat of a mental impasse. Was it wrong to be excited over a headless dead man riding a horse through the park? Since he'd been killed days before, I wasn't sure where the line between respect for the dead and intrigue over the Headless Horseman routine was drawn.

Merlin was feeling especially irritable and had run across my forehead at 6:00 a.m. Then he'd proceeded to pounce on imaginary bugs—mostly on my body—until I'd gotten out of bed to give him breakfast and then let him out for a bathroom break. I knew he was aggravated at his limited outdoor time, but I'd already been warned that black cats sometimes disappeared around Halloween. So it was best to keep him inside more than out, especially after dark. Unfortunately, only one of us understood the reasons.

I poured coffee and sat down at my kitchen table, mulling over everything Ida Belle and Gertie had told me the night before. Carter hadn't come by or called but that didn't surprise me. That crime scene must have been a bear to try to work, and he had the crowd, the body, and the horse to deal with. And that was just in the park. I didn't even want to imagine how informing the widow about her husband's night ride had gone.

I figured he'd be into work early but I wasn't about to call. Since he had a job reporting to other people and the hours could be erratic, I mostly let Carter call me. So if I called him up at the crack of dawn, he'd know I was poking my nose into police business. And since I didn't have a viable client to put it back on, then he'd take his usual line and tell me to butt out.

No way was I butting out of this one.

When a dead man rides a horse through the Halloween festival and loses his head and Celia ends up holding it, that was entirely too much temptation for someone like me to resist. My phone signaled a text. Ida Belle.

*You up?*

I texted back that I was up and dressed. Her reply was immediate.

*At Francine's.*

Since breakfast at the café sounded light years better than the somewhat stale bread I'd been considering for toast, I polished off my coffee, then wrangled Merlin back inside, which was getting progressively harder every time I had to do it. I'd started with cat treats but now I was up to canned tuna. Before the end of the week, I might have to offer up raw fish and a sacrifice.

It took me ten minutes and a disgruntled stare that should

have turned me into a pillar of salt before I got him back inside, then I grabbed my keys and wallet and hurried out the door. The café was always busy on a Saturday, but it usually picked up a bit later in the morning. It wasn't even 7:00 a.m. and I had to park at the other end of the block. I figured more than the usual customers had ventured out to get the gossip about the Headless Horseman, which was probably why Ida Belle and Gertie had headed out so early.

"I see the masses are ready to descend," I said as I slipped into my seat, trying to avoid looking people in the eye.

"They always think we know something," Gertie said.

"That's because we usually do," Ida Belle said. "Add to that Fortune is hooked up with Carter and I'm married to his uncle, and they really think we have the inside track."

Gertie sighed. "If only that were true. Heck, we'd get more random information if that wasn't the case. Carter probably expends twenty percent of his daily energy trying to figure out how to keep Fortune in the dark about his cases. And Walter would definitely prefer you stayed out of that line of work as well."

"Sadly, all true," I agreed.

"Speaking of the closemouthed devil," Ida Belle said, "I don't suppose you've heard anything from Carter."

"Not so much as a text," I said. "But that's not surprising."

Ally popped over to our table and grinned down at us. "Aunt Celia called me last night ranting about pressing charges against Gertie for throwing a head at her. She said two years in a row is intentional, not coincidence."

"She threw first last year," Gertie said. "Besides, since I didn't behead either of them, I hardly see how this was my fault."

"You know Aunt Celia," Ally said.

"Unfortunately," Gertie said and we all laughed.

"You guys want your usual?" Ally asked. "Francine has a Halloween special today."

"What is it?" I asked, always interested in new food offerings.

"Lobster and cream cheese crepes," Ally said.

"I might have just gotten a little woozy," I said. "Hook me up with that. Do you have any muffins?"

Ally nodded. "Blueberry and banana nut."

"Blueberry, please," I said and leaned back in my chair, already anticipating an excellent meal.

"I'll have the same," Gertie said.

"Ida Belle?" Ally asked. "You want the same?"

"No way," Ida Belle said. "Only sweet things belong in crepes. Just give me some eggs, biscuits, and bacon."

"Got it," Ally said and then leaned in. "Rumor is the Headless Horseman was Gil Forrest. The sheriff's department isn't announcing anything, but one of the paramedics said he recognized him."

Gertie nodded. "So did I. Although I'll admit it happened a bit after the whole head-catching fiasco."

Ally shook her head. "But that doesn't make any sense. Gil was killed in New Orleans days ago, and there was no mention in the paper about his head being removed."

"Interesting, isn't it?" I asked.

She smiled. "You three are about to poke your nose into police business, aren't you? Well, I won't bother to try to tell you not to and I know you'll be as careful as you're ever going to be, so I'll just say watch your back. Because whoever did that isn't sane."

She headed off to the kitchen to place our order.

"So how are we going to play this?" Gertie asked.

"Technically speaking, we don't have a client so we can't play it at all," I said.

"But we're still going to, right?" Gertie asked.

"Of course," I said. "It's a headless dead man riding a horse. I can't just let that one slip away into the sunset like a news story on the biggest bass caught or something."

Ida Belle grinned. "That curiosity level of yours must have caused you problems with the CIA."

I thought about that for a moment. "You know, it probably did, but it wasn't nearly as bad as it is here."

"It's because the people are no longer strangers," Gertie said. "I mean, you don't know everyone that we've investigated, but it's your community now. That gives you a vested interest."

"Unfortunately, it still doesn't give me a legal one," I said. "So can I assume we'll be doing a food run to the child bride?"

Gertie nodded. "That's what I figured. I pulled out a chicken casserole last night to let it thaw. All she'll have to do is pop it in the oven and she'll have meals for days."

"Great," I said. "Then we should probably do that as soon as is proper so that she's not exhausted by the thrill seekers before we get there. What about the son? Is he still local?"

"Local-ish," Ida Belle said. "He works up the highway near the motels and that strip mall. I think he lives nearby. We never see him in town, though. Not since his dad and Tiffany got together."

"What does he do?" I asked.

Gertie smiled. "He's a butcher."

I stared. "Well, isn't that interesting. Would he think it odd if you paid him a visit?"

Gertie shook her head. "I taught and tutored him. He knows me well. And I took out two casseroles this morning, anticipating the need."

Ida Belle nodded. "Best I know, he's a single guy, so he's not likely to turn down free food, even if he's not exactly over-whelmed with his father's death."

"Awesome," I said. "So we have a plan. After breakfast, we head to see the widow, then up the highway to see Liam."

"There's one other person we might want to talk to," Gertie said.

"Who's that?" I asked.

"Judith Trahan," Gertie said.

"Oh!" Ida Belle said. "I hadn't even thought about Judith."

"Who is she?" I asked.

"She was Gil's best friend since they were in grade school," Ida Belle said. "Probably the only one who could tolerate him enough years to remain friends. He was a bit much for most people, especially as a kid."

"Friends." Gertie rolled her eyes. "Judith's been in love with Gil since he stepped into the elementary school."

"You think?" Ida Belle asked. "Hmmm. I guess I never paid attention."

"It's not like you saw them together in school like I did," Gertie said. "And Judith didn't and still doesn't spend much time in town, so not much opportunity to observe her in adulthood."

"Why doesn't she come to town?" I asked.

"She's a farm girl," Gertie said. "Crops, free-range chickens, and dairy cattle. She was an only child and had to work it from a young age, so she wasn't out much. She inherited the farm when her parents died and kept it running herself with a little help from a local or two."

"She's also a huge introvert," Ida Belle said.

"Do you think she'll talk to us?" I asked.

"I think so," Gertie said. "She always seems happy to see us, the few times a year we happen to run into her."

Ida Belle nodded. "We shouldn't have a problem."

"Okay, then, that's three interviews today," I said. "Sounds like a good start to me. Hey, here's a question—do either of you know who the horse belonged to?"

They both shook their heads.

"He was a nice-looking steed, though," Ida Belle said. "There's a couple people nearby who breed horses. But anyone could pull up with a trailer and make off with a horse if they planned it right."

I nodded. "But it's beyond just access. That horse stood still while someone strapped a body onto it, then was guided to the park and sent into the fray. And why did he stop all of a sudden? It's almost as if he was trained to do so."

"Maybe it's just coincidence," Gertie said. "I know, I know, you don't believe in that. But look what happened right after you arrived in Sinful—your inherited dog dug up a bone in your backyard. That wasn't staged."

"Okay, I'll give you that one," I said. "And maybe we just happened to be in the right place at the right time, but I still reserve the option to remain suspicious."

"I wouldn't expect anything else," Gertie said. "But even you have to admit that sometimes you just get lucky."

Ida Belle laughed. "We're the only people in Sinful who would call coming into direct contact with a headless body lucky."

"Yes, but that's why we're friends," I said.

# CHAPTER THREE

As we headed out of the café, I spotted Carter coming across the street. He caught sight of us and hesitated for just a split second, but I still noticed. He must have resigned himself to the conversation that was coming because he waved and continued up as we stopped and waited on the sidewalk.

"Did you get any sleep?" I asked.

The dark circles under his eyes told the story, but I figured an inquiry into his health would be the appropriate way to start the conversation.

"Not a lot," he said. "The forensics team didn't finish up in the park until around 3:00 a.m."

"I can imagine that was a real nightmare," Ida Belle said. "Especially with it happening right in the middle of the festival. Is anything closed off? If so, I can rearrange some things for the opening today."

"Nothing will be restricted," he said. "We did ask them to push back the opening until this afternoon, just to give forensics a chance to look it over in the daylight, but I think they were thorough. So the whole thing is closed for now, but you should be good to go as it was before by one or so."

"Thanks," Ida Belle said. "I'll just make a couple phone calls and make sure everyone knows."

"Did you get that poor horse taken care of?" Gertie asked. "I swear I couldn't stop thinking about him. He must have been scared to death. If you need a place to keep him, I'm resodding my backyard next year anyway..."

I had to hold in a grin. It wasn't a stretch that Gertie loved animals, and I had no doubt she'd let the horse stay in her backyard and probably cook for it, but that wasn't the real reason for her inquiry.

"We located the owner and the horse is back home," Carter said.

"Well, that's a relief," Gertie said. "He looked expensive. He wasn't injured, was he?"

"Not that I could tell," Carter said. "But I'll be following up with the owner, of course. Unless she was the one who strapped the body to the horse and sent him off in the park, I'm assuming she'll want to file a theft report."

"I would," Gertie said. "If someone stole Francis, I'd come down on them like hellhounds."

Carter smiled. "I have no doubt about that. Well, if you ladies don't mind, I'm going to grab a bite to eat before I get started unraveling this mess."

We said goodbye and started down the sidewalk.

"Nice try on the horse thing," I said to Gertie. "He wasn't about to give you anything."

Ida Belle and Gertie grinned.

"But he did," Gertie said.

Ida Belle nodded. "Only a breeder would have a horse of that quality, especially a stud. And there's only one woman in the area who breeds horses."

"Great," I said. "Then I guess we have another person to talk to. Are we on the list for any chores at the festival today?"

"Not a thing," Ida Belle said. "I told you, I cleared us off the operating schedule. We only had setup duties. Of course, I did that thinking that after last year, no one would be able to blame us if something went wrong, and danged if another head didn't fall in our laps."

I grinned. "Lucky."

"Let's go get those casseroles and see just how lucky we are," Gertie said.

"I'll go get the food with Gertie," Ida Belle said to me, "then swing by your house and pick you up."

"Sounds good," I said.

Fifteen minutes later, I hopped into Ida Belle's SUV, giving the back seat a once-over.

"You put a cover on the back seat," I said.

"A *pet* cover," Gertie said.

"If the shoe fits," Ida Belle said. "I got tired of steam cleaning the upholstery after Gertie's escapades."

"You always make me do the cleaning," Gertie said.

"You don't do it good enough," Ida Belle said. "Which means I end up doing the bulk of the work."

"She means going over every inch with tweezers and a toothbrush," Gertie said. "It's a car—not a priceless work of art."

"Says you," Ida Belle said as she pulled up to the curb and parked.

I looked over for my initial view of the late Gilbert Forrest's house. It was in a cul-de-sac that backed up to the woods and was completely typical of the others in the neighborhood. Quite frankly, it was a little disappointing. The only standout item was the flashy red Mustang convertible in the driveway, which I assumed was Tiffany's since Gil's car had been stolen.

"I was expecting something bold," I said as we exited the SUV. "From the house, I mean."

"I'm sure he would have if he could have gotten away with it," Gertie said.

"I forget about all of Sinful's rules," I said.

Gertie nodded. "There's that, and he probably didn't want the house detracting from him."

"True," Ida Belle said. "He didn't like competition. He hated Ronald."

"That's probably because Ronald has a better wardrobe," Gertie said as we made our way up to the house.

"Ronald has a better wardrobe than a lot of women in Hollywood," Ida Belle said. "I'd hate to see his credit card bills."

I frowned. "You know, I hate to even ask questions about the man because I'm afraid it's like summoning him or something, but what does he do? Did do? I never see him leave to go anywhere, but he's paying for all that couture somehow."

"Inherited," Ida Belle said. "His grandmother was a Texas oil baroness. The story is Ronald's father was her only son and he always took issue with Ronald's...unique personality. The grandmother was apparently a bit ahead of her time when it came to the 'whatever floats your boat' philosophy, so she cut the son out of her will and left everything to Ronald."

"Really?" I asked.

"That's the rumor, anyway," Ida Belle said. "Seems to fit with what we see here, so I don't think anyone ever questioned it beyond that."

Gertie nodded. "God knows, no one is crazy enough to ask Ronald and in Sinful, that's saying a lot."

Ida Belle rang the doorbell and we waited. I was starting to wonder if anyone was home when the door finally swung open and a young woman peered out.

*Midtwenties. Five foot four. A hundred thirty pounds, a considerable amount in boobs. No sign of grief or lack of sleep. Zero threat unless you were dating her and had a father with money and no ethics.*

"Good morning, Tiffany," Gertie said. "You remember Ida Belle and me, right? And this is our friend Fortune. We brought you a chicken casserole."

She looked surprised and a little dazed.

"Oh," she said. "I'd completely forgot about the food thing. It's been a long time since I was around someone...anyway, come in."

We stepped inside and I paused, taking in the living room as Tiffany headed off down the hall. Apparently the normalcy of the outside of the house was the cover for the inside. It was very modern—bright yellow walls and shiny black furniture with metal hardware, and a red velvet couch and love seat with the occasional leopard-print throw draped across them. I could see why Gil hadn't liked Ronald. Compared to this mess, Ronald had the best taste in Sinful.

"Is that a painting of dogs playing poker with Jesus?" I asked and nodded toward the painting leaned up against the wall above the fireplace.

Gertie nodded. "Wait until Celia drops by. She's going to have a conniption fit."

The kitchen was another room of shiny black and metal, with more gold than Fort Knox. Except this gold wasn't real. We took seats at the kitchen table in strange bright red chairs that seemed to be designed for small cats to sit in them. Tiffany took the casserole from Gertie and offered us something to drink. I declined, hoping we could get something out of the widow and get out before I needed a chiropractor. Apparently, we all felt the same because Ida Belle and Gertie shook their heads, and Tiffany finally perched uneasily on the edge of one of the chairs.

"How are you doing?" Gertie asked.

Tiffany shrugged. "Fine, I guess. I mean, it was all a shock, really. He was at a rehearsal, like always, and then he was gone. I just got everything set with the funeral home yesterday. They had to hold the...uh, body for forty-eight hours for all the police stuff in New Orleans, so I couldn't do anything before that."

Ida Belle nodded. "That's common and part of the reason we didn't come by sooner. In fact, we didn't even hear about it until day before yesterday, and then we figured you might have to go to New Orleans to take care of things and then address the other stuff."

"And here I thought everything was done," she said. "I did all that picking things with the funeral home. My God, that was awful. And then the deputy shows up last night and tells me Gil was...well, I still can't believe it."

"If I hadn't seen it, I wouldn't believe it either," Gertie said.

Tiffany's eyes widened. "You were there?"

"Front-row seats, so to speak," Gertie said.

Tiffany bit her lower lip, looking more like a teenager than a young woman.

"And it happened just like he said?" Tiffany asked. "I mean, I'm sure the deputy was telling the truth. but I just can't see why..."

"Yeah, I think that has everyone stumped," Ida Belle said. "But I'm sure the police will figure it out."

"I don't mean to pry," Gertie said, "but are you okay with finances and the like? Because I know a man who's really good at helping people restructure when there's a change in familial status."

"Oh, I'm okay, I think," Tiffany said. "I mean, Gil had

money and life insurance. Would have been kinda silly if an insurance salesman didn't, right? The house is paid for, so I think I'm all right. I mean, I guess I'll have to find a job at some point because I'm young and the money won't last forever, but I should have some time to figure it out."

"That's good," Gertie said. "Well, you let me know if you need any help with your planning and I'll get you that guy's number."

"Have you talked to Liam?" Ida Belle asked.

Tiffany blushed. "No. Liam and I haven't talked in years. Not since I married Gil. I thought maybe I should call, but then I'm probably the last person he wants to hear from."

"Did Liam and Gil still talk?" Gertie asked.

"No," Tiffany said. "Gil would call every once in a while, but as far as I know, Liam never answered and never returned his calls. Not that I blame him, mind you. What Gil and I did really hurt Liam, but I had to do what was right for me. Liam was great and all, but we were both young. He couldn't support me like Gil."

I blinked, unable to process marrying a man old enough to be my father just to be financially secure, but then I didn't know anything about Tiffany's background. However, it sounded like I needed to. If Tiffany had only married Gil for his money, and now it was all hers, then that left her free to pursue the younger Forrest again.

"We all make choices that seem best for us," Ida Belle said. "At the time anyway. And then we hope they are the right decision."

Tiffany just stared down at the table.

"Do the New Orleans police have any idea what happened?" Gertie asked.

Tiffany looked back up and shook her head. "The security cameras in the parking lot weren't working. There were a couple cameras on a nearby street, but they were low quality. All they got was a guy in a hoodie walking down the street around the time Gil was killed, but I mean, it could have been anybody, right?"

"Have they found the car?" I asked.

"Not that I know of," she said. "There's a liaison who calls daily to update me, but they haven't really had anything more to say. When he called yesterday, he said they'd be moving that to once a week. Of course, I don't know if the situation last night changes things."

"Did Gil have a beef with anyone?" Ida Belle asked.

Tiffany shrugged. "Gil had a beef with almost everyone unless he was trying to sell them insurance. He wanted everything his way because he was certain it was the right way. I think he rubbed people wrong a lot. But I can't think of anyone who would kill him over that. Besides, if it was just someone with a grudge, why did they take the car and his wallet?"

"Did he seem distracted or worried about anything recently?" I asked.

She frowned. "You know, he did. I noticed one night when we were watching our favorite TV show that he wasn't even paying attention. And he always paid attention to everything on that show and watched every episode multiple times. I asked him if something was wrong, but he said no. Still, he would blank out sometimes, you know?"

"How long had he been like that?" I asked.

"A couple weeks maybe," she said. "All my days kinda run together. Being here, the same thing to do all the time. Or nothing to do, I suppose."

Ida Belle glanced at me and I gave her a nod.

"Well, we're going to get out of your hair," Ida Belle said

and we all rose. "Please let us know if there's anything we can do to help."

"Thanks," Tiffany said. "I really appreciate the offer and the food. Gertie's casseroles are legendary in Sinful. It will be nice to finally have one."

She walked us to the door, and we headed out and climbed into the SUV. I glanced back at the house and saw the blinds in the front window snap shut.

"That was awkward," I said as we drove away.

"Incredibly," Gertie agreed. "That girl acts like she's fifteen, not twenty-five."

"She didn't seem very upset," I said.

"Not upset at all," Ida Belle said.

"I got the impression she married Gil for the money," I said. "Is that the local take?"

"There was talk," Gertie said, "that her family situation wasn't all that grand. Mind you, I don't have a reliable source for that and was never curious enough to ask, but the general consensus was she married Gil to get away from her stepfather."

Ida Belle frowned. "It wouldn't be the first time a young woman married an older man to escape an abusive situation."

"No," I agreed. "But it gives her motive. Now that the money is hers, she's free to have a relationship with whomever she wants."

"Including making another run at Liam," Gertie said.

"That definitely occurred to me," I said. "But where I get stumped is the body in the park. That girl is small and doesn't spend any time in the gym. No way she could have gotten Gil's body on that horse. And anyway, what point would it serve? The carjacking case will go cold quickly with no leads, and insurance and the estate will settle up. This whole Headless Horseman thing could delay all of that."

"That's a good point," Ida Belle said. "And really the crux of the matter. I think if we knew *why* someone put Gil up on that horse, we'd have the whole thing solved."

Gertie sighed. "Have you ever noticed that we're always chasing down the why? It's exhausting. I'd like to have just one case where someone is killed, we know why, and it's a matter of tracking down the killer."

"That wouldn't be much of an investigation," I said. "When would we run from bears, or have car chases, or get shot at, or knock butthead cops into porta-johns?"

Gertie brightened. "That's true. I would definitely miss the action. I mean, things have picked up a bit on the personal end since I started dating Jeb but there's no way his bad hips could offer up the workout I get when we're on a case. Or the creativity, for that matter. I was thinking about buying a book—"

"Nope!" Ida Belle held up a hand. "We had an agreement."

"That was only for the first date," Gertie said. "And I still haven't talked about it, except for the ending up in the hospital part."

"That's not how I remember the agreement," Ida Belle said. "Sexy-time talk is banned. We are *not* those kind of girl-friends."

Gertie sighed. "But that means Fortune will never tell us about Carter."

"I wasn't going to tell you those kinds of details about Carter even before Ida Belle brought down the ban hammer," I said.

"You guys are no fun," Gertie said.

"Well, you'll never really know that, will you?" Ida Belle said.

"Tease," Gertie said.

"I can tell you some good gossip on the personal side of my

life, though," I said. "Assuming you still want to know why Emmaline and Carlos are no longer dating."

"Why?"

"Heck yeah!"

They both responded at once.

I laughed. "You two want to bet on it?"

Ida Belle shook her head. "We'd both be betting on it being Carter."

"That's what I thought, too," I said. "But apparently, it was both more mundane and yet more interesting than Carter putting the strong-arm on the man. You remember I told you about those paintings I saw when I went through Emmaline's house after the break-in?"

"Yeah," Gertie said. "You thought they were really good."

I nodded. "I don't know crap about art but they looked awesome to me. Well, apparently, they *were* really good. So good that a gallery in New Orleans is going to put on a show for Emmaline."

"Wow!"

"That's incredible!"

"It is," I agreed. "Emmaline told me that before she met Carter's dad, she was going to be an artist, but then she got married and put all that aside. So when she took the class and met Carlos, she liked him well enough, but said as time went on, she realized her first love was actually painting and every time she had a date with Carlos, she wished she was in her art room instead. So she cut him loose."

"I'm not sure if that says a lot for painting or very little for Carlos," Gertie said.

"I'd go with a lot for painting," Ida Belle said. "Carlos seemed nice enough, but if a person doesn't do it for you in the beginning, it's unlikely they'll do it for you later on."

Gertie rolled her eyes. "Says the woman who married the man pursuing her a hundred years after the fact."

"Preparation time was required," Ida Belle said.

"What preparation time?" Gertie asked. "Aside from giving the man half your practically empty closet and cleaning out one small corner of your freezer, you didn't change a thing."

"*He* needed preparation time," Ida Belle said.

"That I can see," Gertie said. "The way you two do things, Fortune won't be marrying Carter until her next life."

"Something to look forward to in death," I said cheerily.

"Hopeless," Gertie said and shook her head.

"Speaking of hopeless and relationship issues, how are we going to handle Liam?" I asked. "I don't know him, so I figured I'd let you guys take the lead. Maybe jump in if I see an opening that makes sense for me to fill but otherwise do the polite nodding thing."

"If you manage only polite nodding through the entire conversation, I will check your pulse," Gertie said. "You always come up with good questions."

Ida Belle nodded. "You're definitely a natural at investigation. But Gertie and I can take the lead. Men are a lot harder to get relationship information out of, in general, but if he's going to talk, it will likely be to old ladies like us. We come across as sympathetic."

"I *am* sympathetic," Gertie said. "And I have no idea who you're calling old."

"He's twenty-five," Ida Belle said. "Everyone is old as far as he's concerned."

She turned into the strip mall and parked in front of the butcher shop.

"That's him at the counter," Gertie said.

# CHAPTER FOUR

I took a look through the picture window at the man at the counter.

*Six foot two. Two hundred pounds of mostly lean body mass. Excellent biceps. Strong jaw. Disgruntled look on an otherwise handsome face. The meat cleaver he was slamming onto a side of beef was somewhat concerning. Threat level medium until confirmed otherwise.*

"No customers," Ida Belle said. "Maybe we'll get lucky and he's working alone."

"Then let's do this," Gertie said and hopped out with the casserole.

We headed into the shop and Liam looked up as the bell rang on the door. He narrowed his eyes for a moment, then gave Gertie a small smile.

"Ms. Hebert," he said. "It's been a long time."

"Too long," Gertie said and stepped up to the counter. "But I swear, you still look just like that boy I taught in school."

"Hopefully, I'm smarter now," he said. "How can I help you?"

"We're actually here for you," Gertie said. "You remember my best friend Ida Belle, right? And this is our friend Fortune."

39

"Of course," he said, and gave Ida Belle a nod, then he looked over at me. "Nice to meet you."

"You too," I said.

Gertie put the casserole on the counter. "I'm sorry we didn't make it by sooner, but I made you up a chicken casserole. The instructions are on a sticky on top."

He looked down at the casserole, clearly confused, then his expression shifted into slightly irritated.

"That wasn't necessary," he said.

"Still," Gertie said. "There are Southern lady requirements that must be met when someone passes."

He relaxed a bit and nodded. "You're right, and I appreciate the thought. My grandma would have done the same thing."

"Your grandma had class," Ida Belle said. "Unfortunately, it's a diminishing art."

He nodded. "She was strict as heck but she was a good woman. I'm lucky I had her, especially since my father couldn't be bothered to raise his only kid."

"You've had a difficult time," Gertie agreed.

His face flashed with anger again and he shook his head. "And then that man goes and creates drama and aggravation in my life from the grave. I told the police that his death didn't affect my life one way or another and then they go tell me about last night. Do you know about it?"

"We saw the whole thing," Ida Belle said. "It was rather surreal."

"Well, the cops knocked on my door early this morning," he said, "questioning me like I had something to do with it. I was quick to tell them that I didn't have anything to do with my father when he was alive, so it was rather a long shot that I'd want to hang out with him dead."

He threw his hands in the air. "Then they show up here an

hour ago, wanting to look around the place. I told them no way unless they came with a warrant. This isn't my business and I'm not about to let them railroad me over something I had nothing to do with. They seem to think since I have some fancy knives that I run around cutting up people with them. What would be the point of that?"

"It really seems a completely senseless thing to do," Gertie said. "And quite shocking. But then his death was as well."

Liam shrugged. "That's the luck of the draw in the city. I had an offer from a butcher shop there, you know? But all the noise and the crime turned me off. Then the owner of this shop offered me this gig. He's setting himself up to retire and when that happens, the shop will be mine. I've been working for a down payment and will give him a cut of business until the rest is paid off."

"That sounds like a good deal," Gertie said.

"It is," he said. "The shop does a good business. I have a lot of regulars and I supply for several restaurants in New Orleans. I've got access to some good ranchers. They produce excellent product. As long as I keep people happy, I'll have a good living until I decide to retire."

Gertie smiled. "I think that's great."

"Maybe your dad left you something and you can buy the owner out early," I said.

"Ha!" Liam said. "That man never cared about anyone but himself. He probably didn't even bother to leave a will. Why would he care what happened after his death? First off, he probably thought he'd never die, and if he did, then he figured it wouldn't be his problem."

Ida Belle frowned. "Well, that hardly seems fair given that I'm sure a lot of your father's money came from your grandma. I wish she would have left a will and taken care of you in it."

Liam sighed. "My grandma went to the grave pretending

that my father was a good person. She couldn't face the truth. I'm sure she thought her beloved son would take care of me. Well, he took care of me all right. She's probably rolling in her grave."

The phone rang and Liam excused himself to answer it.

"I'm sorry, ladies," he said when he hung up, "but I have to go check on a couple invoices for a client."

"Well, if you need anything from us, please don't hesitate to call," Gertie said. "My phone number is on the sticky."

"I appreciate it," he said. "And the casserole. I remember them from before and I'm in for some good eating. You ladies stay safe. I don't know what's going on in Sinful, but it sounds like someone is completely off. You can't be too careful."

"We will be," Gertie assured him and we made our way out.

"So what do you think?" I asked as we drove away.

"He's definitely angry," Gertie said, "but I can't say that I blame him. His father treated him horribly and now he's got the police bearing down on him."

I nodded. "If I was in his position, and didn't have anything to do with it, I'd be mad too."

"It does seem like his father keeps stepping in to ruin his life, even in death," Ida Belle said.

"He'll be fine as long as he didn't do it," I said. "And honestly, what reason could he have?"

Ida Belle shook her head. "I don't even have a guess as to why someone pulled the Headless Horseman prank, but if word gets out that the police are questioning Liam and going over the butcher shop, the gossip alone could ruin him. Even if it's not true."

"That sucks," I said.

"Which means we have to work harder than ever to figure out what happened," Gertie said. "Or Liam is going to end up taking the fall for something that he probably didn't do. He didn't have a reason to do this."

"What reason did anyone have?" I asked. "Since the motive on the Headless Horseman is altogether murky, we can't really eliminate anyone. Not even Liam."

"Maybe he was right," Ida Belle said. "Maybe there *is* a crazy person among us."

"Sinful is *full* of crazy," I said. "But there's crazy and then there's this."

"Well, that doesn't let Tiffany off either," Gertie said. "I know she couldn't have done it alone, but she might have had help."

"That's a heck of an ask," Ida Belle said. "And Tiffany doesn't have any close friends that I'm aware of. You don't just ask someone to tea, then pitch your idea of stealing a body and a horse, then cutting off a man's head and strapping it all to the horse to send through the festival. I can't imagine what kind of person would actually say 'All right. Sounds like a good time.'"

Gertie frowned. "Someone helplessly in love might do it."

"You think Liam is still in love with Tiffany?" I asked.

"I don't know but it's possible," Gertie said.

"But again, we come back to what the point was of sending Gil through the park." Ida Belle said.

"Maybe cutting off the head of the monster who ruined his life was cathartic," I suggested. "And the ride was a mockery of Gil and his acting, which seemed to be the only thing he cared about."

"That's a lot of hate to be carrying around," Gertie said.

"How badly do you think he hated his father?" I asked.

Gertie blew out a breath. "A lot. Gil was never a good father to begin with, but that thing with Tiffany left the boy devastated. He fled town for a couple months right after."

"Really? Why?" I asked.

"The rumor mill said he went to stay with a cousin so there would be someone keeping a watch on him," Ida Belle said.

"Were people afraid he was suicidal?" I asked.

"That's the indication I got," Ida Belle said.

I looked at Gertie. "You think Liam was capable of that?"

"I guess most anyone is, given the right circumstances," Gertie said. "And Liam was an emotional boy. What others considered 'soft.' He took a lot of grief in school because of it. Tiffany was the only person outside of his grandmother who played a prominent role in his life that I'm aware of."

"And then his father stole Tiffany from him," I said.

Gertie nodded. "A year after his grandma died. But why wait all this time to get revenge?"

"Because his father didn't die until now?" I suggested. "If he's not that emotionally strong, then he might not have had the spine to do it when his father was alive."

Ida Belle shook her head. "It's crazy but not the strangest thing I've ever heard. Gil was very concerned about how people perceived him. Liam could have thought it was a way to make a stab at his father's ego and hurt Tiffany at the same time."

Gertie slumped in her seat. "This sucks. I don't want it to be Liam."

"Neither do I," I said. "It sounds like he deserves a break."

"Well, a forensics team should be able to clear him, right?" Gertie asked.

"I'd be surprised if they could," I said. "That butcher shop is blood central. And I imagine they clean it all the time. It would take them a hundred years to collect and test every specimen they found in there. And even if they did find something, it would be diluted or damaged from the cleaning."

"And even if Gil's DNA was there, it would be a partial

match for Liam," Ida Belle said. "The defense could easily blame a lower match percentage on degradation."

"Then why sweep the place at all?" Gertie asked.

"Because they have to follow the logical path," I said. "Even if they can't find anything that makes their case, a lot of perps cave from the pressure of an investigation, especially if they're not normally criminals."

"Well, I really hope Judith knows something worthwhile," Gertie said. "Because I don't like the direction this is going."

I nodded. I didn't either.

————

WE WERE ALMOST TO THE EXIT FOR JUDITH'S FARM WHEN I saw the red Mustang on the opposite side of the highway, moving at a fast clip.

"I guess Tiffany decided to bail before the rest of Sinful could descend on her," I said.

"I wonder where she's going," Gertie said.

I have no idea why the thought came to me, but I pointed at the car.

"Follow her," I said.

Without saying a word, Ida Belle yanked the steering wheel left and drove into the grass median. Gertie flew up and hit the roof as she launched into the dip, then fell on the floorboard, only to be shot up again as Ida Belle jumped the shoulder back onto the highway. I turned around and shook my head as Gertie crawled back up onto the seat.

"When are you going to learn to wear your seat belt?" I asked.

"Is it too much to ask for a warning?" Gertie complained. "She didn't have to tear through the median so violently. There's nothing coming for miles."

"I didn't want to lose her," Ida Belle said.

"Spaceships couldn't lose you," Gertie said.

We followed from some distance, easily keeping the bright red car in our sights. When she took the exit for the strip mall, I felt my pulse tick up a notch. I glanced back at Gertie, who frowned. Ida Belle kept her distance, but it was easy to spot the Mustang pulling up in front of the butcher shop.

"Go around back," I said.

Ida Belle entered the strip mall on the opposite side from the butcher and headed down the side to the back. The rear parking lot had a couple dumpsters and cars scattered around, which I figured belonged to the people who worked there.

"Park on the side of the dumpster," I said. "That way, if Liam walks out the back door, he won't see your vehicle."

"What are you going to do?" Gertie asked.

"I'm going to sneak in the back and see what I can hear," I said and jumped out of the SUV.

"What do you want us to do?" Gertie asked.

"Same as always," I said and grinned.

Hopefully, I wouldn't run into an issue but if I did, I knew I could count on Gertie to create a diversion. I hurried down the side of the building to the back of the butcher shop and leaned against the door. I couldn't hear anything and there was only one old truck parked directly behind the shop, so I hoped that meant it was still only Liam inside. An ancient moped leaned against the wall and I wondered if Liam used that in lieu of his truck when he didn't have to haul anything. It would certainly be better on gas.

I twisted the knob and was happy to find the door unlocked. I eased it open and peeked inside. The back room of the shop was where the heavy lifting and cutting went on. A side of beef was hanging from a hook in the middle of the room, blood dripping onto an area with a drain in the middle of the floor. Stainless steel tables lined the walls containing an electric slicer, hand tools, and stacks of steak that had my mouth watering.

I could barely make out voices at the front of the shop, so I eased forward until I reached the swinging door that led to the front of the store. I pushed the door just a tiny bit and listened to the exchange.

"You can't be here," Liam said.

"But I need to talk to you," Tiffany said.

"What do you want from me?" Liam said.

"You know what I want," Tiffany said.

"Well, it's a little late for that," Liam said. "The police were all over me this morning. I don't need that kind of grief."

"I'm sorry, Liam," Tiffany said. "I didn't send them."

"You didn't have to," Liam said. "Just being born to that man has made my life miserable, and now I'm in hot water. It's only a matter of time before they come back with a search warrant. Just go, Tiffany, before you make things worse. You might not have told them to come here, but you're the reason they did."

I heard a half cry, half sob along with retreating footsteps, then the bell over the front door rang, signaling her departure. I crept back across the room, ready to slip out, but when I eased the back door open, a guy carrying what looked like a whole pig came staggering toward me.

I bolted back inside, scanning the room for a place to hide, but there wasn't one. All the tables were open underneath, the only other door in the room led to the front, and the back was covered by a pig farmer. The only option was the walk-in freezer, and I had no way of knowing if that's where the pig was going.

With no other options, I dashed into the freezer and placed a sausage link in the door to keep it open. Then I ducked behind a shelf stacked with ribs and pulled a sheet of plastic over me. I'd no sooner gotten the plastic in place when the door opened and I heard someone huffing inside. A second later, the pig hit me square in the face and knocked me back into the wall. I couldn't see over the massive body, so I just held my breath and hoped the pig guy wouldn't be taking a closer look. He must have been satisfied because I heard him walking away and then a couple seconds later, the door slammed shut. I managed to shove the pig off of me and ran for the door, but it was one of those old styles that locked automatically from the outside.

Crap!

There wasn't even a ceiling to climb through.

I pulled out my phone and sent a text.

*Need a diversion and a rescue. Locked in freezer.*

Gertie: *On it.*

Ida Belle: *Good God.*

# CHAPTER FIVE

I HEARD THE BACK DOOR OPEN AGAIN, AND THIS TIME LIAM greeted the pig guy and they started discussing weights and prices. I ducked back behind a shelf on the opposite side of the cooler from the pig in case Liam came inside to check out the product.

Out back, I heard a small engine fire up and rev.

The moped!

"What the heck!" Liam shouted, and footsteps ran for the back door. "Someone's stealing my moped!"

"And my boudin!" the pig guy yelled.

I heard scrambling for a minute and the sound of jiggling keys, then a vehicle fired up and I assumed either Liam or the pig man were going after Gertie, who was undoubtedly the boudin thief. I tugged on the door handle, silently willing the thing to open, but it wouldn't budge. No way was Gertie going to outrun a truck with a moped.

The back door opened again, and I let go of the door handle, hoping whoever had entered hadn't heard me trying to escape.

"Who's there?" the pig man called out.

Double crap!

I grabbed the plastic sheeting from behind the pig and pulled it over my head. It had barely hit the floor when the door flew open and the pig man stomped inside. I couldn't see much with the thick plastic over me, but there was no mistaking the dark object in his hand. Well, this had gone south fast.

I had totally Gertied.

I waited until he took a step in my direction, then launched. As I tackled him, I threw the plastic over his head and he went flying into a heap in the corner. I sprang up and ran out of the freezer, slamming the door shut behind me. I just hoped he didn't start shooting. Those freezers weren't cheap.

No way was I running out the back door, so I headed to the front of the store, texting Ida Belle that I was out of the freezer as I went. The coast was clear in the entry, so I eased up to the windows to stare outside. I heard an engine racing and barely ducked behind a fake ficus tree when Gertie shot by on the moped, wearing an ET mask and with a trail of boudin links around her neck, flying behind her like a scarf. Liam's truck was right behind.

The pig farmer pounded on the freezer door, yelling and threatening to open fire, so I bolted out the door and in the opposite direction of Liam and Gertie. The lot next to the strip center was wooded, and I dashed into the trees for cover so I could take a moment to figure out what the heck to do. I'd barely gotten into the trees when I heard a huge boom that shook the ground and then saw debris flying up and over the strip mall.

Gertie had gotten onto the service road with the moped, Liam still hot on her tail, but as soon as the blast went off, he slammed on his brakes, made a U-turn and headed back for the shop. I stepped out of the tree line near the access road and waved wildly at Gertie, trying to get her attention. She saw me at the last minute and decided that was a good time to make a hard right onto the grass.

It wasn't.

The moped was airborne for a moment as it launched off the curb. The ET mask looked strangely appropriate in that instant. Gertie lost her grip and her ride midair and fell into a mudhole. Miraculously, the moped kept going, but I was too busy staring at Gertie to realize it. By the time I realized it was still in motion, diving was my only option for escape, so that's what I did.

Right into a blackberry thicket.

I sprang out of the thorny bushes as if I'd bounced off a trampoline. Gertie had climbed out of the mudhole and was limping toward me, clutching the mask. I pulled out my cell phone and sent Ida Belle a text.

*In woods east of strip mall.*

Ida Belle: *On my way.*

I watched down the access road, waiting on Ida Belle's SUV to appear, but when I heard the approaching engine, I realized it was coming from in front of us. Seconds later, the SUV flew out of the woods, went into Reverse, and backed to where we were standing, sliding to a stop. Gertie and I ran for the SUV and didn't even manage to get the doors completely closed before Ida Belle took off, staying on the grassy area. About fifty yards down, she took a hard turn into the woods and I realized there was a road there.

Sort of.

A Sinful-type road, anyway.

It was mostly two runners of dirt with weeds in the middle that ran into the woods. Ida Belle's face was tight in concentration on maintaining warp speed while racing on a non-road in the middle of a forest. I just held on for the ride and about a hundred yards away, she took a hard left and we flew out of the woods and into a parking lot behind the higher-end motel.

Ida Belle increased speed as soon as she hit pavement, and the SUV screamed out of the parking lot and onto a side road. But instead of turning left, back toward the highway, she took a right and floored it. When we'd done a good five miles at over a hundred miles per hour, she finally let up and looked over at us, shaking her head.

"I'm going to have to backtrack to the darn Gulf of Mexico to get home," she said.

"Did Liam see your SUV?" I asked.

"He drove right by me chasing Gertie out of the parking lot," she said. "But I don't think it registered with him. I took some dynamite from Gertie's purse and set it with a long fuse. Then I hauled it out of there and onto that logging trail when he chased Gertie to the front of the building. Some people might have come out of the back doors of their shops to see what the commotion was about, but if they did, I was too far away to get a license plate."

"Then all they know is that a black SUV was fleeing the scene," Gertie said. "So we're good."

Ida Belle stared at her in dismay. "A moped stolen by a boudin-eating ET, dynamite set off in a dumpster, and a black SUV leaving the scene. Yeah, Carter won't figure that one out at all, especially when he gets there to question Liam and sees Gertie's casserole on the counter."

Gertie blew out a breath. "Busted."

Ida Belle shook her head. "Did you get anything to make all of that worthwhile?"

"I might have," I said and repeated the exchange I'd heard between Liam and Tiffany.

"Do you think they did it together?" Ida Belle asked. "It

sure doesn't sound like they were completely done with each other. At least, not on Tiffany's end for sure."

"It didn't sound that way to me either," I said. "Although Liam is clearly hacked about the police involvement, so we're back to what would that stunt gain them?"

Ida Belle shook her head. "I don't know. Seems like if they were starting up again before Gil's death, the last thing they'd want is to draw unnecessary attention to themselves."

A rush of air hit the back of my head and I looked back to see Gertie dangling the boudin out the window, pouring a bottled water on it to get the mud off. She popped back inside the SUV and took a bite.

"This is great," she said. "Anyone want a piece?"

———

WE COULDN'T EXACTLY HEAD TO JUDITH'S HOUSE GIVEN that Gertie was covered in mud and I had tiny spots of blood all over my arms where I'd wrestled with the blackberry thorns. Plus, we probably needed to go home and appear to be doing normal stuff for when Carter called or came by. And there was no doubt he'd be by. So Ida Belle hauled it on the back roads until she could cross back over to the highway and hurry home. Her phone rang just before we got to Sinful.

"It's Myrtle," she said.

Myrtle was one of the Sinful Ladies and, more importantly, worked dispatch at the sheriff's department. Normally, she worked nights, so I wondered what had her calling now.

Ida Belle put the call on speaker.

"It's Myrtle. Got a situation down here at the sheriff's department."

"What kind of situation?" Ida Belle asked.

"The kind that usually means you guys were up to something," Myrtle said. "A call came in about a stolen moped, an alien, and an explosion."

"Crap," Ida Belle said. "Is Carter coming for us?"

"No. He's out looking into that Headless Horseman thing. Deputy Breaux took the call and is on his way to the butcher shop now. I had to wait until he left to call and warn you."

"What are you doing there right now anyway?" Ida Belle asked.

"That idiot Gavin pulled a muscle in his leg," Myrtle said. "I told Carter if he bothered to get some muscle tone, he could have limped in here and done his job. It's not like you use your legs for dispatch."

"What if he needed to pee?" Gertie asked.

"He's a man," Myrtle said. "We got Dixie cups. Anyway, I'm sure Carter will hear about it soon enough, but you've got a little time to get an alibi in place."

"Thanks, Myrtle," Ida Belle said and disconnected.

"Well? Anyone got a good cover story?" Gertie asked.

"I don't even know where to start," I said.

"I have an idea," Ida Belle said. "But it's going to require some verbal fabrication."

Gertie shrugged. "It's not Sunday, so I'm good."

"I'm going to stop by our houses, and we all need to grab a swimsuit and a beach towel and haul it back out," Ida Belle said.

I had no idea where she was going with it, but I didn't care. At least she had an idea.

And how much trouble could we get in wearing swimsuits?

Twenty minutes later, I found out.

"What if Nora shoots us for trespassing?" I asked.

"I don't know that she owns a gun," Ida Belle said as we slipped into Nora's backyard.

"Everyone in Louisiana owns a gun," I said.

"True, but Nora knows us," Ida Belle said.

"Didn't you tell me that she'd been drunk for fifteen years?" I asked.

Ida Belle nodded. "That's the genius part of my plan. Gertie, get that bottle of wine and those plastic glasses out."

Gertie pulled four plastic glasses from her purse along with a huge bottle of wine while I helped Ida Belle shove back the top on Nora's hot tub. Gertie poured up the wine and we all climbed in.

"Now, start laughing and talking loud," Ida Belle said. "And Gertie, dip down and get that mud off."

I felt ridiculous but I did my best fake laugh, which led to real laughs from Gertie and Ida Belle. Sure enough, a minute later, the patio door to the house opened and Nora came out with a shotgun.

"What are you people doing in my hot tub?" Nora yelled.

"Nora, it's Ida Belle and Gertie, remember?" Ida Belle said. "You invited us over for a dip. You've been in here with us for an hour already. Why did you get dressed? Gertie just poured you another glass of wine."

Nora frowned, then looked at the glass of wine and shrugged. "Heck if I know. Let me go see where I put my suit."

Five minutes later, Nora was in the hot tub with us, regaling us with tales of her trip to Amsterdam, where apparently anything goes, and Nora went right along with it. We'd polished off the first bottle of wine—most of it going to Nora —and had moved on to the second by the time my phone rang. I leaned out of the hot tub and answered.

"Where are you?" Carter asked and I could hear the aggravation in his voice.

"At Nora's house," I said.

"Nora's?" he repeated, clearly confused.

"Yeah, we're in her hot tub."

"I'll be right there."

I dropped the phone back on my towel and slipped back into the steamy water.

"We're up," I said and reached for my glass.

Five minutes later, Carter stomped into the backyard, glaring at us.

"You want to tell me what you were trying to accomplish over at Liam's butcher shop?" he asked.

We all put on our best confused look. Except for Nora, who really *was* confused.

"We dropped off a casserole," Gertie said. "Dropped one off for Tiffany, too. It's kinda what we do."

"Gil died Monday night," Carter said.

"But we didn't hear about it until day before yesterday," Ida Belle said. "And since we had festival prep, we didn't have time to address it before today."

"I'm supposed to believe that?" he asked.

"Gil died?" Nora asked.

Ida Belle raised her eyebrows and waved a hand at Nora, who was making her point.

"Gil died in New Orleans," Ida Belle said. "Tiffany has nothing to do with the townspeople. Liam left years ago and never looked back. Josephine is dead. Who do you think we would have heard it from so quickly? A carjacking doesn't exactly rate a nightly news slot in New Orleans."

"Fine," Carter said. "The problem isn't the casserole. You stole a moped and boudin, blew up a dumpster, and assaulted a pig farmer."

We all put on our blank faces.

"I once dated a pig farmer," Nora said. "He grew the best weed. There was this one time we got in his best pigsty—"

Carter cringed.

"We don't know anything about all that," Ida Belle said,

cutting Nora off. "We left the butcher shop and came straight to Nora's. Been here for over an hour already."

Gertie nodded and held up her hand. "See, I'm starting to prune."

I struggled not to laugh because even with no water, Gertie's fingers were starting to prune.

Carter looked over at Nora. "That true, Nora?"

"Heck yeah," Nora said. "We've been drinking wine and I've been telling them all about my trip to Amsterdam. Brought some great drugs back with me. Didn't even get caught in customs."

Carter stared at her in dismay.

"Look," I said. "I don't know what happened at the butcher shop after we left—although it sounds like something we'd all like to hear—but it wasn't our doing. Gertie's been fighting a backache since she twisted around trying to get rid of that head last night, and Ida Belle was complaining about her knee. I just like sitting in hot bubbly water and drinking. In fact, I'm seriously considering getting one of these."

Carter threw his arms in the air, whirled around, and stalked off. I'm pretty sure he knew we were lying but with a witness that placed us in her hot tub while all the drama was going on at the butcher shop, there wasn't much he could do.

"That was genius," I said and clinked my glass against Ida Belle's.

"I met a genius in Amsterdam," Nora said. "He figured out how to get an awesome high from soybeans and plastic milk jugs."

# CHAPTER SIX

BY THE TIME WE MADE IT OUT OF NORA'S HOT TUB, WE ALL needed a shower, some food to absorb all the alcohol, and a nap. Otherwise, we weren't going to be in any shape for the festival that night, and I intended to walk that maze this year as a customer since I wasn't part of the scaring crew. Hopefully, it wouldn't become another crime scene.

Ida Belle dropped me off at home and I trudged in and up the stairs. Lord knows, I'd already had my fill of hot water for the day, but I turned on the shower because the smell of chlorine combined with all the wine was about to knock me out. I did the whole wash the hair gig, wrapped it up in a towel, and pulled on one of Carter's T-shirts and some underwear before heading for the kitchen. If anyone decided to drop by, they'd just have to wait for me to find pants.

I had some leftover hamburger patties from grilling with Carter a couple nights before, so I popped a bun in the toaster and set a patty to heat in the microwave while I munched on potato chips. Soon, I was at the table with my burger and making notes on my laptop about the case. I'd gotten halfway through the meal and not quite that far into the notes when I heard my front door open and Carter call out.

"Don't shoot," he yelled.

"Are you coming to arrest me?" I asked.

"No."

"Then I won't shoot."

I closed my laptop and a couple seconds later, he walked into the kitchen and took a seat across from me. He eyed my burger, then gave me a once-over.

"You look half asleep," he said. "Too much assaulting ranchers today? Or were you the alien on the moped?"

"Too much wine and even more of Nora's conversation combined with the hot tub," I said and hopped up from my seat.

I ran into my office to retrieve some papers off my printer and handed them to Carter.

"See?" I said. "I've been doing some research."

He flipped through the papers, frowning. "These are all sales ads for hot tubs. You were serious about that?"

"Heck yeah. I feel like I had a deep tissue massage all over my body, but no one had to touch me to get it."

"Then why didn't you keep the one Ida Belle and Gertie gave you for Christmas?"

I shrugged. "I wasn't completely sold on the idea then, and when the senior center's broke and they didn't have the funds for a new one, I figured they needed it more than I did."

He shook his head. "I don't know why you continue to surprise me, but you do."

"Don't pretend like you wouldn't love a sit in a hot tub after a day like today."

"I suppose I would. I'm just not braving Nora's house to do it."

"Yeah, I found it a bit rough, and it wouldn't work for you

at all given that Nora is always on the prowl—for men and a high."

"I don't need that visual. I'm still trying to forget that mud and the pig farmer comment."

"I would have thought you'd be more concerned about her drug stash from Amsterdam."

"Not in this case."

I laughed. "Well, I'm calling a couple of these places to see if they have displays I can see. Then I'm going to check them out and have one put right behind the house."

"Why not toward the bayou where you can get the breeze and watch moonlight on the water?"

"I could do that, but I'm planning on hot-tubbing naked. It's a pretty big backyard to cross."

"Then behind the house it is. That way you only have to worry about Ronald showing up."

I waved a hand in dismissal. "He won't be interested if I'm not wearing clothes. I'm pretty sure that's all he notices about people. So anyway—tell me about this situation at the butcher shop. Someone stole a moped?"

He nodded. "It was Liam's moped that he kept behind the shop. Someone wearing an ET mask grabbed a bunch of boudin links off the farmer's truck and took off on the moped."

"I gotta tell you, that sounds like kids."

"Or someone who acts like a kid. They also blew up the dumpster behind the strip mall. Does that sound like kids?"

"This is southern Louisiana. Gertie's not the only person who carries more dynamite than chewing gum. Probably half the fishermen on the lake have a stash."

"Don't remind me."

"Anyway, why does any of that matter? Is Liam a suspect in the Headless Horseman thing? I mean, I don't know the guy, but Ida Belle and Gertie filled me in on his story before we got there to deliver the casserole and I have to say, while he was polite and appreciated the food, he didn't even look remotely bothered that his father was dead. Actually, he was more annoyed than anything since apparently someone from your office questioned him."

"I questioned him myself," he said. "And yeah, the chip on his shoulder was definitely there, but I have a hard time holding it against the guy. Still, everyone's a suspect until they're not."

"Who else are you looking at?"

"I just said everyone until they're not. You know I'm not going to discuss it with you."

I sighed. "Fine. But you could save me from my boredom. I need something to do."

"I thought you were working that disability case for the insurance company."

"That took all of one day. That idiot went fishing, put a new roof on his shed, and then played football in his backyard with his buddies."

Carter frowned. "Wasn't that the guy who claimed he couldn't walk?"

"That's the one."

"Maybe you should expand your territory more."

"Nah. I don't need much business to pay basics. And I don't want to get into city crime. It's all so mundane. No one ever sends a headless dead man riding a horse through a festival in New Orleans. Seriously, though, why would someone do that? I know, I know, your case and all that, but come on, Carter, that's really weird. Even for Sinful."

He nodded. "I agree. And honestly, I can't see the point."

"I would say maybe it's just a crazy person but this is Sinful so that doesn't narrow things down much."

"I know."

"Well, since you're here, do you want something to eat? I have some more burgers."

"I thought you'd never ask."

I tossed another bun in the toaster and patty in the microwave and retrieved him a bottled water as he was still officially working.

"Are you working the festival again tonight or are you on detective duty?" I asked.

"I'm working the festival. I tried to recruit some backup from neighboring towns but anyone close enough to cover is running shorthanded. Hey, maybe that's something for you to consider. I know Mudbug is hiring a deputy."

"Hard pass. I got out of government work for a reason. I don't like the oversight."

"You also don't like following the law."

"There you go. It's not a good fit."

I put the burger together and slid it in front of him before sitting back down.

"What was your take on him—Gil, I mean. And I'm not getting into your investigation. I just wondered what a guy's perspective is given the description I've gotten. You can't blame me for being interested. He did ride headless through the festival. And it sounds like that wasn't necessarily the biggest eyebrow-raising event he was involved in."

Carter took a bite and thought while he chewed. "I didn't like him much. He was one of those guys who was always talking just a little louder than necessary. He'd walk right up in the middle of anyone's conversation and just start talking over them until everyone else shut up and had to listen to him. And obviously, the situation with Liam's girlfriend didn't get him many fans."

"But Ida Belle said he did well with the insurance sales."

"Oh, he was a natural salesman. When he was in insurance mode, he could convince even the cheapest of people that they had to have insurance right then or their entire life was going to fall apart."

"A bit dramatic, which stands to reason, I guess. Ida Belle and Gertie told me about his acting thing."

Carter nodded. "The problem with people like Gil is he spent so much time in character that I think he forgot who he really was."

——————

NONE OF US BOTHERED WITH COSTUMES THAT NIGHT. Nothing we put on could top the Headless Horseman and besides, we were all tired. Between the Mad Moped Dash, all the wine, and listening to Nora's many drug-induced man conquests, we probably all needed to stay home and sleep. But come sundown, we were all back in the park, hitting up the corn dog vendor even though we'd all eaten at home. Even Ida Belle had indulged in a corn dog but balked when Gertie and I moved on to caramel corn.

"Too much sugar," Ida Belle said and pointed a finger at Gertie. "You don't need it and it will catch up with Fortune one day. There's a reason I'm still in good shape."

Gertie rolled her eyes. "If they were selling Ally's cookies, you wouldn't have that opinion."

"That's a completely different situation," Ida Belle said and I laughed.

"So do you guys want to go do the maze?" I asked.

"I do!" Gertie said. "We've already had our headless guy at the festival this year, so it ought to be safe."

"That's quite a disturbing and unfortunately accurate statement," Ida Belle said.

We headed toward the maze, Gertie and I munching on our caramel corn, when suddenly Gertie stopped short and pointed to a barbecue stand about thirty feet away.

"Look, it's Judith Trahan," she said.

I looked over.

*Midfifties. Five foot six. A hundred fifty pounds. A good bit of it muscle mass. This was a woman who spent a lot of her day doing manual labor. Given she was a farmer, probably also deadly with a shotgun and a thresher. Threat level low for me, high for crops and chickens.*

We set off in her direction and she looked up as we approached and slipped her cell phone into her jeans pocket. Then she gave Gertie and Ida Belle a smile and me a curious look.

"Ladies," she said. "It's been a while."

They both nodded.

"Have you met our friend Fortune yet?" Gertie asked.

Judith raised her brows and extended her hand. "The lady spook. I've heard about you but haven't had the pleasure. How are you getting by in Sinful?"

"I really like it here," I said.

"Not quite as fast-paced as CIA work, though," Judith said.

"I don't know," I said. "It has its moments."

She smiled. "We're nothing here if not interesting."

"Definitely," I agreed.

"How have you been?" Ida Belle asked. "I assume all the rain this year did you some good."

"It did," Judith said. "My best crop to date, actually. I was finally able to get a new tractor. Not sure the old one would have made another year."

"That's great," Ida Belle said. "I have to say, I'm surprised to see you here. Crowds aren't usually your thing."

"No, they're not," Judith said. "And that hasn't changed one bit. But Marie called me up and asked if I'd make some of my chocolate pies for the children's charity auction. Between the kids benefiting and Marie asking, I couldn't say no. So I was just dropping off my contributions."

"Your chocolate pies will bring top dollar," Gertie said. "Marie was smart to hit you up."

Judith looked pleased with the compliment. "Thank you. I still can't bake a casserole I'd put up against yours, but the chocolate pies and I seem to get along."

"I hate to bring up sad things," Gertie said, "but I wanted to say how sorry we are about Gil. His death was a shock. I know you guys have been friends since you were kids."

Judith's expression shifted from jolly to sad. "Yeah, that was a big blow. I mean, ever since Gil married Tiffany, we haven't spent as much time together. Not appropriate and all that, I suppose. You know how people around here can talk. But it was a real shock. Seems unbefitting him going out like that."

Gertie nodded. "It was dramatic, I guess, but not the kind of drama Gil would have appreciated for his curtain call."

"Exactly," Judith said then frowned. "I guess Tiffany is probably gleefully counting her chickens. She didn't have to wait a lifetime to cash in and be free again."

"You think she married Gil for his money?" Ida Belle asked. Judith snorted. "Who doesn't?"

Ida Belle nodded. "Yes, I suppose that's the general consensus. Have you talked to Liam?"

"Not since I picked up steaks a couple weeks ago," Judith said. "I'm thinking I should go by but honestly, I keep making excuses not to. What the heck do I say to the boy?"

Gertie shook her head. "We took him a casserole earlier today. Said we were sorry, but that's about it."

"How'd he take it?" Judith asked.

"As well as can be expected, I suppose," Gertie said. "He thanked us for the food and the sentiment but said it didn't matter to him."

Judith sighed. "He's lying, of course. I don't believe for a second that Liam didn't still love his dad. He just didn't like him overly much. And he's still carrying around a whole lot of mad. Not that I blame him, mind you. Hell, Gil's dead and I'm still carrying around some mad at the way he treated Liam."

"It was a really bad situation," Ida Belle said. "It's a shame Gil died before they could reconcile."

Judith sadly shook her head. "I doubt it ever would have happened. Gil would have had to leave Tiffany and apologize for a hundred years before Liam forgave him. He tried to talk to Liam, you know?"

"No," Gertie said. "Liam didn't say and we rarely talked to Gil."

Judith nodded. "Tried several times over the last couple years but Liam wouldn't have it. He even threatened to call the cops on Gil once to get him out of the butcher shop. Liam ended up calling me and I convinced Gil that accosting the boy at his place of work wasn't the way to go about things."

"I guess you heard about what happened last night," Ida Belle said.

"I heard," Judith said, "but I'm not sure I believe it. At least, not the way it was told to me."

"If you heard that someone strapped Gil to a horse and he rode into the middle of the festival, then lost his head, that's pretty much the story," Gertie said. "The horse stopped right in front of us, so we saw it all."

Judith's eyes widened. "You're serious? Good God! What in the world?"

"I wish we knew," Gertie said. "Doesn't make much sense."

Judith looked over at me. "Don't you date Carter? What's he saying?"

I laughed. "Carter never says anything to me about his investigations. He's afraid I'll get in the middle of them."

"Probably because you do," Ida Belle said. "Not that I'm complaining, mind you."

Judith stared across the park, silent for several seconds, then looked back at us. "You know, the whole thing feels off to me. Not that stunt last night. Obviously, that's way off. I can't even imagine where that came from or why, and I'm not even going to try. But Gil's death, I mean. It doesn't sit right."

"I thought it was a carjacking," Ida Belle said. "Sounded like standard fare for New Orleans."

"It did," Judith agreed. "But the last time I saw Gil, he was worried about something. I thought it had to do with Liam but when I asked, he dismissed it completely and I could tell he was telling the truth, at least about that. But something was bothering him. Then he asked me to recommend a good pistol and I knew for sure something was up."

"Gil didn't own a gun?" I asked. "I thought everyone in Sinful owned a gun."

"He had a shotgun for home defense," Judith said. "But he never was much for local sort of pastimes. Didn't like to hunt or fish. Mostly he was into his acting and not a lot else."

"Did you ask him why he wanted a pistol?" Gertie asked.

"Of course!" Judith said. "When a man you've known your whole life, who's never shown an interest in guns, is suddenly asking you for advice on acquiring one, you take notice. But he just said that he figured it was smart to have one with all the late hours he kept with rehearsal in New Orleans. And they traveled to different cities. It's not like I could argue with him in theory, especially now. Maybe if he'd followed through with the purchase, he wouldn't be dead."

"But you don't think that's why he wanted it?" I asked, because something in the way Judith delivered the information said that what she heard from Gil wasn't exactly what she thought was the truth.

She stared at me for a couple seconds then shook her head. "You know, I don't know that I do. There was an undercurrent—something was going on that Gil wasn't talking about. Then he turns up dead and I can't help wondering, even though it seems aboveboard. I mean, as aboveboard as a carjacking can be."

She blew out a breath. "It's probably just nerves or me being upset over him being gone. Pay no mind to me. Well, it was good to see you ladies and good to finally meet you, Fortune. But I think I'm going to head home and soak my feet. They did a lot of walking today."

We said our goodbyes and watched as she crossed the park and disappeared down the dark street. I watched the dark spot where she'd gone from view, then finally looked over at Ida Belle and Gertie.

"Is Judith prone to drama like her good friend Gil was?" I asked.

"Lord no," Ida Belle said. "She's a farmer. They're usually the opposite of drama."

Gertie nodded. "Farmers kinda own practicality."

"Then maybe we're looking at this all wrong," I said

"What do you mean?" Gertie asked.

"Take the horseman thing out of the equation and what do we have?" I asked.

"A man who was killed in a carjacking," Gertie said.

"Exactly," I said. "A man who was killed and a young wife, who used to be in love with his son and who will inherit a lot of money. A man who was recently inquiring about firearms for protection."

"You think the carjacking could have been staged?" Ida Belle asked.

"Why not?" I asked. "It would push suspicion away from the wife. After all, it happened in another town, not their house. And wives usually go for poison."

"But surely you don't think Tiffany drove to New Orleans, killed Gil, and managed to get his car stashed. You met the girl."

"I don't think she did it alone," I said.

They both frowned and I knew they were thinking about the conversation I'd overheard between Tiffany and Liam.

"But then why pull the Headless Horseman thing?" Ida Belle asked.

"That is where my theory departs from logic," I said. "Unless the car is found."

"Lots of places to hide a car in this state," Gertie said.

"I think we need to redirect our focus for a bit and find out everything we can about that carjacking," I said. "Just to be sure."

"And apparently about Tiffany and Liam," Gertie said and frowned.

I nodded. "I'm afraid so."

"Well, we can't do it tonight," Gertie said, "so I vote we head for the maze."

"Sounds good," I said.

The maze was in full swing with a line when we arrived. We took our places at the end and waited as we heard the screams of terror and joy and spotted people running out the exit where the monster with the chain saw chased them. That had been Ida Belle's usual gig.

"Are you missing your role?" I asked when I spotted her wistfully staring at a pair of teens running away from the maze.

"A little bit," she said. "Removing us from the maze was the smart thing to do after last year—puts some distance on things even though we weren't responsible."

"First on the scene always gets the blame," Gertie said. "But since we weren't working the maze, I was available to catch another head, so we're right back in the hot seat. I'm really tired of catching heads."

"Yes, it does appear that my calculations were wrong," Ida Belle said. "We wound up front and center for another morbid display."

"A morbid display of another man already deceased," I pointed out.

"Good God," Gertie said. "I hope we don't have some weird copycat, thinking it's a lark to put a dead body in the festival every year."

It was a thought that had already occurred to me, but I wasn't ready to go there yet. Going down that path left the door wide open, because then the only motive was a twisted mind. There would be no logic behind the act. And twisted minds were harder to pin down than one might think, especially in a place like Sinful where hardly anyone seemed normal.

"Well, the first place that needs to up their game is the funeral home Gil was stolen from," I said. "Do you have any idea where his body was?"

"No," Ida Belle said. "But it shouldn't take much to find out. I can tell you, though, neither of the ones closest to Sinful have security systems. At least not that I'm aware of. Stealing coffins isn't much of a thing."

"Much?" I frowned.

"Well, there was an old fisherman who got hacked over the cost to bury his wife," Gertie said. "He stole a coffin and the body and had a pretty good hole dug in his backyard when Sheriff Lee got there."

"I have no words," I said.

"I'll make some calls," Ida Belle said. "It won't take long to find out. Are you going to call the Heberts to get the police report on the carjacking?"

"Yeah, I guess I will," I said. "Although I doubt it's going to tell us much short of the exact location and a range of time."

"Probably not," Ida Belle agreed. "But you tend to see things that the cops don't. It wouldn't hurt to check out where it happened."

"Definitely," I agreed.

"We're up!" Gertie said.

We handed over our tickets and headed into the maze. They'd done a great job, although I sort of missed the guillotine display. It had been replaced with an *Anaconda* theme, which was done well but wasn't as scary as the way it was before. But then, no one could lose a head, so there was that. The mummy display was the same but the mummy itself wasn't nearly as good as Gertie's. She took one look and shook her head.

"That's what we get for allowing people who aren't committed to play these roles," she said as we exited down the hay bale path. "Playing the mummy correctly requires sacrifice, discomfort, and the ability to hold your bathroom needs for hours on end."

I grinned. "Some people just don't have the dedication."

"Got that right," she agreed.

We were approaching the last scene—the chain saw killer—when crap hit the fan. Or the hay bales.

I could hear the chain saw revving but knew it was perfectly safe because the blade had been removed. Quite frankly, everyone in Sinful knew that, but people loved to be scared so they screamed and ran and generally had a great time with it.

Except Celia.

Why Celia felt the need to go into the maze after what had happened last year, I have no idea. But then, Celia regularly showed up in places she had no business being. I heard a scream and was pretty sure I recognized it and looked over at Ida Belle and Gertie. It wasn't the scream of someone having a good time. It was a real scream.

And it was coming straight for us.

Celia burst around the corner, her mouth wide open and the scream still echoing. It took me a second to recognize her, because she'd ditched the Rose Kennedy costume and was dressed as a pioneer girl—dress, apron, bonnet, and carrying a lantern.

And a skunk was chasing her.

# CHAPTER SEVEN

I PIVOTED AND BOLTED BACK DOWN THE PATH TOWARD THE mummy display. I could hear Ida Belle and Gertie running behind me and Celia's mouth, locked in a permanent scream. When I got to the mummy scene, I jumped on top of the coffin and launched onto the top of the hay bales. Ida Belle followed suit and then Gertie gave it a whirl.

Kinda.

She made a sort of hopscotch jump onto the top of the coffin and yelled "Parkour!" but didn't have the velocity to make the next jump onto the bales. She crashed into the side of the bales, then bounced backward into the coffin. The coffin wobbled for a second, then tipped over, spilling the mummy out into Celia's path. Celia's feet connected with the mummy and she went flying face-first into a hay bale wall, where her lantern broke.

Her lantern with a real fire!

The hay bale went up in flames as the confused skunk ran into the middle of the scene and decided everything looked like a threat. He turned around in circles, letting out a toxic stream as he went. Gertie leaped up, jumped over the coffin, then dropped and rolled inside, closing the lid behind her. The poor mummy was so wrapped up he couldn't even stand and finally resorted to rolling facedown, probably to protect his eyes from spray. Celia pushed herself up and half ran, half hobbled out of the scene, the skunk hurrying after her.

Walter and Scooter ran into the maze with fire extinguishers and sprayed foam on the blaze, getting Ida Belle and me in the fray. When only the lantern remained burning, Ronald ran in, wearing a Thor costume, and smacked it with his giant hammer. He looked up at us and shook his head.

"You guys are so rough on clothes," he said. "I'm never lending you anything."

Ida Belle and I jumped off the hay bales and shook the foam off our arms and heads. Walter and Scooter helped the mummy up and he shuffled off, probably high from the fumes on all that wrapping.

"I'm pretty sure I'll never have the need for your level of finery," I said to Ronald. "Although this outfit is a departure. What's up with that?"

"Thor is awesome," Ronald said.

"So is Chris Hemsworth," Gertie said as she crawled out of the coffin.

We all nodded.

"You know," Gertie began, "there was this almost-nude picture—"

"Nope!" Walter said and held his hand up. Then he and Scooter shook their heads and left before Gertie could finish her comment. Ronald looked disappointed but decided he needed to get home to fumigate his costume before the smell of burnt hay and skunk set in.

"Looks like our night is over since Ida Belle and I need a shower," I said as we made our way out.

"Finally, I'm the one with clean clothes," Gertie said.

"It was a fluke," Ida Belle said. "Don't get used to it."

"I wonder how far that skunk chased Celia," I said.

"Hopefully into the next parish," Gertie said.

We scanned the area as we exited the maze. A crowd that had gathered was starting to wander away and I couldn't hear any more screaming, so I assumed Celia had either collapsed somewhere and the unfortunate paramedics were dealing with her again, or she'd run all the way home.

Because we knew how Ida Belle felt about her SUV, we elected to walk home, and as we left the park, I saw a familiar woman duck into a big pickup truck.

"Whose vehicle is that?" I asked. "The big blue truck."

"That's Judith's," Ida Belle said. "I thought she was leaving a while back."

I nodded. "That's what she said."

"Must have gotten caught up with someone," Gertie said. "At least she got to see the show this time. Or hear it. Judith loathes Celia almost as much as she does locusts."

"That's pretty stern words when it's a farmer you're putting them on," I said.

"Celia's tried to cause trouble for farmers before," Gertie said.

"What a shocker," I said. "Celia trying to make trouble for people."

"That's not the big reason, though," Gertie said. "You see, Judith's family is Catholic and when her dad died, Celia raised hell over them having his funeral service in the church."

"Why in the world would Celia care where the man's funeral was held?" I asked.

"Celia claimed Judith's dad cheated on her mom and shouldn't be allowed a 'Godly' service," Gertie said.

"Good Lord, if you denied sinners a funeral service in the church, there wouldn't be any," I said.

"Which is exactly what the priest told her," Ida Belle said. "But Judith has hated Celia ever since."

"Can't say that I blame her," I said. "That's pretty low. The woman's dad dies, and Celia tries to sully his reputation and take away his right to a religious funeral. That's crappy even for Celia."

Gertie nodded. "We always figured there was something else going on there that we didn't know, but whatever it was, Celia wouldn't tell what the bug up her butt was over."

"Probably something imagined or lied about," I said. "Celia's not a fan of seeking the truth, especially if it doesn't suit her narrative."

Gertie grinned. "It's like you've been here all your life."

I laughed. "People like Celia are easy to spot coming. They're miserable and seek to bring everyone down into the mudhole they're wallowing in. It's the quiet ones who are always pleasantly smiling that make me nervous."

"Me too," Ida Belle agreed.

We reached the intersection where we all needed to head different directions and Ida Belle looked at me.

"I'll pick you up tomorrow morning for church," she said.

"I don't suppose we can get out of it," I said.

"Not this week," Gertie said. "If you don't go to church Halloween week, everyone will think you're a devil-worshipper."

"And that's a bad thing?" I asked. "Hey, will Celia be going all skunked up then?"

Ida Belle shrugged. "Probably. But since she's not Baptist, we don't have to care."

I laughed. "I'll text Mannie and request the police report when I get home."

"So what's on the agenda tomorrow after church?" Gertie asked.

"I'm not sure yet," I said. "We already talked to Judith and I want the police report before we head to New Orleans. I guess we should try to talk to that horse breeder."

Gertie nodded. "And maybe we should spy on Liam and Tiffany some more."

"Because the last time was such a success," I said.

"Hey, we got a bit of information, some boudin, and a couple hours in a hot tub out of it," Gertie said.

"As much as I hate to agree," Ida Belle said, "she's probably right. That conversation between Liam and Tiffany bothers me a lot. They warrant a closer look."

"Okay, but no stealing things," I said.

"No getting locked in the meat cooler," Gertie said.

I smiled. "Touché."

I heard a burst of thunder overhead and a couple drops of rain splashed on my face.

"Now it rains," Gertie said. "Could have used it back at the burning maze."

"Oh well," I said. "At least it will wash off most of the foam. Maybe I won't have to mop my floors."

————

I HAD A NICE LONG SHOWER AND SENT A TEXT TO MANNIE explaining what I needed while I heated up some beef stew. He promised me something the next day, which worked perfectly. My corn dog and caramel corn had worn off ages ago and the smell of the stew heating up had me practically salivating. For extra measure, I heated up some garlic breadsticks and gave a piece of cheesecake the side-eye as I closed the refrigerator.

"I'm coming back for you," I said, then turned around to see Merlin staring at me.

"Don't give me that look," I said. "You already had your dinner and you're not going out again. You're going to be fat as a horse before Halloween is over from all those bribes. And I don't have any more fish thawed, so head into the living room and take a seat."

I pointed to the doorway and I swear, if a cat could give you the finger, he would have. Finally, he stalked by and I heard him jump onto what I was certain was my recliner. I had no doubt that when I got up to go to bed, he'd dash upstairs to lie on my pillow. Living with a disgruntled cat was worse than living with a teenager. I was just getting ready to dig in when there was a knock on my door and Carter called out.

"Kitchen," I yelled.

He came back looking exhausted and dripping all over my floor. Since I hadn't mopped it after my own drenching, I figured it didn't matter. He stepped into my laundry room and grabbed a towel, then plopped down at my table.

"You want me to heat up some more stew?" I asked. "I have another serving."

"No thanks. The vendors loaded up Deputy Breaux and me with their leftovers when the rain cleared everyone out. I have enough food for a week. I'll bring some over tomorrow when I can get it all sorted because I'll never finish it before it goes bad. They just sort of threw stuff into big containers."

"That's a good score. I guess being the last one standing and getting wet has a few advantages."

"*Very* few." He ran the towel over his head and his face. "I hate to say it, but I was kinda happy to see the rain. Those two hours gained are going to feel good on my pillow, and hopefully tomorrow will be a slow day, it being Sunday."

I nodded. "The festival has been a bit challenging this year."

He raised one eyebrow.

"Okay," I said. "So last year wasn't exactly a picnic. What happened to Celia, anyway? Did she run all the way home and have a heart attack? Please, please, please."

"I'm going to give you a pass on that somewhat horrible comment given who it was about. And no, unfortunately for all of us, Celia did not run home. Instead, she stood around braying about filing a police report and making everyone within a ten-foot radius's eyes bleed. I finally told her I wasn't even going to listen to her a second longer until she'd bathed in tomato sauce for a week."

"What the heck is she going to file a report on—the skunk?"

"She's insisting that someone tossed the skunk into the maze."

I held my hands up. "We were behind her."

"I know where you were. I got a detailed report with much laughter from Walter and Scooter and a somewhat disturbing recount of Thor worship by the three of you and Ronald. Besides, there's fire extinguisher foam in your living room to back up their story."

"Crap. I'm going to have to mop, aren't I?"

He shrugged.

"So how did Celia propose that someone tossed a skunk into the maze?" I asked.

"She said as she was headed for the exit, that the skunk flew into the maze, right at her. Like someone had done a low toss of him into the last tunnel."

"But that's crazy. If someone was carrying around that skunk, they'd be as stinky as Celia."

"Exactly. And since Gertie doesn't smell, I figure it's all bunk."

I shook my head. "We get blamed for everything around here. And why? This town is full of crazy people."

"Oh, I never said it was crazy. Risky, yes, but if someone could manage to throw a skunk at Celia for a good laugh without getting sprayed themselves, I'm not sure I'd call that crazy at all."

"Yeah, but even if someone let that skunk loose, they couldn't guarantee it would chase after Celia."

"And that's where her 'I was targeted' theory falls apart." He rose from his chair. "Anyway, I'm going to head out, get a shower, eat some food, and try to get eight solid hours."

"Well, I'm not going anywhere but to the living room to watch TV and then to bed, so you won't be getting a call about me."

"You know, most boyfriends would hear 'you won't be getting a call *from* me,' not '*about* me.'"

"You're not most boyfriends."

He laughed and leaned over to give me a kiss. "'Night, Fortune. Turn on your alarm after I leave."

I waited until the front door closed behind him and heard the lock click into place, then grabbed my phone and armed the alarm. I knew he'd be standing out there in the rain waiting to hear the beeps. A more determined woman would have let him stand there a bit, but I took pity on him. It couldn't be easy dating me. I looked at Walter and Ida Belle and thought Walter deserved sainthood. Carter would probably be sitting on the right-hand side of God after putting up with me.

I polished off my dinner and headed into the living room, ignoring the foam on the floor. Then I moved Merlin to the couch and sank into my recliner. I clicked through the channels and stopped when I saw Thor.

What the heck. Ronald was right. Thor *was* awesome.

# CHAPTER EIGHT

I HAD AN EXCELLENT NIGHT OF SLEEP, FOR A CHANGE, probably because I locked Merlin out of the room and turned up the stereo so I couldn't hear him. I was careful exiting the next morning, though. He'd paid me back before by leaving small objects on the stairs. And since I usually put on my shoes downstairs, that meant anything from stepping on a sharp object to plummeting down the stairs from slipping on a smooth object was on the menu.

But suspiciously, nothing was out of place.

I went into the kitchen and saw Merlin sitting calmly on his cat bed, licking his paws. Uh-oh. Somewhere, he'd done something. I just hadn't found it yet. I let him outside to do his business and went on the hunt. In the half bath next to my office, I found his handiwork. He'd unrolled an entire roll of toilet paper onto the floor. I just scooped it all up and dumped it on the counter next to the toilet. Little did Merlin know that I'd dealt with far worse bathroom situations before. He was going to have to up his game to get the best of a former CIA assassin.

I headed back into the kitchen and fixed his food, then opened the back door and called. He came fairly quickly but he always did when it was time to eat, which is why I'd started letting him out for business before feeding him rather than after, which had been our usual routine. He gave me a hard stare as he strolled in, probably wondering if I'd seen his mess, then sauntered over to the food bowl for breakfast. I pulled on my navy tennis shoes that matched my skirt and striped top, grabbed my wallet, and was on my way to the front door when I heard Ida Belle honk.

Gertie had been right about church. The place was packed. Ida Belle was doing her thing in the choir, so Gertie and I squeezed into a back pew, ready to make our break for the café. I wondered if Celia had shown up across the street to stink them all out, but figured I'd know in an hour when I went sprinting out.

Even though I'd gotten a good night's sleep, I found myself nodding off during service. Pastor Don was a nice man but made watching paint peel look attractive. Finally, Gertie elbowed me and we rose to sing the final hymn. When Pastor Don started the prayer, I readied myself for the run.

As soon as he got the 'Amen' out, I bolted for the door. Across the street at the Catholic church, the doors flew open and Celia ran out, a determined look on her face. I just shook my head when I felt a hand on my arm and turned to see Gertie standing there.

"Let me get this one," Gertie said.

I looked down and realized she'd changed into tennis shoes and waved her on. "Go for it."

Celia had gotten a tiny jump on Gertie but I wasn't worried. Besides, if things went sideways, I could always tag in and take over. Celia's only backup was Dorothy, and she wasn't going to ever win a footrace, not even against a turtle. I jogged behind them, leaving a fifteen-foot gap, and watched as Gertie turned on the afterburners as they neared the café. Surprisingly, so did Celia.

Someone had been practicing.

I readied myself to make the pass when I saw Judith Trahan pull something large and white out of the bed of her pickup truck just as Gertie and Celia got near the café. The large white thing flew out of her arms and right into Celia's face and I realized it was a chicken. Celia flung her arms out, striking Gertie in the face, and Gertie barreled body-first into Judith's pickup truck. I slowed to a walk and strolled past Celia, who was on the ground wrestling the chicken, gave Judith a high five, and waved at Ally, who was just inside the doorway, to secure our table and banana pudding.

Ally was laughing so hard she was crying but she managed a nod before heading off.

I helped Gertie up and made sure she hadn't dented Judith's pickup truck, but there were so many dents already that I couldn't tell if Gertie had added to the mix. Francine walked outside, shaking her head. No way I was going to miss the end of the show, so I stayed put.

"Good Lord, someone save that chicken," Francine said, glaring down at Celia, who was still flailing about with the poor chicken. "And you are not coming in my café. I could smell you when you left the church. Maybe head back there and see if a bath in holy water can fix that."

Judith grabbed the chicken and shoved it into a cage in the bed of her truck, and we watched as Celia scrambled up and glared at Judith.

"You did that on purpose," Celia said.

"I was taking the chicken out to show Francine," Judith said. "You ran right into it. This is totally on you. And since you shouldn't even leave your house before the EPA clears you, that makes it further your fault. If you hadn't been out running, it wouldn't have happened. Now, if you'll do us all a favor and leave before my chickens start dying from the smell."

"My eyes are watering," Gertie said.

"Leave or I call the cops," Francine said. "I have the right to refuse service, and this is me doing just that. I won't have you driving my customers and my staff out of my café."

Celia's face was flushed so red I thought she was going to pass out, but she knew she didn't have a leg to stand on.

"You'll pay for this," she huffed. "All of you."

We all waved a hand in dismissal and Francine walked back into the café. Ida Belle strolled up, holding her nose as Celia passed, and we filled her in on the finer points.

"What the heck are you doing here with these chickens?" Gertie asked.

"Francine is interested in some of my stock," Judith said. "Some of the older hens are sneaky and managed to hide a nest. They've multiplied so much that I have to get rid of some or build a bigger coop. Since I'm not much interested in the latter option, I talked to Francine. She'd mentioned getting some chickens before and you can't beat free and already laying. Plus, it's getting harder to keep the varmints away. They seem to have multiplied tenfold this year like the chickens."

I pointed to a cage thing with a trap door behind the chicken cages. "What is that?"

"It's for catching varmints," Judith said. "Easier to trap them and relocate than shoot them and hope you don't hit anything else, especially as they're mostly out at night."

I stared at her for a moment. "Varmints...like skunks?"

Judith grinned. "Yeah, they seem to be the biggest offender."

Ida Belle and Gertie started to chuckle.

"How in the world did you get the skunk to chase Celia?" Gertie asked. "Or was it just good luck?"

"I might have spilled a tray of fish juice from the fish fry booth on the bottom of her dress when she wasn't looking," Judith said.

"How did you get the skunk out of the trap and into the maze without it spraying you?" I asked. Skunks as a weapon was something I'd never considered, but I was considering it now.

Judith shrugged. "You mess with them as many years as I have, and you learn how to get around them. And they only spray if they feel threatened. I guess there's something about me that calms them. Well, until I tossed him into that maze. I'm glad you guys didn't get caught in the fray. If I'd known you'd were right behind her, I would have set the thing on her when she got out."

"We weren't right behind her," Gertie said. "In fact, we didn't even see her going in, so she must have lollygagged around in there."

Judith nodded. "She was in there a long time."

"Probably making notes on everything that was done wrong," Ida Belle said. "Celia files a list of complaints with the mayor every year after the festival."

"Well, then it serves her right, now doesn't it?" Judith said.

"I really like you," I said.

———

LUNCH WAS A GOOD TIME, CHATTING WITH THE SINFUL Ladies, especially the recounting of the skunk escapade. And the banana pudding seemed particularly excellent. But maybe I was just in a good mood since I'd actually gotten decent sleep the night before and the dead person wasn't someone I knew or liked. In fact, it seemed from the chatter that a lot of people weren't particularly fond of him. Marrying his son's girl-friend seemed to have put off the majority of the women in the town, anyway.

"Do you think we can catch the horse breeder today?" I asked.

"River Hayes rarely leaves her ranch unless she's showing or selling a horse," Ida Belle said. "The bigger question is whether or not she'll talk to us. She's a huge introvert approaching recluse. I expect she'll go full-on prepper when she retires and we'll never see her again."

"Great," I said. "She's not going to shoot at us when we pull up in her driveway, is she?"

"It's possible," Ida Belle said.

"Probably not on a Sunday, though," Gertie said. "She *is* Southern."

I shook my head. "There is a lot to unpack south of the Mason-Dixon. Well, let's give it a whirl. I'm not going to say a 'shot' because that might be too accurate."

We were headed up the highway when I got a text from Mannie letting me know he'd emailed the police report from Gil's carjacking. I accessed the file and scanned it.

"Well, the police report on the carjacking doesn't have anything worth noting," I said. "Like Tiffany said, the security cameras for the theater were broken and there weren't any witnesses, as Gil was the last to leave. There are no residential buildings that look into the parking lot. Just a bunch of busi-nesses and warehouses that would have been closed already."

"Who found him?" Gertie asked.

"A taxi driver who was new to the area and got off in the wrong district," I said. "Noticed a heap in the parking lot as he drove by and stopped to see what it was."

"Probably wishes he'd kept driving," Gertie said.

"Probably," I agreed. "But he's definitely in the clear. Had fares all night. Doesn't seem to be much else."

"We figured it would be unremarkable," Ida Belle said. "If the cops sniffed anything off about it, they would have come down on Tiffany like a pack of wolves."

"That still doesn't mean it wasn't intentional," Gertie said.

"Oh, I'm not saying that," Ida Belle said. "I'm just saying that if it was intentional, whoever did it was prepared and waiting for the opportune moment. No one could know for certain that Gil would be in the parking lot alone, so that meant waiting for the right moment at the right location."

"But even if they waited for the perfect moment," Gertie said, "they couldn't have known the security cameras were broken."

"Which is why they were probably wearing a hoodie and mask and parked blocks away in a busy area," Ida Belle said. "Remember, Tiffany told us that was the only figure caught on nearby cameras."

I nodded. "And an empty parking lot with no occupied buildings at night meant that if it hadn't been for our lost taxi driver, no one would have found him until the next day. If this was a setup, someone really patient and clever pulled it off."

"Well, I suppose there was no hurry if it was Tiffany and Liam, right?" Gertie asked. "I mean, there was no ticking time clock on it."

"There was no time clock as long as Gil intended to remain married to Tiffany," I said. "But I assume he was smart enough to insist on a prenuptial, especially given the circumstances. So what if their marriage was on the rocks? What if the urgency was because of something *Gil* was up to?"

"You think Gil was sniffing around other fence posts?" Ida Belle asked.

"Maybe," I said. "You said he was full of personality and

acting mattered to him more than anything else. So what if he joined up with this NOLA group and found someone who was a better fit than someone with no interest in acting and who wanted to stay hidden in her house."

Ida Belle nodded. "I like it."

"Me too, except for the part where Liam is involved," Gertie said. "But it has intrigue and drama and a solid motive if we can prove Gil had his eye on another woman."

"That shouldn't be overly difficult to ascertain," Ida Belle said. "We'll just head to New Orleans tomorrow and have a word with this acting troupe. You and I can spot a floozy at a hundred paces and Fortune knows a liar before they even speak. If Gil was looking to change up his romantic situation, we'll know."

"But it wouldn't give us proof against Tiffany," Gertie said.

"No," I agreed. "That might be harder to come by. But if she and Liam colluded on this, or even if she hired someone to take care of it for her, she'll slip eventually. Most criminals do, and Tiffany doesn't strike me as sociopathic. A conscience changes everything."

Gertie sighed. "I've got no particular loyalty to Tiffany, especially after how she treated Liam. But I like Liam. I really hope he's not involved."

I nodded. I understood her sentiment. Liam was the wronged party, and no one wanted to slide him from victim to perp status. I didn't either, truth be told. He'd seemed like a nice guy. But if that nice guy had colluded with his former girl-friend to kill his father, then I was going to take him down.

Ida Belle turned off the highway and we headed down a gravel road. A heavy group of trees lined the access road, but after about twenty feet, the woods turned into open pasture with nice pipe fencing. Several horses grazed in the field and even though I knew very little about horses, I suspected they were well bred. They had that muscled and shiny look that you saw with horses on television.

We turned off the gravel road onto another gravel road and then had to stop at a huge iron gate. There was an intercom on a post, so Ida Belle lowered her window and pressed the button.

"Yeah?" A woman's voice came over the intercom.

"River? This is Ida Belle and Gertie and a friend. We'd like a couple minutes of your time if we could have it. We won't be long."

"What about?" River asked.

"A horse," Ida Belle said.

Hey, it wasn't a lie. And besides, only Gertie had a rule about not lying on Sunday. I'd never heard Ida Belle make that sort of claim.

The intercom went silent and a couple seconds later, the gate started to swing open. Ida Belle pulled through and we followed the winding drive until it finally ended at a ranch-style house with a huge barn. I could see a bayou in the distance and more horses in paddocks around the barn. As we climbed out of the SUV, a woman walked out of the barn.

*Midfifties. Five foot ten. A hundred fifty pounds. Mostly muscle. A tiny limp on the right side—probably an old knee injury. Threat level open, depending on how fast she could draw that gun strapped to her hip.*

She wiped her hands with a towel as she approached and gave us a nod.

"It's been a long time," she said.

"Years, I think," Ida Belle said. "This is our friend Fortune. She moved to Sinful last year."

River's eyebrows went up. "The lady spook?"

"That's me," I said.

"Well, I'm just dying to know what you three could want with me," River said. "One of you looking to buy a horse?"

"Not exactly," Ida Belle said. "I'm sure the police filled you in about what happened in the park the other night."

River nodded. "Kinda had to as some ass—body used my horse Shadow for their stunt. I was mad as heck. That horse is worth a mint in breeding rights. If he'd been injured..."

"I don't blame you," Gertie said. "My bird isn't even worth anything, but I'd shoot someone who tried to hurt him."

"So what's your interest in this?" River asked, looking directly at me. "The police already asked everything they could think of. Not that I had any answers. You don't work for the cops now, do you?"

"Nothing like that," I said. "My interest is more personal, I guess you could say."

"How's that?" River asked.

"The head fell off in front of us," Gertie said. "Actually, I caught it."

River frowned. "That's horrible. But I still don't see what that has to do with me or Shadow. Or why you're here asking about it."

"We're just nosy," Ida Belle said.

River stared at her for a moment, then let out a laugh.

"I like direct," River said. "And truth be told, if that had happened to me, I might be asking some questions myself. But I don't think I can help you. The last time I saw Shadow was when I turned him out in the front pasture around noon. I didn't know he was gone until I went back to collect him that evening and couldn't find him. I scoured every inch of that fence looking for a break and couldn't find one. Then I figured he'd gone over and started to panic. I saddled up and rode myself into a frenzy trying to find him, and here he was running through the park with a dead man strapped to him."

Ida Belle nodded. "It does seem a bit surreal."

"A bit?" River asked. "It's the most absurd thing I've ever heard in my life, and that's saying a lot for someone who was born here."

"I've only been here a little over a year and I get it," I said. "I assume there was a gate that someone could have taken Shadow out of?"

"Sure," River said. "Can't have this much pasture without plenty of gates. You never know when you'll need to access a sick animal or have some other emergency. Don't have time to go cutting and rewelding fences all the time."

"I notice you have a good security system here," I said and pointed to the cameras on the barn and house. "But you don't have any in the fields?"

"No," River said. "Never thought I had to. I only turn the horses out during the day. They're all inside at night and the security for the barn is top-notch. Now I've been rethinking everything. Might have to shell out some cash to get more cameras installed."

"Why put such a valuable horse in that front field in the first place?" I asked.

"Space," River said. "He's a stallion. If he doesn't get to run out some of that energy and attitude, he will tear my barn down. The other pastures aren't big enough for him to get in a good flat-out run. And he needs to—for his physical and mental health."

I nodded. "Seems brazen to take him in broad daylight."

"Brazen doesn't begin to describe it," River said. "I don't go anywhere that I'm not strapped. Hell, I carry this thing into the bathroom when I shower. If I'd caught someone stealing that horse, there'd be one more body in the morgue and I'd be in jail."

"Is Shadow trained?" I asked.

River shrugged. "He's green broke, but I don't spend much time on him. Shadow is here for one thing and that's making more little Shadows. I ride him just enough for him to remember the process."

"So whoever stole him was taking a huge risk that he would even cooperate or not run and hurt himself," I said.

"Which is exactly why I'm so mad about it," River said. "I already told Carter if he figures out who took that horse, I'm not responsible for what I do. Now, if you ladies don't need anything else, I've got stalls to clean."

"I think that's it," I said. "Thanks for talking to us. And I'm glad Shadow is all right."

She nodded and headed for the barn. We trailed back to the SUV and drove off.

"Why *that* horse?" Ida Belle asked. "Who steals a stallion who's barely under saddle and uses him for a stunt like that? The number of things that could have gone wrong is astronomical."

Gertie nodded. "True, but he did look the part. Are there any other solid black horses around?"

"Probably not that look like Shadow," Ida Belle said.

"I assume River knew Gil, right?" I asked.

"They were in school together," Gertie said. "But they ran with completely different crowds. Or I should say Gil ran with a different crowd. River preferred crowds of one."

"Did they ever have any beef with each other?" I asked.

"Not that I saw," Gertie said. "More like they didn't know the other existed. The only people I ever saw River talking to were a couple of guys who did rodeo and Judith. I figured that was because they were both girls working their fathers' businesses. It wasn't exactly the norm for women to take over farming or ranching. They caught a lot of flak for it—'manly girl' and all that crap."

"I wonder if River and Judith still talk," I said.

Gertie shrugged. "She's talking to someone, because she knew about you. But I don't know that they hang out. Neither has the time. I know Judith hires some locals to help when things are really busy, but for the most part, she does it all herself. I've never known River to hire someone, and the care alone of that many horses is a ton of work. Then add the breeding, raising and training so she can sell them, and you've got another two full-time jobs."

Ida Belle nodded. "River's always been an independent cuss. Walter said she's ordered parts for machinery and her vehicle, but she never lets Scooter fix anything. Always says she'll do it herself."

"How much money is in horse breeding?" I asked.

"Not nearly as much as people would imagine," Ida Belle said. "It's hard to make a living, so River handling things herself doesn't surprise me. One good stud, like Shadow, can keep you in the black, but I've never known anyone who got rich off of it. Honestly, unless you just love the work, I can't see why anyone would do it."

"And obviously River loves the work," I said.

"She's always preferred horses to people," Gertie said.

"Well, this visit didn't tell us much," I said. "The butcher shop is closed today, right?"

They both nodded.

"Maybe we could keep an eye on Tiffany's house," Gertie said.

"I don't think that would do any good," I said. "Unless we're planning on following her if she left. If Tiffany and Liam have anything going on, they're not going to meet at her house, especially now that all of Sinful is focused on her."

"You think they'd meet at Liam's place instead?" Gertie asked.

I shook my head. "That seems risky as well. What if Carter has more questions and shows up or even worse, has a search warrant? Unless Liam lives in a busy apartment where Tiffany could hide her car and exit out a back window, it would be a big risk."

"What about your microphone thingy?" Gertie asked. "We could listen in and see if she calls him."

"Phone calls and email would be the kind of thing an amateur would do," Ida Belle said. "Especially now that Carter is sniffing around. My guess is that's why Tiffany showed up at the butcher shop. Either she knew better than to call or Liam was refusing her calls."

Gertie threw her hands in the air. "So what now?"

"Oh, to heck with it," I said. "I'm not interested in going back home, especially with Merlin there plotting ten ways to kill me. Let's find out where Liam lives and see if we can listen in on him watching television or whatever else he's doing on his day off."

I pulled out my phone and did a quick search. Sometimes you didn't get a good hit but this time, we lucked out. At least, there was a physical address. Assuming Liam still lived there, then we were in business. I pulled up the address on maps and passed the phone to Ida Belle.

"It's near the butcher shop," she said. "Looks like a small neighborhood of houses—maybe twenty or so, and his is on the outside perimeter."

"That's good," I said. It would be a lot harder to watch the house if we had to park in the middle of a neighborhood. People in small towns were very aware of what was going on down their street. A strange vehicle just sitting would attract attention. And since Liam had seen Ida Belle's vehicle, we couldn't afford to jaunt around in full view of his entire neighborhood.

"Maybe we should switch cars," Gertie said. "I've had my Cadillac forever so Liam might recognize it, but he wouldn't know Fortune's Jeep. Or wouldn't know it belonged to Fortune anyway, even if he remembered Marge had one."

"What's across the road from his house?" I asked.

"Woods," Ida Belle said. "There's a laundromat a little farther down but it wouldn't have a clear view of his house."

"But we could park there and hike it," I said.

"You think the microphone will reach across the road?" Ida Belle asked.

"We won't know until we try," I said.

"I suppose we don't have anything better to do," Ida Belle said.

Gertie shook her head. "The two of you are something else. Ida Belle is recently married and Walter closes the store on Sundays. Fortune has a hot boyfriend and he's got the day off. And yet the two of you claim you have nothing better to do than stalk around among the red bugs and mosquitoes. Don't get me wrong, I'm happy to be out stalking, but I don't have a man waiting for me since Jeb's got his hip thing going again."

"If I go home, Walter will want to talk about replacing the kitchen floor," Ida Belle said.

"That floor is as old as you are," Gertie said. "Why not do it?"

"Because it's working just fine, that's why," Ida Belle said. "I can't see wasting money on something that isn't necessary."

"Didn't you just pay several thousand dollars for hop-ups on that motorcycle I gave you?" Gertie asked.

"Exactly my point," Ida Belle said. "Necessary."

"You're going to fall right through that floor one day," Gertie said, then looked over at me.

"Don't drag me into this," I said. "I'm still trying to avoid the third degree on the alien-moped thing. Trust me, I only got off last night because he was soaking wet and tired. Besides, we need you to stay far away from Carter until midnight at least since it's Sunday, so better that we stick around and buffer just in case we cross paths."

Gertie sighed. "Mosquitoes it is."

## CHAPTER NINE

WE COLLECTED THE EQUIPMENT, THEN HEADED BACK OUT. Since we were planning to park at the laundromat, we stuck with Ida Belle's SUV. It had more room for the equipment and unless Liam didn't have a washer and dryer in his house and decided he needed clean clothes, we were probably okay. We'd just park as far off to the side as possible, and next to a large truck. The beautiful thing about Louisiana was that there was always a large truck.

We were halfway to Liam's house when my cell phone rang. Carter. Crap! I tried to come up with a good cover but Sundays in the South limited things somewhat.

"Hello," I finally answered, still searching my mind for a reason to not be home.

"Hey," Carter said. "I came by earlier to drop off that food, but you weren't home. I let myself in and left it in the kitchen."

"That's great! Thanks."

"So what are you up to today?"

"On my way to New Orleans with Ida Belle and Gertie," I

said. "Gertie has a date coming up with Jeb and had a wardrobe emergency."

"And she thought you and Ida Belle were the best people to help?" he asked.

"No, probably Ronald is, but she can only handle him in small doses," I said.

"Uh-huh. Walter said Ida Belle tried to pass off that story too. But when he pressed for details, she wouldn't give them."

I glanced over at Ida Belle, who put her hands up. Great minds, but this time it wasn't flying.

"Fine," I said. "You want details—we're shopping for bras and undies. Sexy stuff. But when you get old, things start to droop so you need a lot of support. And without trying things on, you don't know if that support is going to return you to 1980 or 1940. We're looking for 1940, even if it has steel braces to go along with the lace."

There was complete silence on the other end, then he cleared his throat.

"Then I'll talk to you later," he managed, then disconnected.

"That was a thing of beauty," Ida Belle said.

"I wasn't even wearing a bra in 1940," Gertie protested.

"You're not wearing a bra now," Ida Belle said.

"I have this heat rash—"

"No one wants to hear about your heat rash," Ida Belle interrupted. "The point is, Fortune is a genius. Carter and Walter won't dare ask about your underwear, so we won't be asked to prove anything."

Ida Belle exited for Liam's neighborhood and pulled into the laundromat parking lot. As predicted, an enormous pickup truck with tires the height of Gertie was parked close to the end. There was a shrub on the other side, so the only thing visible would be the back end of the SUV. Perfect.

I grabbed the parabolic microphone from the back of the SUV and Ida Belle handled the suitcase with the receiver. Gertie peered around the gigantic pickup truck and declared us clear, so we set off down the side of the building for the woods. I scanned the back of the building as we went and was relieved to see only one door and no windows. No one would see us pass.

We hiked it through the woods parallel to the road until we reached the point across from Liam's house. Ida Belle indicated which one it was, and I recognized the truck from behind the butcher shop as the one in the driveway.

"At least he's home," I said.

"Alone, though," Gertie said. "So unless he's talking to himself, we're not likely to get anything."

I pulled out the receiver and got it all attached to the microphone, then slipped on the headphones and pointed it at the big window on the front of the house to see if we were close enough to get anything. The signal crackled a bit at first, then I could hear a television playing car racing.

"I can hear the television," I said and pulled the headphone off one ear. "If he takes a phone call in the front room, we might be able to get something."

Gertie located a tree stump and plopped down, then opened her handbag and pulled out a sub sandwich. "Roast chicken, anyone? I also have peanut butter and jelly."

"That sounds good but not without something to drink," I said.

Gertie stared. "What am I—an amateur?"

She hauled a soda out of the bag and passed it to me.

"I have another soda, water, orange juice, and some mini vodka shooters," Gertie said to Ida Belle.

"Water please," Ida Belle said. "You know that's why your

shoulder always hurts. Between ammo and half your kitchen, that thing probably weighs thirty pounds."

I propped the microphone up against a log and made sure it was pointed in the right direction. Since the television was still coming through loud and clear, we were good. I was just about to ask for that peanut butter sandwich when a truck pulled up in Liam's driveway. I lifted my binoculars.

"That's Judith," I said.

"I'm glad she's finally visiting Liam," Gertie said. "She always had a soft spot for the boy, and you could tell he really liked her."

"Should we be listening in on their private moment?" I asked.

"Absolutely."

"Heck yeah."

"Alrighty then," I said. "Just thought I'd ask."

I didn't figure there would be anything to learn in a conversation between Liam and Judith, but I supposed it didn't hurt to maintain position. It wasn't like they were going to have sexy-time or anything. But I'd really been hoping that Tiffany would show up, even though I knew it would have been the dumbest thing ever. Still, criminals often indulged me.

"Judith," Liam said when he opened the door, and I could tell he was surprised.

"Hi, Liam," Judith said. "I've been meaning to come by since...well, since everything, but I chickened out every time because I didn't know what to say."

Liam reached out and hugged Judith and she wrapped her arms around him.

"Please come in," Liam said when he broke the hug. "You know you're always welcome here."

Judith went in and he shut the door behind her. Now, as long as they stayed in the front of the house, I could continue to pick up what they were saying. I filled Ida Belle and Gertie in on what was said so far, then I heard Liam offer Judith some iced tea, then silence. If he went to get the iced tea and served it in the living room, we were still in business.

It wasn't long before I heard Judith thank him for the glass. There was a long silence and for a minute, I thought they'd moved to the back of the house, then Judith cleared her throat.

"I thought you were supposed to be out of town," Judith said. "Some conference?"

"Fell through. The boss got sick at the last minute and we had commercial accounts to be delivered this week."

"I see," Judith said. "Look, I know how you felt about your father and I'm not about to try to change your mind. The past is what it is and he's dead and gone now and nothing could change any of it anyway. But I wish you'd consider forgiving him. For yourself. Living with a grudge is hard work. I had one for my daddy and it weighed on me until it almost broke me. I don't want that to happen to you, Liam. You're the closest thing to a son I've ever had and ever will. I don't want you carrying that burden around like I did for so long."

"I know you don't," Liam said. "You're the only person who's ever cared about me except my grandma. But I still don't know that I can get there. Hell, he's causing me more trouble dead than he did alive."

"What do you mean?" Judith asked.

"The cops have come twice already—once to my house, once to the business. They asked to search both places. I let them search my house but said they have to have a warrant for the business or permission from the owner."

"You shouldn't have let them search your house," Judith said.

"What difference did it make? There's nothing here to find.

Nothing at the butcher shop either but since I don't own it, I can't say what's done there, even though the owner will agree to anything to keep the shop's name out of the papers. And even if he doesn't, they'll just come back with a search warrant anyway."

"Is your boss giving you any trouble?"

"He's not happy. He hasn't said anything about firing me or cutting out of our deal, but the bad publicity something like this might bring could put him out of business. If my name heats up with the cops, he won't have a choice."

"Oh, Liam. I'm so sorry," Judith said, her distress clear.

"It just pisses me off. What the heck do they think—that my father screwed me over years ago, so I waited this long to get back at him? And what sort of revenge was that anyway? He would have loved being the center of attention. I bet there's not a person in Sinful who isn't talking about him today. He's probably smiling in hell."

"I agree that it is all very strange. I can't really see the point to any of it. But Liam, I came today because I wanted to let you know that I'm always here for you but also to tell you something important. I don't want you to be surprised by it."

"What now?"

"Your father changed his will a year ago. He split everything between you and Tiffany."

"What?! No way!"

"I witnessed the document myself down at the attorney's office. He said he knew it wasn't enough but it was the least he could do."

"Yeah, well, I don't want his dirty money."

"Come on, Liam. He earned his money and your grandfather earned it before him. His personal decisions might not have been aboveboard, but his business decisions were. Hell, I wasn't even happy with him only leaving you half and told him so. Most of it belonged to your grandmother, and I see no reason that Tiffany should take away a huge chunk of it, especially after what she did."

"What she and my *father* did. And I hold him more responsible than her. He owed me better. But then why should I be surprised? He put himself first my entire life."

"I'm really sorry. I hope this doesn't cause you more problems."

"I'm sure the cops will love it. I'll have even more reasons to be happy the man is dead. I'm guessing they'll see the whole headless thing as insulting in some way."

"It *was* a rather gruesome thing to have happened. I just can't help but think it's someone crazy, you know?"

"Yeah, that was my thinking as well, but what kind of crazy do you have to be to pull a stunt like that?"

"I don't know. You heard about what happened last year, right? Maybe someone thought they'd copy it and it would be a lark. It's not like your dad was killed at the festival."

"That other guy wasn't either. Man, the more I think about it, this whole thing is just weird. Look, I appreciate you coming by and letting me know about the will, but if you don't mind, I think I'm going to get good and drunk until I pass out."

"Please call me if you need anything. Here's the number for an attorney. If the police come after you again, call him. I've already explained the situation to him and told him I was going to give you his card."

"Thanks, Judith."

The front door opened and Judith came out. I picked up my binoculars and watched as she wiped her nose with her finger. Her eyes were red.

"She looks upset," Gertie said.

"With good reason," I said. "Let's head back to the car so I can play this for you."

We got everything loaded up and off from the laundromat without incident. I kept looking behind us, waiting to see Liam, or Carter, or maybe a team of assassins. We never got away this easy. It was a little unnerving.

"What now?" Ida Belle asked as she stopped at the highway access road.

"We can't go home yet," Gertie said. "We won't have had time to go to New Orleans, shop, and get back. Heck, we've barely had time to get to New Orleans."

"Maybe we should go ahead and go," I said.

"But I don't need new underwear," Gertie said. "I found this website called Sexy at Sixty and—"

"Nope!" Ida Belle said and held up her hand. "You are *not* sixty and even if you were, I still don't want to hear about being sexy."

"We don't have to go shopping," I said. "You know I'd prefer we didn't, anyway. I was thinking maybe we could check out the parking lot where Gil was killed while there's no one around. Then maybe late lunch and a movie."

"Oh, it's been a long time since I've seen a movie," Gertie said. "What's playing?"

"*Not Getting Caught by Carter*," Ida Belle said. "It's really popular."

I queued up the audio and played it as Ida Belle drove. When it was over, they both looked troubled.

"No wonder Judith looked upset when she left," Gertie said.

"I'm a little upset myself," Ida Belle said. "This inheritance thing has a serious impact on our faked carjacking theory."

"But Liam didn't know about the inheritance," Gertie said.

"Are you sure?" Ida Belle asked. "Because maybe he just

pretended to be surprised because he didn't want Judith to know that he knew about the change, especially since the cops are certain to ask her about it since she was a witness."

"Crap," Gertie said.

"Things are definitely getting messier," I said. "Since Judith said Gil had tried to contact Liam recently, it might be that he told Liam about the change in his will, using it to try to prompt a meeting."

"Or it could be that Tiffany was told or found out about the change and told Liam," Ida Belle said.

"Or didn't tell him but figured she'd try to pursue that angle again so she'd still have the whole lot in her kitty," I said.

"That's a really low opinion of the girl," Ida Belle said, "but you're right. People have done worse for less."

"So how do we sort it out?" Gertie asked.

"I don't know that we can necessarily," I said. "I suppose the attorney might know what Gil's intentions were with regard to telling Liam and Tiffany about the change, but he wouldn't talk to us. Did Gil have any other friends that he might confide in?"

They both shook their heads.

"Not that I'm aware of," Ida Belle said. "Judith was his only friend in town. Everyone else seemed more surface level. That being said, I don't know anything about his acting buddies in New Orleans."

I nodded. "I think a trip to New Orleans is in order tomorrow to meet those actors and see what we can find out. Rehearsal is Monday nights, right?"

"Another trip to New Orleans?" Gertie asked. "How many bras do I need?"

I waved a hand in dismissal. "I want to look at a hot tub and they're not open today. We're good."

"Is Carter really going to buy that we drove all the way to New Orleans to look at a hot tub?" Gertie asked.

"He will when I buy it," I said. "If it's everything they advertised, I'm going to put that thing on order."

Gertie hooted and Ida Belle grinned.

"I guess you can't argue with a sales receipt," Ida Belle said.

"Especially not when you're going to benefit from the purchase," Gertie said. "I can't wait. That hot tub sitting yesterday worked wonders for my back but good Lord, the stress of listening to Nora is not something I can endure very often. She's kinda the opposite of relaxing, even with all the drugs."

Ida Belle nodded. "Plus you have to be suspect about anything she gives you to eat or drink. I would definitely BYOB if Nora's involved."

"Nora is what, sixty or so?" I asked.

"Try ten years younger," Gertie said. "That's what drugs and booze will do to you."

"And all those random men," Ida Belle said.

"Men keep you young," Gertie said.

"Says the woman who's not married," Ida Belle said.

I laughed. "Okay, so I have to ask, did she work before she fell into a career of finding the best drugs and men all over the world? Was she married to a dealer who passed and left her his fortune? Because her house is well kept and professionally landscaped, her car is new, and all that travel isn't cheap."

Ida Belle grinned. "You're not going to believe me."

"Try me," I said.

"She invented some sort of pipe for weed that went viral," Ida Belle said. "I don't pretend to know anything about it, but she patented it and licensed the patent to some company who sends her money off every sale."

I stared. "Good God. She probably has enough money to buy Amsterdam. What's she still doing in Sinful?"

"People in Sinful leave her alone," Ida Belle said. "If she lived somewhere else, there wouldn't be people she could trust around, and probably everyone would be hitting her up for money."

"Or weed," Gertie said.

I grinned. Sinful never stopped surprising me.

# CHAPTER TEN

THE PARKING LOT WHERE GIL WAS KILLED WAS AS unremarkable as I'd figured it would be. The police report had contained photos, so we knew exactly where his car had been parked and which door he'd exited the building from, even where the body was. The shot was fired at close range straight into his chest. There had been no indication of defensive injuries, so he hadn't had time to react.

"Maybe he was about to get into the car when the perp walked up," Ida Belle said. "Gil didn't hear him until the last second, then turned around and that was it. That would explain the lack of defensive wounds."

"You're probably right," I said. "If the cops had found the car that might have helped clarify positioning given blood spatter."

I scanned the surrounding buildings, trying to find any sign of life, but it was all warehouses and other industrial-type places that weren't open on Sundays and closed down in the evening. Unless somebody was pulling a late night making tools or stocking inventory, it was unlikely anyone would have been in the area that night, much less just happen to be looking out a window when Gil had been shot.

"It looks pretty dead," Gertie said. "So to speak."

I nodded. "The police canvassed the building employees the next day, but no one was working that late, and they suspect the night guard for the building across the street was sleeping on the job. So without witnesses or cameras, let's think about where the killer would have approached from."

"Too many options," Ida Belle said. "Could have parked on another street and walked up. Could have been dropped off by an accomplice. I assume the cops tried to track the car as it left?"

"The report says they canvassed the neighboring blocks for security cameras to attempt to track, but there's no other notation about them so I'm assuming that was a dead end," I said. "I guess short of asking the entire city to check their security footage for that night, they don't really have a way to spot it."

"The city has cameras in a lot of places," Gertie said. "I wonder if they're checking those."

I shrugged. "Maybe, but who knows at what rate. They probably have one or two poor people sitting at desks watching security video all day looking for a needle in a haystack. We don't even know what kind of priority Gil's case would get, even with it being a murder."

Ida Belle nodded. "Unfortunately, there's not exactly a shortage. And if there's a live victim situation, like a kidnapping or missing person, especially a child, that will take priority."

"Exactly," I said. "Add to that, if someone changed out the plates in the parking lot, they wouldn't even know the car was Gil's unless they're running the plates on every silver Mercedes that drives down the street."

Gertie blew out a breath. "And even if they were doing exactly that, it only means the amount of time involved with this and every other case they have to do it for probably pushed Gil's case back to twenty years before anyone touches it."

I nodded. "All this technology but no way to put it together quickly in so many cases."

"Well, I don't know that there's anything else to see here," Gertie said.

"I agree," I said. "Let's grab something to eat and see about that movie. We'll come back tomorrow and talk to some people in the building across the street and then wait for rehearsal and talk to the actors."

And hope they know anything.

———

WE WERE ALMOST FINISHED WITH LUNCH WHEN MY PHONE rang. Carter.

"I'm surprised it took him this long," I said and answered.

"Still in New Orleans?" he asked, and I could tell by his tone that he didn't buy our story at all.

"Yep," I said. "Just about to finish up lunch and head back to the shops."

"Lunch, huh?"

Again with the tone.

"I'm going to switch you to FaceTime," I said.

Once the video pulled up, I flipped my phone around to show Ida Belle and Gertie, who waved, then turned it back on myself.

"Are you at Mother's?" he asked, his tone almost reverent.

"Yes, and I just had the best soft-shell crab ever," I said as I switched back to a regular call. "It's a shame you think I'm a big fat liar or I might have considered bringing you something."

"Fine, so you're really there, but you can't blame me for thinking you guys are up to something."

"Like what?"

"Like poking your nose into my investigation."

"Well, we can't do that at Mother's, so it looks like you're in the clear. And what in the world is up your craw? And why are you at the sheriff's department? I thought you were off today."

"I got called in for a situation."

"What kind of situation?"

"The kind I'm not telling you about."

"Oh, I see. Something happened that you figured we did so this phone call is about trying to prove you were right and we were up to shenanigans."

He sighed. "That's not true. I don't think you had anything to do with this. It's not your style."

"You might as well tell me because if it happened in Sinful, we'll know in probably ten minutes or so."

"Someone left a headless chicken on Tiffany Forrest's porch."

I frowned. "What the heck?"

"I don't know, but it's beyond tasteless and now the girl is scared half to death."

"That sucks. Any idea who would do such a thing or why?"

"I can't begin to think of a good reason why and without a reason why, I have no idea who."

"I don't suppose you can identify the owner of the chicken, right?"

"It was a basic chicken. It's not like people brand or tag them. Anyway, I guess I better start talking to people and see if they're missing one. Assuming they'd even know."

"Okay. I'll talk to you later."

I disconnected and filled Ida Belle and Gertie in. They looked as confused as I felt.

"What is the point?" Gertie asked.

"Got me," I said.

Ida Belle shook her head. "The only thing I could think of is maybe it's someone who really doesn't like Tiffany. Trying to scare her out of town, maybe."

"You'd think they would have tried that before she went through with her marriage to Gil," I said. "What's the point in scaring her away now?"

"Maybe she did it herself," Gertie said.

"To distract the police?" Ida Belle asked.

I stared at Gertie for a moment, then nodded. "A lot of times, if you're a victim, you don't get as hard a look."

"This is Carter we're talking about," Ida Belle said. "He wouldn't cut his own mother slack."

"But does Tiffany know that?" I asked.

"Okay," Ida Belle allowed. "But unless she killed Gil, why does she need to be a victim?"

I shook my head. "That's a good question."

"Do you think it could have been Liam?" Gertie asked.

"But if Liam and Tiffany are in on something, why would he do that to her?" Ida Belle asked.

"Maybe so she'd leave town," Gertie said. "And not try to contact him anymore. If Carter sees the two of them together, he'll start digging deeper, and my guess is he'll get on the same track we are."

"Especially when he hears about the will," I said.

"Could be Liam and Tiffany cooked up this plan," Ida Belle said. "For whatever reason, I can't picture Tiffany cutting off a chicken head, but clearly Liam wouldn't even blink."

"And he has access to chickens," Gertie said.

"Someone else has access to chickens too," I said. "And doesn't like Tiffany."

Gertie's eyes widened. "Judith?"

I shrugged. "Why not? She's already worried that Tiffany is going to set her sights back on Liam now that Gil is gone."

Ida Belle nodded. "That would be the double blow to Judith if Liam took back up with Tiffany. I'm sure she'd like nothing better than for the girl to cash her check and get out of Dodge."

"Enough to risk a stunt like that?" Gertie said. "I don't know. It just doesn't seem like something Judith would do, especially knowing the cops have got to be watching."

"Hard to say," Ida Belle said. "Woman scorned and all. And with Gil gone, she might figure she doesn't have anything to lose."

"You think she's been waiting on him to dump Tiffany all this time?" Gertie asked.

"She wouldn't be the first to waste her life on a man who was never going to give her the romance she was looking for," Ida Belle said.

"Then let's muddy the waters even more," I said. "What if Judith told Gil how she felt, and he told her it was never going to happen? What if she decided that if she couldn't have him, Tiffany darn sure wasn't going to either?"

Ida Belle shook her head. "We really need to figure out this carjacking thing. Do you think the detective assigned would talk to us? I know they're not fond of PIs."

"It wouldn't hurt to try," I said. "Since this case isn't likely to win someone a promotion, he might be willing to talk. Let me call and see if he's working today."

I called the main number and asked for Detective Casey. I expected to get voice mail and was surprised when a woman answered the phone.

"Casey," she said.

"Hi, Detective Casey," I said. "My name is Fortune Redding and I'm a private investigator looking into some odd business concerning Gilbert Forrest. I understand you're in charge of the investigation concerning his death."

"Yes, I am," she said, her voice clipped, but I didn't hear any underlying derision.

"I was wondering if you'd be willing to chat with me," I said. "It shouldn't take longer than a couple minutes."

There was silence for several seconds and I could just imagine her weighing the options of whether to blow me off or meet in case I had something relevant to her investigation.

"I'm about to break," she said. "If you can meet me at Mo's Coffee in ten, then I can give you a few."

"Sounds great," I said. "Thanks."

I smiled. "We're on."

# CHAPTER ELEVEN

Mo's Coffee was only a five-minute drive away in Sunday traffic and we found a parking spot about half a block away. Detectives wore street clothes, but I figured I'd still be able to pick her out of a crowd. Cops had a certain look. Other cops and criminals knew how to spot it. I figured I fell under the sort-of-a-cop designation. I scanned the place when we went in but didn't see anyone who fit the bill and no one studied us, so we headed for an empty four-top in the corner to wait. About five minutes later, Detective Casey walked in.

*Midthirties. Five foot ten. One hundred forty pounds. Excellent physical conditioning and a walk that had purpose. Threat level high for criminals.*

I waved to her as she scanned the room. She hesitated a second after taking in Ida Belle and Gertie but headed our way. I rose and stuck out my hand as she approached.

"Fortune Redding," I said. "Thanks so much for meeting with us, Detective Casey. These are my assistants, Ida Belle and Gertie."

"Call me Casey," she said. "Everyone does. I have to say,

you and your assistants are not the usual fare for PIs. What's your background, if you don't mind my asking?"

"I worked for the CIA," I said.

She raised her eyebrows. "Nice."

"And we're just nosy and old, so we know a lot," Ida Belle said.

"Who are you calling old?" Gertie asked.

Casey smiled at Gertie. "You remind me of my great-aunt. Nothing goes on in her town that she doesn't know about. I take it y'all are from Sinful?"

We all nodded.

"So what's your interest in Gilbert Forrest?" she asked.

"Has anyone contacted you about a recent event concerning him?" I asked. "Besides his death, I mean?"

She shook her head. "Do you have some information for me?"

"More like I have a situation I'm trying to get an explanation on," I said and told her about the Headless Horseman ride.

She stared at me when I finished and glanced at Ida Belle and Gertie, probably waiting for one of us to yell that she was on one of those practical joke shows, but when we all just sat silently, she finally broke her silence.

"Oh my God," she said. "You're not making this up."

"I'm not that creative," I said.

"That's one word for it," she said. "So who hired you to look into this?"

"Technically, no one," I said. "But since the head literally fell into Gertie's lap, we've been asking why."

She shook her head. "I would be too. So what do you think that has to do with the carjacking?"

"I don't know that it has anything to do with it," I said.

"But it got us thinking and we wondered if maybe the carjacking was a cover."

She frowned. "You think someone intended to kill Forrest and they made it look like a carjacking."

"Is that a possibility?" I asked.

She shrugged. "As good a one as anything else, I suppose. Unfortunately, I haven't made much headway. No witnesses. No working security system. No recovery of the car, so no forensics to speak of."

"What about the car leaving the parking lot?" I asked. "Were you able to track it at all on other streets?"

"Not exactly," she said.

"What do you mean?" I asked.

She glanced around, then leaned in. "Look, I never told you this, but the department is really low on staff to review hundreds of hours of camera footage. I collected it but the backlog is bad. Really bad. So...so I have my kid working on it. She's a criminal justice major and intending to follow in my footsteps, but if the department knew I had a civilian looking at footage..."

I blinked. "You have a kid in college? Holy crap! You don't look old enough."

She grinned. "I'm forty. Clean living."

Gertie snorted. "That explains my wrinkles."

"So did your daughter find anything?" I asked.

"She found a car the same as Gil's on a couple blocks, but the plates didn't match," Casey said. "I ran the plates and they belonged to a total loss that went to the junkyard years ago. She lost the car on the highway, though."

"What about the owner of the total loss?" I asked.

"Died in the car wreck," she said. "The junkyard claims the plates weren't on the car when it came there, but who knows. I spotted four sets of plates just standing in the drive. The owner is old and doesn't seem to care much about what's going on at his business. Is there anything beside the Headless Horseman thing that makes you think this wasn't a regular carjacking?"

"Did you do much background work on Gil?" I asked.

"I know his wife's a lot younger than him," she said. "She ID'd the body. But she didn't strike me as someone who had the mind to plot a murder."

"And maybe she doesn't," I said. "But before she married Gil, she'd been dating his son for years. I guess it just calls some things into question."

Casey whistled. "Yeah, that puts a different light on things. Man, I wish I had something to go on, but I honestly don't. I mean, except for gut feeling."

"Gut feeling is good enough for me," I said. "What's it telling you?"

"That there's more to this than what I see," she said. "I can't tell you why but it just doesn't sit right. Never did. And then you tell me about this incident at the festival and the wife and Gil's son, and I have that feeling all over again. But unfortunately, I don't have an avenue to pursue in that direction."

I nodded. "I understand and agree. There's a lot of movement under the surface. I just wish some of it would come up for air."

She checked her watch and stood. "I've got to get back. I've got an interview, but here's my card with my cell number. Let me know if you find anything. You've got my mind going in a million directions."

"Can I ask a favor?" I asked as I gave her one of my cards.

She raised an eyebrow. "Another one?"

"Yeah, well, you see, I'm sorta poking my nose into police business without an actual client, and my boyfriend tends to get aggravated when I do that, so if we could just keep this conversation between ourselves, I'd really appreciate it."

She frowned. "You don't strike me as the kind of woman who would let a man tell her what to do."

"Oh, I don't, which is why we have issues. You see, he's a deputy in Sinful—kinda runs the place really since the sheriff is a hundred and eighty-two years old."

She laughed. "A deputy and a PI who is former CIA. Yeah, that relationship isn't going to have any bumps. But don't worry. Your secret is safe with me unless I have to go on record with any of it."

"Thanks," I said and she left.

"What do you think?" Gertie asked.

"I think Detective Casey is one smart cookie," I said. "And if she doesn't like the feel of this then there's probably something to it."

---

It was evening before we arrived back home. I took pity on Carter and had a box of pralines in tow. The movie had been a good action flick and we'd all enjoyed it, but I was glad it hadn't required much concentration since I couldn't stop my thoughts from wandering back around to the carjacking, the headless chicken, the stunt at the festival, and the conversation between Liam and Tiffany. I knew it must all tie together but I just couldn't figure out how. I needed more information, and I was hoping the acting troupe could fill in some gaps.

Carter swung by my house shortly after I got home. I was heating up some of the food he'd brought over when he called out from the front door. I yelled him back and he trudged into the kitchen and sank into a chair, looking mentally and physically exhausted.

"A person really shouldn't look that bad on his day off," I said and grabbed him a beer.

"I shouldn't feel this bad either."

"You look like you've been on a CIA mission. All of this is not over a headless chicken."

"That was just the start of my fun day. After the headless chicken, I got a call from two fishermen whose boat was stuck on something submerged in one of the bayous. Deputy Breaux and I set out in the sheriff's department boat because it has the biggest engine, figuring we might be able to pull them off whatever they were hung on."

"But you couldn't?"

He shook his head. "By the time we got there, the tide had been going out for an hour and they were even more stuck than before. I told them to tie off their boat and we were going to give them a ride home and then address it again when the tide was in tomorrow morning. But then Deputy Breaux poked an oar into the water below the boat and said it wasn't something natural, like a tree."

"Another boat?"

"I wish. I looked over at the bank and a little ways upstream, I saw tire tracks leading down the embankment."

"If the tire tracks were still visible in the marsh grass, they were fairly fresh."

He nodded. "I got a bad feeling about the whole thing, so I called for a recovery vessel. And you'll never guess what we hoisted out of the bayou."

"Gil Forrest's car."

He stared at me for a moment, then shook his head. "You don't think his death was a carjacking, do you?"

"Let's just say it sounded sketchy before and now I don't buy it at all."

"Just once, I'd like someone to die normally in this town."

"There was that guy who had a heart attack last week."

"While walking down the road wearing his granddaughter's tank top—and that's it—and carrying a toilet plunger like an Olympic torch."

"Okay, so not exactly normal but it *was* natural causes. That might be as good as you get."

He sighed.

"You want me to heat you up some of this food?" I asked. "I was just about to eat."

"No. I've got plenty more at home and after being in the bayou all afternoon, I really want a shower more than anything else."

I grabbed the box of pralines off the counter and set them in front of him.

"So I guess Tiffany and Liam just topped the suspect list," I said.

"You know I can't talk about it."

"Whatever. I'm not an idiot. Young wife who married for money. Son who got thrown over by the young wife and his own father. It's not exactly a Hallmark movie. And if that carjacking was even remotely legit, that car stolen in NOLA wouldn't have wound up in a bayou in Sinful."

He rose from the table. "I'll leave you to your speculation. I shouldn't have even told you about the car, but the recovery guys are regulars at the Swamp Bar, so it will be all over by tomorrow morning."

My cell phone rang and I showed Carter the display. Ida Belle.

"You're underestimating the Sinful grapevine," I said.

He leaned over to kiss me, then headed down the hallway. "I don't know anything about that phone call or what you're about to do."

I waited until he'd left and then called Ida Belle back.

"Carter just left," I said when she answered. "He told me about the car."

"Was he drunk or ill?" she asked.

"Neither. He said the recovery guys would have it all over by tomorrow. I told him he was shortchanging the speed of gossip."

"By a good half a day," Ida Belle said. "Looks like we were on the right track."

"You know, I wish being right made me happier."

"I guess we have to take a harder look at Tiffany and Liam. Do you still want to talk to the actors tomorrow?"

"Yeah. If any of them had gotten close to Gil, they might know something about his personal life that casts a different light on one of them."

"You're still thinking he might have been fooling around."

"It's a possibility. And if Tiffany found out and thought that meant she was going to be kicked off the money train..."

"A dead husband is worth more than a divorced one."

# CHAPTER TWELVE

GERTIE AND IDA BELLE PICKED UP PASTRIES FROM Francine's the next morning and we cooked some eggs and bacon at my house because we needed to meet without being overheard. Gertie said it had been a good call on my part as she'd had a time getting out of Francine's with the box of pastries. Everyone had wanted to talk about Carter finding Gil's car, what she'd heard, and what it meant.

"I swear they were waiting to pounce on me when I walked in the door," Gertie said as she served up the eggs and bacon.

"This is big news," Ida Belle said. "Everyone in Sinful has opinions on things and most aren't afraid to air them, but everyone had strong opinions on the Gil-Tiffany-Liam situation."

"Anyone on Gil's side?" I asked.

"I wouldn't say necessarily on his side but some of the more questionable men were high-fiving him behind backs," Ida Belle said.

I rolled my eyes.

"Carter didn't," Gertie said. "Which you probably already assumed. Carter was disgusted with the entire thing."

"So was Walter," Ida Belle said. "He told me he was glad Gil was cheap and preferred to shop up the highway because then he didn't have to worry about forcing politeness every week."

"I imagine most decent people were outraged," I said. "It's one thing for an older man to hook up with a younger woman. God knows we've seen that one since the dawn of time. But when it's your son's girlfriend, it adds this whole layer of wildly inappropriate and disgusting to it."

My cell phone rang and I glanced at the display.

"Detective Casey," I said when I answered.

"I just got off the phone with a Deputy LeBlanc from Sinful," she said. "Is that your man?"

"He is."

"Did he tell you about finding Gil's car or is he trying to keep you in the dark?"

"He told me. No point in trying to hide it. The recovery guys had it spread across town an hour after they pulled the car up."

"Ha. I guess that's the advantage and disadvantage of living in a small town."

"Definitely."

"Well, it looks like both our guts were right."

"Yeah, and unfortunately, it looks like the killer is from Sinful."

"I've already talked to my captain and changed the scope of the investigation. Deputy LeBlanc didn't sound overly pleased that he wouldn't be taking point, but that can't be helped. The murder happened in New Orleans, and we already had an open case for it. The location and suspects are all that's changed."

"Well, if there's anything we can help you with, just let us know."

"I appreciate it. And unfortunately, from this point on, I can't really speak to you about the investigation until I've reached some sort of conclusion. But I figure I know your type well enough to know you're not going to stay out of this—especially since you know the people involved. So I'll just give you a warning—don't get caught. My captain has a real beef with PIs. He wouldn't hesitate to jail you over here for interference."

"Thanks for the warning. We'll be careful. Good luck."

I hung up and relayed the conversation.

Gertie sighed. "How come everyone has a problem with PIs? No one wants us to have any fun."

"I'm sure we're welcome to have all the fun we want as long as it doesn't involve police investigations," Ida Belle said.

Gertie waved a hand in dismissal. "Where's the fun in that? All these insurance things and women thinking their husbands are cheating isn't fun. Nothing makes the adrenaline rush like chasing down a killer."

I nodded. "Well, it's not going to stop us, but we definitely have to be careful. The good thing is that Casey's captain doesn't know us or our MO, so it should be easier to fly under their radar. The bad thing is that he's not Carter so we're not likely to get even a hair of a pass on anything they *do* catch us doing."

"What about the acting troupe?" Ida Belle asked. "You still want to question them?"

"I do," I said. "With Casey focused on getting the dirt on Sinful suspects, she won't be looking at the acting troupe right away. But I'd still like to see if any of them got close enough to Gil to know his personal business."

"Like if Gil was hound-doggin'," Gertie said.

Ida Belle nodded. "According to Tiffany, rehearsal starts after regular work hours. So what's our cover for not being at the festival tonight?"

I frowned. "Crap."

"We're still going to look at hot tubs, right?" Gertie asked. "What time do they close?"

"Six, I think," I said.

"Do you think it's going to take long to buy the thing?" Gertie asked.

I shook my head. "If I like it, I'm buying it. No financing."

"Then let's just say we got there midafternoon but the sales guy you talked to on the phone had to bounce for an emergency and wouldn't be back for a couple of hours. Since you didn't want someone scamming his commission, we stuck around until he got back and then we decided to grab some dinner and wait for work traffic to die down before heading back. We figured we'd just skip the festival because we weren't working it anyway. And besides, the two nights we *have* gone we had run-ins with a dead man and a skunk."

"That's very detailed and logical," I said, trying to keep the surprise out of my voice.

"Yeah," Ida Belle said. "What gives?"

Gertie shrugged. "Maybe Fortune is rubbing off on me."

"I carry a wallet in the pocket of my jeans and admit my real age," I said.

"Okay, so you're not rubbing that much," she said and we all laughed.

"So what now?" Gertie asked. "We have the morning to kill."

"It's time to do some legwork on Tiffany," I said.

---

Since I figured Casey would make a beeline for Tiffany first thing, we decided to start our legwork with a background check. That meant making a trip over to Mudbug, a town I referred to as Sinful's equally colorful cousin. Gertie had an old schoolteacher acquaintance there and figured she'd be up for a gossip session, especially given all the recent drama. Gertie also knew the teacher favored good whiskey in her coffee, so I'd retrieved a bottle of the quality stuff from my stash and we were armed and ready.

We elected not to call first because people had a harder time declining company when you were standing on their doorstep, especially when you were holding good booze. And I preferred people have no warning because then they couldn't think about what they might say and what they shouldn't say. I wanted people to say everything that came to mind. A lot of it might be nonsense, but I could parse through that.

The teacher's name was Brenda Randolph, and she lived just a couple blocks from Mudbug's downtown area. Her house was typical of the same fare in Sinful, was painted white with yellow shutters, and had yellow flowers in the beds with the shrubs. A black Lab with a silver muzzle looked up from his sleeping spot on the porch as we approached. His tail thumped twice, then he dropped back off to sleep.

Gertie rang the doorbell and we waited a bit, but there was no movement inside. An old Toyota Corolla was in the driveway in front of the garage door, so we assumed she was home. Gertie rang the doorbell again and this time I heard a woman's voice inside, ranting about salespeople interfering with her game shows. A couple seconds later, the door flung open and the woman I assumed was Brenda glared out at us.

*Mideighties. Five foot three. A hundred pounds, maybe. So little muscle content that I wasn't sure what was holding her upright. Only a threat to the whiskey Gertie was holding.*

Brenda stared for a couple seconds, then blinked and scrunched her brow.

"Gertie?" she asked. "Is that you?"

"It's me," Gertie said and held up the whiskey. "How are you doing, Brenda?"

Brenda broke into a smile as she turned around and started walking. "Oh hell, I'm fine. You and your friends come on inside. Here I was thinking somebody was ruining *The Price Is Right* and instead, it's angels bringing holy water."

"Celia would love her," I whispered as we followed her into the kitchen.

"Take a seat," Brenda said. "I'll get some glasses. I assume everyone wants a round?"

"Maybe not for us yet," Gertie said. "We've got to make a trip to New Orleans after we leave here and don't want to get into any trouble on the way."

Brenda nodded. "That's smart. I've always had a firm policy of not drinking and driving."

"I see you still have the old Corolla," Gertie said.

"Yep," Brenda said. "Sixteen years now and only seven thousand miles on her."

I grinned.

"So what can I get you?" Brenda asked. "I can put on some coffee. I made some sweet tea last night. Should be good and cold by now."

"Tea would be great," Gertie said, and Ida Belle and I nodded.

Brenda served us up large glasses of tea and a tea glass for herself, but full of whiskey, and sat down at the table with us.

"Pardon my lack of manners," Gertie said, "but do you remember my friend Ida Belle? And this is Fortune, a new friend of ours, who moved to Sinful a little over a year ago."

Brenda nodded and took a big sip of whiskey. Gertie took that to mean that introductions were acknowledged and proceeded with the purpose for our visit.

"So did you hear about our excitement over at the Halloween festival Friday night?" Gertie asked.

"Sure enough," Brenda said. "I don't think there's a person in a hundred-mile radius of Sinful who hasn't heard. What the heck is in the booze over there?"

"That's a good question," I said.

"Anyway," Gertie said, "the whole thing stirred up all the talk about Tiffany and Liam and since Tiffany was from Mudbug, it made me think of you. So I figured I'd pay you a visit before we headed to New Orleans as we haven't talked in a while."

Brenda took another gulp and shook her head. "Tiffany and Liam...boy, wasn't that a mess? Being a teacher for so long and having all these years behind us...Gertie, *you* know how it's hard to be surprised anymore, but I have to say, that one threw me for a loop."

Gertie nodded. "It definitely stood out."

"I just remember thinking, what the heck was wrong with that man," Brenda said. "Gil, I mean. Not Liam. Heck, Liam was just a boy and a nice one at that. He didn't deserve what they did to him."

"No, he didn't," Gertie agreed. "You know, I never asked you, but why do you think Tiffany did it? I mean, I know sometimes women are attracted to older men, but I never got that vibe from her. Everyone in Sinful figures she did it for the money, but I didn't know her before or anything about her situation with her family. Did she come from a poor family?"

Brenda shook her head. "Not at first. Her daddy worked the oil field and made good money, but he died when she was fifteen or so. Didn't have much of an insurance policy, which surprised me a little, but you know how some men are."

"Thinking they're never going to die," Ida Belle said.

Brenda nodded. "Anyway, Tiffany's mother took up with

this guy—I'd call him a drifter, really, and that's being polite about it. He came through here claiming he was looking for work but all he cared to do was odd jobs—basic labor like painting and simple carpentry. From the moment I met him, I got a bad feeling. Like he was hiding things, you know?"

We all nodded.

"Well, it was hardly any time at all before Tiffany's mother up and married the guy and moved him into her house," Brenda said. "All of it took a toll on Tiffany. She lost weight that she didn't really have to lose. Her eyes had dark circles under them and were sunk in, like she'd been ill for a long time. Mind you, she started to decline when her father died. It was a big life change. The money that used to support them in a decent middle-class style was gone. And her mom didn't have any job skills. She took a job cleaning rooms at the motel after her dad passed and that's what they had to make it on. The only plus was that the house was paid for. Her first husband had inherited it from his parents."

"Was Tiffany dating Liam when her father died?" Gertie asked.

"I don't know that I'd say dating, as such, as they were still kids," Brenda said. "But there was a group from the area that hung out together and Liam was part of it. Hang on a second."

She got up and retrieved a photo album from a hutch and flipped the pages.

"There you go," she said. "I took these at a local rodeo right before Tiffany's dad died. There's Tiffany and Liam on the right."

We all leaned in to look at the photo. It was a group of teens standing in front of a fence. There were horses in the background, and the name of each teen was carefully penciled in below their image. I didn't need the names to spot Liam and

Tiffany, though. They looked the same but younger—that kind of young in the face that you lose when you hit your twenties.

"Who's the sourpuss off to the side?" I asked, pointing to a woman frowning at the teens.

"That's Emilia, Tiffany's mother," Brenda said. "If I remember correctly, Tiffany was supposed to be on punishment for her grades, but she'd sneaked out to go to the rodeo."

Brenda tapped the photo where Liam and Tiffany were. "I think most people could see Liam and Tiffany were sweet on each other, but in a good way—an innocent young teen way. I didn't see any cause for concern back then and trust me, I know the signs of a toxic teen relationship. You know what I'm saying, Gertie."

Gertie nodded. "Oh yeah. So when her father died, did Tiffany keep hanging out with the group?"

"No," Brenda said. "That was probably the second big blow to hit her. That group of kids were big into rodeo and Tiffany had been an up-and-coming barrel racer. She really loved her horse, but after her father died, her mother said they couldn't afford to keep him as they were paying stable fees, food, vet, and entry for all the competitions. When her mother sold the horse, Tiffany stopped hanging out with the group. Stopped hanging out altogether that I could see. I'd spot Liam's truck at her house on weekends, but I never saw them out anywhere from then on...until her mother remarried. Then it got so her mother was always looking for Tiffany because she didn't want to come home."

"What do you think was going on?" I asked. "Abuse? Because I get depression over losing her father and her horse, but that look of long-term illness you described plus the complete shift in behavior says something went very wrong."

Brenda blew out a breath. "I suspected as much. Even asked Tiffany about it a time or too—in a roundabout way, you know. Just trying to get her to open up a bit about the man and what was going on with her life. But every time I brought him up, her face went blank and she bolted."

"Because that's not a red flag," Gertie said.

Brenda nodded.

"Did you try talking to her mother?" Ida Belle asked.

"Of course," Brenda said. "But I could tell straightaway that woman wasn't going to hear anything about anything. She'd always been weak, you know? Had to have someone propping her up. She'd found a replacement and by God, wasn't nothing I or anyone else said going to shift her thinking on the matter."

"So she stuck her head in the sand and ignored the fact that her daughter was likely being abused by her husband," I said. "What a piece of—you know what, that's even too kind."

Brenda nodded. "I talked with the principal and social services and all of them had a go. Just so you don't think I left it at trying to talk to her mother. But Tiffany wouldn't say a thing so there was nothing they could do. The girl just moved like a zombie through high school until she turned eighteen mid senior year. All the teachers wondered if she'd drop out and take off. Well, you could have knocked us all over with a feather when she up and married Gil. No one had seen that one coming."

"I can't imagine you would," Ida Belle said. "No one in Sinful saw it coming, either. I mean, we knew Tiffany spent a lot of time over at Gil's house, but we always assumed she was there to see Liam and preferred it to her own situation as Gil wasn't exactly an involved parent."

"Not as much supervision," Brenda said. "And that's the logical road to take. I wish that had been all it was, but I suspect it wasn't."

"Well, what you've told us explains a lot," Gertie said. "Is Tiffany's mother still with that guy?"

"No, but not by her own choosing," Brenda said. "Shortly after Tiffany married Gil, the state police showed up and arrested him. Seems he was wanted for a series of assaults of high school girls back in Mississippi."

"How did they find him?" I asked.

"Luck. The regular food delivery driver for one of the local restaurants was injured and a replacement was filling in," Brenda said. "Turns out the fill-in driver was from that town where the assaults occurred, and he made a delivery the same day that criminal was doing some painting downtown. He recognized him from the news bulletins and called the cops."

"It's a shame it didn't happen years sooner," Gertie said. "Could have spared that girl."

"Do you know if she talks to her mother anymore?" Ida Belle asked.

"I'm not aware of Tiffany having a word to say to her mother since even before she left," Brenda said. "And I can't say that I blame her. After the arrest, I guess the mother couldn't face the truth of it all. I heard she went into the hospital right after for a spell. Rumor was she had a nervous breakdown. She sold her place shortly after all that and moved up the highway somewhere. The local gossip says she never leaves her house, but I don't have any firsthand knowledge on what she did after leaving here, so that could be drama made up by the bored. Don't care what happened to her, truth be told. It's women like her make the rest of us look bad."

Gertie shook her head. "What a sad, sad thing. All the way around."

"And then Gil gets killed for his car, which wasn't necessarily surprising given the times and he was in the city," Brenda said. "But that stunt at the Halloween festival...well, I just don't know what to think."

We all nodded. Apparently the news of finding Gil's car in a Sinful bayou hadn't made it to Brenda yet, but I saw no point in bringing it up. Brenda had told us everything she knew.

"We don't know what to think either," Gertie said. "It seems so pointless."

Brenda sighed. "Well, at least this time the tragedy struck when the girl is of age and I assume she'll have some money to get on with things. It's better than she had before."

# CHAPTER THIRTEEN

WE CLIMBED INTO IDA BELLE'S SUV AND HEADED BACK FOR Sinful. As soon as we drove off, we were all exclaiming at once, clearly outraged by what we'd heard.

"It certainly explains a lot," Ida Belle said.

I nodded. "It does. I wonder if Tiffany ever told Liam what was going on."

"I doubt it," Gertie said. "Liam wasn't much of a tough guy, per se, but I can't imagine him knowing something like that and doing nothing."

"Even the weak can fire a gun," Ida Belle said. "And besides, if Liam had known, he would have told his grandmother, and there's no way Josephine would have let that lie. She'd have raised the roof off of Louisiana."

"True," Gertie said. "And the first thing she would have done is moved Tiffany in with her."

"I just don't get why Tiffany didn't tell someone the truth," I said. "If Josephine would have taken her in, then she had an option. A good one, it sounds like."

"She was still a kid," Gertie said. "One who'd lost her father and had a mother who'd basically thrown her to the wolves for her own gain. I imagine there were all manner of threats involved if she talked. There usually are."

I sighed. "I know you're right, but it still hacks me off."

"The real question is, does this information change our stance on Tiffany as a suspect?" Ida Belle said.

I shook my head. "If anything, it makes it worse."

"How do you figure?" Gertie asked. "All we got was confirmation of our suspicions about why she married Gil."

"There's that part where Tiffany was a rodeo girl," I said. "Which meant she potentially had the skill to handle Shadow."

Ida Belle nodded. "You're right. And since Liam was close with Tiffany and hung out with the same crowd, I imagine he spent a decent amount of time around horses as well."

"So the two of them could have done this," Gertie said. "But why?"

"That's the question," I said.

"That's been the question since this started," Ida Belle said.

"Are we still going to spy on Tiffany?" Gertie asked.

I glanced at my watch. It was approaching eleven, but we didn't need to head to New Orleans for hours.

"Might as well since there's nothing else on our list," I said. "Unless you think the funeral home director will tell us how he lost a body."

Ida Belle laughed. "Last night, I heard from one of the Sinful Ladies who had a connection on that end that the director almost had a heart attack over the whole thing. They had to call the paramedics, who gave him a shot to calm him down. The back door looked like it had been jimmied with a crowbar. But since he's always been too cheap to install a security system, that's all they know."

"Guess he'll be coughing up the money now," I said. "People aren't likely to use his service if they can't be guaranteed they'll have a body for the viewing."

"That definitely wouldn't fit into an advertising campaign," Gertie said.

I nodded. "I noticed Gil's house backed up to the woods. Do you guys know a way around so we can spy from the back? I want to get close enough to use the microphone, but we can't park anywhere near on the street because Casey might be there already or be coming back. And lurking in peoples' bushes is ill advised in a place like Sinful."

Ida Belle nodded. "About fifty yards away is a service road that the utility company uses. Poachers are known to frequent it as well but that's at night. I can pull off where there's a clearing and park. We're not likely to run into anyone."

"Sounds good," I said. "Then let's go get the equipment and head out."

We loaded up and headed for the site Ida Belle had mentioned. As explained, it was a narrow, mostly grass-and-dirt road that ran through the woods. She found a small area cleared of trees and pulled the SUV off the road.

"Looks like we're not the first to park here," I said, motioning to a set of fairly recent tracks.

"Probably poachers," she said. "There's some good deer in these woods, but no hunting allowed, even in season. Protected land and all."

I nodded but walked up to get a closer look at the tracks. Something wasn't completely right about them. On closer inspection, I realized that the larger set of tracks had another laid within it, then separated where the vehicle would have turned around and headed out of the woods.

"Someone had a trailer in here," I said. "Do poachers use trailers?"

Ida Belle frowned. "Not usually. They only take what they can carry out, so it's not like they'd need a trailer for the haul."

I walked forward more to an area just past the tracks that was clear of grass and knelt down.

"This is horse prints," I said.

Ida Belle and Gertie came up beside me and peered down.

"Sure is, and recent too," Ida Belle said.

"You think this is where the killer unloaded Shadow?" Gertie asked.

"The park is only a hundred yards or so through the woods," Ida Belle said. "And where you'd come out is the direction Shadow came from. So it's definitely a possibility, and a good one, really. Especially since everyone knows that no one really uses the road except the utility company and poachers."

"Then it's possible someone saw the vehicle," I said.

Gertie shook her head. "Wouldn't matter if they did. If poachers saw another vehicle already here, they would turn around and head to another spot. And even if they knew the make, model, and the license plate number, they'd never tell the cops."

"Because they'd have to explain why they were here," I said and sighed.

Ida Belle walked ahead of us a ways and pointed. "There's a fairly wide trail here headed in the direction of the park."

"Big enough for a horse?" I asked.

She nodded. "Plenty big enough." She bent over, frowning, and came up with a handful of shrubbery. "It's been cut and recently."

"Someone cleared a path," I said. "So this definitely wasn't some last-minute rush of crazy. This was planned."

Gertie shook her head. "This keeps looking worse for Tiffany. I'm sure she knows about this road. It's practically in her backyard."

"Then let's go see if we can get anything from her," I said.

"The house should be straight through the woods that direction," Ida Belle said and pointed.

We headed back to the SUV and I grabbed the parabolic microphone. Ida Belle took care of the electronics suitcase. Gertie already had her purse so we didn't ask her to help with anything else. And we weren't about to ask what was in the purse, either. Some things were better left unknown, but still, I was sorta hoping she had some snacks. I'd forgotten to grab some at home and my breakfast was burning off fast.

We headed into the woods, following Ida Belle's lead. I had a good idea where the house was in relation to where we'd parked but until I had as many years tromping through Sinful as Ida Belle did, it was more efficient to put her in front. Then Gertie was in the middle and I was rear. That way Ida Belle and I were covering front and back and Gertie was, well... Gertie. This way I could see if she got into trouble and immediately respond versus if she was behind me and my reaction delayed.

It didn't take long to get to the tree line behind Gil's house —or, I supposed, I should start referring to it as Tiffany's house—and we located an old log behind a large bush and sat on it while we unpacked. We got everything set up, and I stuck the microphone in the bush and directed it at the kitchen window.

"Interesting that Gil didn't fence his backyard," I said.

The neighbors on each side of the cul-de-sac had fences that bordered his property so that just left it wide open in the back. I mean, I didn't have a fence either, but I left mine open for the view of the bayou. Gil's view was just a bunch of trees and brush.

"He was probably too cheap to do it," Gertie said. "He didn't like to spend money on much besides himself."

Ida Belle nodded. "And Gil wasn't exactly the outdoorsy

sort. You see that tiny patio and only one lounge chair on it. I guarantee you Tiffany is the only one who's been out that back door in years."

"Explain to me again why Judith has been pining for this guy her entire life?" I asked. "I mean, he didn't like the outdoors and she's a farmer. He didn't shoot guns, and my guess is Judith is probably James Bond with a handgun and a pitchfork. He was only interested in acting and constantly playing a role, and Judith is completely what-you-see-is-what-you-get."

"Attraction is often one of life's great mysteries," Gertie said.

"I guess so," I said. "Well, at least it's convenient for us not to have to try to go over a fence."

"Especially with Gertie's history with fences and trees," Ida Belle said.

"I'm fine with fences and trees," Gertie said.

"Until you climb up on one," I said. "Or have you forgotten that fall in Emmaline's lawn?"

"That was a fluke," Gertie said.

"You have more flukes in your life than you have liver spots," Ida Belle said.

Gertie waved a hand in dismissal. "Do you hear anything?" she asked me.

I shook my head. "Not so much as a peep. Could be in another room on the opposite side of the house."

"Or sleeping or not even at home," Ida Belle said. "I guess we should have driven by and looked for her car before coming out here."

"Not sure it would have made a difference," I said. "The house has a single-car garage. I assumed Gil probably put his Mercedes in there and Tiffany stayed parked outside out of habit. But after that chicken stunt, she might be observing stricter safety regimens."

Ida Belle nodded. "Good point. I was thinking—"

I held up a hand to stop her as I'd heard movement in the kitchen and flipped on the recorder. It sounded like the refrigerator opening. I lifted my binoculars and found a spot to peer through the hedge. The room was fairly dark with only the one window and the sun on the opposite side of the house, but I could see a shadow moving around inside. A couple seconds later, I heard Tiffany's voice.

"I don't know what to do," she said. "This whole thing has gotten out of hand."

There was a pause before she spoke again, and I realized she was on the phone.

"Of course I want to leave, but the cops said I can't," she said. "I can't believe this. I already found a great apartment in NOLA, right in the French Quarter. I wouldn't even have to have a car. Everything is walking distance. And the best part is, if I decide I like it, the owner is willing to talk about selling it when the lease is up. But I'm afraid if I can't get going on it soon, he's going to rent it to someone else."

Another pause.

"Yeah, I have the money stashed for the security deposit and first and last month's rent and all that. But if I make a move so soon after Gil's death, how is that going to look? Especially now that the cops found his car. That detective from New Orleans was here this morning asking a million questions about me and Gil and wanting my alibi for the night he was killed. How am I supposed to have an alibi when I lived alone with Gil? One of my nosy, insomniac neighbors verified that I was watering my flowers that evening and my car was here all night, so I guess there's that. But I don't know if it's enough."

Pause.

"I just can't deal with this anymore. First, I was trapped by my mother and my age and married Gil to get out of it, then found myself trapped again by my own bad choices. For the first time in my life, I'm ready to stand on my own two feet, and I've got to sit and wait again."

Pause.

"What if they're watching me? The deputy had my house searched after that horse thing at the festival. And that detective from New Orleans didn't look like she believed a word I said. The last thing I want to do is get them focused on you."

Pause.

"I don't know why they would be watching me. I don't know how any of this works."

Pause.

"No. She hasn't called again. I haven't talked to her and have no intention of doing so. I really need to see you, though. I'm going crazy locked up here in this horrible house in this horrible town. Maybe we could meet somewhere. Away from Sinful."

Pause.

"That sounds good. I'll see you there in a couple hours or so."

That was it.

I turned off the recorder.

"She's going to meet someone in two hours," I said. "My best guess, based on the rest of the conversation, is the meeting place is in New Orleans."

"So shower and change and the drive," Gertie said. "Which puts her leaving here in thirty minutes or so. Are we going to follow her?"

"We can certainly try," I said. "But that means we've got to pack up and get out of here fast. Then find a spot on the highway to pick up her trail. If we try to follow her out of Sinful, it will be far more likely to register with her."

Ida Belle nodded. "We can get ahead and pull off at the Walmart exit close to the city limits. She's not likely to change course before then if she's going into the city."

"And if she's not?" Gertie asked.

"Then we'll miss her," I said. "But since we have to go to New Orleans anyway, I think we should try. And I need to play you guys this audio and see what you think."

Gertie nodded. "Then let's get this show back on the road."

I had just finished packing up the equipment when things went completely south.

"Skunk!" Gertie yelled.

Ida Belle and I froze, then whirled around and finally spotted the black-and-white menace emerging from the bush over to our right. He took one look at us and wiggled his tail. That was all it took for us to clear the area. Gertie whirled around and ran into the tree she'd had her handbag hanging on, and I shoved her ahead of me with one hand while still clutching the parabolic microphone in the other, then sprinted in the opposite direction of the stink machine.

As I burst through a bush, all of a sudden, the ground disappeared from underneath me and I fell a good five feet before jolting back upright as Ida Belle came tumbling over the edge beside me, clutching the equipment suitcase. I whirled around just in time to get tackled by Gertie, who took us both out, then I scrambled back up to peer over the side of the embankment with Ida Belle, trying to spot the skunk.

"Do you see him?" Gertie asked, her glasses crooked and leaves stuck in her hair.

"There!" Ida Belle pointed as the offender went traipsing toward the far end of the clearing and disappeared in a bush.

"I don't think it's safe yet," Gertie said.

"We can take the long way back," Ida Belle said.

"My purse is on the tree," Gertie said.

Then we heard a crack—like a limb splitting off. We all peered back over the edge just in time to see the branch holding Gertie's purse break loose from the tree and hit the ground. There was a loud clank, like metal striking metal, and Gertie's eyes widened.

"Oh no!" she said.

And then there was an explosion.

# CHAPTER FOURTEEN

WE ALL DUCKED AS DIRT AND THE CONTENTS OF GERTIE'S purse blew past us and then a shower began. A glittery pink shower raining down on us.

"What the heck?" Ida Belle said and started brushing off the glitter as it coated her arms.

"Ooops," Gertie said. "I might have forgotten to take that five-pound bag of glitter out of my purse."

"Who the heck needs five pounds of pink glitter?" Ida Belle asked.

"Strippers," Gertie said. "There's this online group—"

"No!" Ida Belle said and glared. "It's bad enough we'll go to the grave wearing this crap because glitter never comes off. Never. But I am not listening to your reasons for buying it."

"You asked," Gertie said.

"Guys, we need to have this conversation some other time," I said. "Because there are probably ten people calling the sheriff's department right now, starting with Tiffany."

"But the skunk," Gertie said.

"We'll have to risk it," I said. "We can't afford to take the long way."

I scrambled over the bank, then grabbed the equipment from Ida Belle and helped her and Gertie up. Gertie hurried over to her purse's final resting place and scowled at the ground.

"Bear trap," she said. "Lucky none of us stepped in it."

I glanced back and saw the back door to Gil's house opening.

"Go! Now!" I said and took off.

I could hear Ida Belle and Gertie behind me and dialed up the speed. When I got to the SUV, I didn't even bother putting the equipment in the back. I just jumped in the passenger's seat and yelled for them to hurry. A couple seconds later, Ida Belle had us turned around and hauling butt down the trail.

"I bet she was calling the cops," Gertie said.

"You think?" Ida Belle said. "I mean, there was only an explosion practically in her backyard."

"That was a fluke," Gertie said.

"Your flukes are going to get us killed someday!" Ida Belle ranted.

"Which fluke of yours caused the explosion?" I asked. "You didn't have anything lit in there."

"The only thing I can think of is that the bear trap pulled the plug on the grenade when it snapped shut," Gertie said.

Ida Belle whipped her head around to glare at Gertie for a second. "Grenade? Seriously? I suppose you just had it tossed in there next to a meatball sandwich?"

"Tuna salad, actually," Gertie said. "But no, it was in a separate pocket so the pin couldn't accidentally get pulled."

"Glad that one worked out for you," I said.

"You idiot," Ida Belle said. "That skunk was after the tuna. He probably smelled it from a parish away."

"It was a really good sandwich," Gertie said wistfully.

I brushed my face and glitter fell into my lap.

"Don't move," Ida Belle said. "And definitely don't shake. My poor vehicle is going to look like a club—and not the kind I'd frequent."

"Maybe you can talk to Hot Rod about installing a pole in the back seat," I said.

"This is not my fault," Gertie said. "Well, not totally my fault. What the heck was that skunk doing out this time of day?"

"I'll bet it was the one Judith threw in the maze," Ida Belle said. "He has to establish a new territory and den. But the identity of the skunk aside, we have a huge problem. I'm certain Carter got a call about the explosion, and he's going to think of us first. All he has to do is take one look at the explosion site and see it's decorated with pink fairy dust, and he'll be on us like stink on crap."

"We can't go to any of our houses," I said. "He'll check them first if we don't answer our phones. But we have to get this glitter off."

"Not to mention that if we go home, we'll create a trail leading him straight for us," Ida Belle said. "I say we take the back roads to the highway. Then head up the road to the hotel and get a room. Shower this crap off and shake the crap out of our clothes, vacuum my car, and pray. A lot."

"I have a lint roller in my—" Gertie started. "Never mind."

"We'll stop at the dollar store on the way and get some lint rollers or duct tape," Ida Belle said.

"How are we supposed to fix our hair without rollers?" Gertie asked.

"Add ball caps to the dollar store list," Ida Belle said.

"And a purse for me," Gertie said.

"What the heck are you going to put in it?" Ida Belle said. "You don't even have an ID on you."

"I have a small revolver and a can of Mace in my bra," Gertie said.

"Stuffing things under your cleavage is why you have a rash," Ida Belle said. "All that rubbing is bad for your skin."

Gertie shrugged. "Either the revolver and Mace rub or my boobs rub. At least with the first option, the girls are propped up a bit."

Ida Belle shook her head and looked upward but I was fairly certain she wasn't going to get any divine intervention on this one.

"What about the audio?" Gertie asked. "Did the equipment get damaged when we fell over that embankment?"

"This is military grade used in a war zone," I said. "I don't think a little drop is going to affect it. Let me queue it up. It was a phone conversation, so only one side."

I passed the microphone to Gertie, then popped open the case containing the audio equipment, plugged it into Ida Belle's car stereo, and hit Play. A few seconds later, Tiffany's voice sounded over the speakers. When it was over, I clicked off the audio equipment and looked at them.

"Well?" I asked.

Ida Belle blew out a breath. "That's a lot of ground to cover."

I nodded. "So let's start at the beginning. Tiffany has already found a place to live in New Orleans. Now, since I doubt seriously that she ran out to look at apartments the day after Gil was killed, that means she was already in the process beforehand."

"Which means she was leaving Gil," Gertie said.

"And she had some money stashed somewhere," Ida Belle said. "So she's been planning this for some time."

"If Gil gave her money to spend on the regular, it would be

easy to put together a decent stash after seven years," Gertie said.

Ida Belle nodded. "And assuming Gil had a prenuptial, my guess is that secret stash would be all she'd get to leave with, hence the comment about not needing a car."

"Okay," I said. "Next question. Do we think she was talking to Liam?"

Ida Belle shrugged. "I wish we could have heard the other side of the conversation. It might be Liam but a couple things don't suit. Like her saying she didn't want to send the cops sniffing around whoever she was talking to."

"Ah," I said, "but her exact words were she didn't want to cause them to 'focus' on this person, which might mean they're already looking at this person, just not hard."

"But aren't they looking hard at Liam?" Gertie asked.

"I don't know," I said. "It's Casey's investigation now, and she has to revisit some of the ground Carter already covered so she can get her own read on things. Maybe she hasn't gotten to Liam yet, especially as she probably doesn't know about Gil changing the will yet."

"Okay, so if it's not Liam, then we could have a mystery man on our hands," Gertie said. "A new boyfriend is a good reason to get rid of an old husband."

"And a really common one," Ida Belle said. "But if it's not Liam she was talking to, then I think it's someone from out of town. I don't think she'd risk an affair in Sinful."

"I don't think she could get away with having an affair in Sinful," I said.

"Things develop online all the time with young people," Gertie said. "Especially on social media."

I nodded. "So next topic—who is the woman Tiffany won't talk to?"

"Given what we know, the only person I could think of is her mother," Gertie said.

"Maybe so," Ida Belle said. "I guess the cops didn't search her house this morning or she would have said so, right?"

"Casey has to get a warrant first," I said. "I'm guessing she's collecting enough information to get one pushed through and will be back for that search when she does."

"A questionable alibi isn't enough," Gertie said, "but the inheritance combined with Tiffany gearing up to leave might be."

Ida Belle nodded. "That goes double if Fortune's theory about Gil sniffing around another woman turns out to be true."

"Well, Tiffany confirmed that she married Gil for the money," Gertie said. "But it sounds like she regrets it. I can't imagine being married to him was a picnic."

"I'm sure it wasn't," I agreed. "But the question is how badly did she want a do-over? And does her do-over include Liam or someone else?"

Ida Belle and Gertie both shook their heads, but none of us were happy. Things didn't look good for Tiffany and unfortunately, that would end up implicating Liam as well, especially after the terms of Gil's new will came to light. I had empathy for both of them, but the biggest piece of that definitely went to Liam. I really didn't want him to be involved, but the more we learned, the harder it was to rule it out.

I was surprised that we made it out of Sinful and up the highway by a good twenty miles before Carter called. I motioned to Ida Belle to exit the highway and told her to pull into the gas station at the pumps. She flew off the highway and skidded to a stop in front of the pumps and I managed to grab the call on the last ring.

"What's up?" I asked.

"Where are you?" he asked.

"Toby's on the highway."

"The gas station?"

"That's usually where you stop for gas."

"Where are you going?"

"New Orleans."

"How many pairs of underwear does Gertie need?"

"We're not going for underwear today. I have appointments to see hot tubs. They were closed on Sunday."

"Uh-huh. Then I don't suppose you know anything about an explosion behind Tiffany Forrest's house?"

"No! Is she all right?"

"She's fine but scared. After the chicken thing, she believes someone is after her, but I have to tell you, I don't think she's right on this one."

"No?"

"Unless she was under siege by a group of kindergartners during craft time, I can't work it out. You see, there's pink glitter all over the area where the explosion happened. There's a skunk back there wearing pink glitter, and Deputy Breaux had the misfortune to make his acquaintance."

"Oh wow! That sucks. Sorry, but we can't help you."

I took a pic of the gas station sign and texted it to Carter.

"Just sent you a pic of the gas station sign. We're nowhere near your kindergarten-glitter-skunk crime scene."

"Of course not. So then you won't mind FaceTiming me."

"I only have one bar. It would never work. Anyway, sounds like you've got your hands full, so I'll let you get back to it."

I hung up the phone and stared at the display for a couple seconds, wondering if he was going to call back. Finally I shoved it in my pocket. Carter knew I'd never cave. He could walk up to me right now and I'd still deny I was in the woods, even though the evidence was all over me.

"Okay, let's go grab some goodies from the dollar store and get a shower," I said.

"Here's the thing," Ida Belle said as she drove. "We can either go to the sketchy motel to shower or pay twice as much at the better motel."

I frowned. Decisions. Decisions.

I'd been in the sketchy motel bathroom more than once and wasn't impressed. But then all we really needed was to shower and leave. It wasn't like we were going to move in. Still, by the time we sprang for toiletries, lint rollers, hats, and potentially new clothes if the glitter refused to come off the old ones, then add the motel room, the expense was rising and we hadn't even had any fun.

"Go to the cheap one," I said. "At least it has the added advantage of no one admitting they've seen us."

———

WE MADE OUR RUN THROUGH THE DOLLAR STORE, THEN headed for the motel. I went inside to rent the room, hoping the new front desk clerk would follow the trend of not wanting to know anything about anything. But I drew up short when the same old clerk we'd tortured with our antics in the past stared up at me, clearly dismayed.

"I thought you were leaving for a job in New Orleans," I said.

"I was," he said. "I did. It didn't work out."

"I thought it was night shift and you would be all alone. How does that not work out?"

"One of the office tenants was an insomniac. He was there every night so that his boss would think he was working. Meanwhile, he spent the entire night talking to me. About the harmonica."

I shook my head. "I don't figure a conversation about harmonicas should be more than a minute or two."

"Exactly. So anyway, I called the motel and they offered me my job back and a raise, so here I am again...and here you are again. What manner of criminal are you looking for now—a serial-killing crafter?"

He waved a hand at me and I assumed he was addressing my glittery appearance.

"No, actually, I need a room. There was an incident, and I need to get this pink stuff off of me."

"There's a car wash around the corner. Might be a better bet for that stuff. And don't you live in Sinful?"

"Yes, but I don't want people there to see me like this."

"Uh-huh. Listen, I'm fine with renting you a room. Heck, I'd rent to Charles Manson if he had cash, but I gotta tell you, if you have to moonlight at that kind of job, then maybe you should reconsider this whole PI thing for something that pays better."

"You're probably right," I said, figuring there was no point in trying to explain, and not that I could without giving away our somewhat criminal behavior.

He told me the price and handed me a key. "Do me a favor and try to brush some of that off in the parking lot. Housekeeping is going to kill me."

"I'll do what I can," I said and headed out.

Ida Belle found a spot close to our room despite the unusually crowded parking lot, and we all hopped out.

"The clerk said to try to shake some of this off outside," I said. "I think he's afraid housekeeping will give notice."

"Sounds like the new clerk is as uptight as the last one," Gertie groused as she shook her head, flinging glitter everywhere.

"Oh, it's the same old clerk," I said and explained why he was back as we headed inside.

While one of us showered, the other two tackled the clothes. I swear, it was like the glitter was covered with glue the way it stuck to fabric. I could see why the clerk was concerned. It would still be in the carpet until they changed it, which was probably slated to happen on the right side of never.

Finally, we'd done the best we could do. Gertie shifted her revolver and Mace out from her cleavage to her new purse, along with the lint rollers, and we stuffed the shampoo, conditioner, and body wash back into the plastic bag. We figured we probably needed to put together an emergency kit and this was a start. Then we did one last inspection. Our clothes were pretty good, but if I dug my fingers into my scalp, I still came up with glitter. And since lint-rolling my hair was out of the question, I figured I'd have a fabulous scalp for some time to come. Hopefully, Carter wouldn't take a close look.

We'd bought beach towels at the store and covered the seats with them to prevent getting glitter on our clothes again when we got back in the SUV. So all we needed to do now was head for the car wash and give the SUV a good vacuum and use the lint rollers to try to get the glitter out. At least Ida Belle was all about utility and had leather seats and rubber floors instead of carpet. That helped.

# CHAPTER FIFTEEN

I HAD JUST OPENED THE MOTEL ROOM DOOR TO STEP OUT when I caught sight of Tiffany crossing the parking lot. I practically shoved Gertie down getting back inside and closing the door, then ran over to the blinds and lifted one to watch. Sure enough, her red Mustang was parked at the back of the parking lot, almost hidden by a dumpster and a big hedge. I couldn't remember if it had been there when we arrived but then, I hadn't been scanning the parking lot like normal as it wasn't that kind of visit.

"What the heck?" Gertie asked as she pushed herself off the dresser.

"It's Tiffany," I said.

Gertie and Ida Belle rushed up beside me to peer out.

"What are the odds?" Ida Belle asked.

"In Sinful?" I asked. "Probably higher than most."

"Did you see what room she came out of?" Gertie asked.

"Not even," I said. "She was already crossing the parking lot. But as soon as she drives off, we need to pull the SUV down some and keep an eye on the rooms in line with her path. Maybe we'll recognize someone coming out."

"You don't want to follow her?" Ida Belle asked.

"I don't think so," I said. "It looks like she met someone here. So unless she has two secret meetings, she's probably headed back to Sinful."

We watched as Tiffany got in her car and drove away and Ida Belle pulled out her cell phone and dialed.

"Yes. May I speak to Liam please?" she said. "Oh, okay. Do you know when he'll be back? He was going to help me with some choice rib eyes for a dinner party I'm having. Okay. I will. Thanks."

She frowned as she hung up. "Liam's out sick."

We all headed outside, and Ida Belle moved the SUV closer to the entrance but back from the motel so we could see all the room doors. We waited a good ten minutes, but no one emerged from the rooms.

"Maybe he's staying put," Gertie said.

"Or left before Tiffany did and we missed him," Ida Belle said. "I don't see his truck anywhere."

"Or he could have ridden the moped over and left it in the woods," I said. "The motel isn't far from the butcher shop or his house."

"So what now?" Gertie asked.

"Well, unfortunately for the clerk, I'm about to go back in there and see if he can identify someone for me," I said.

"Do you have pictures of them?" Ida Belle asked.

I nodded. "One of the first things I do when we're on a case is make a file with pictures of people we're checking out."

"Smart," Gertie said.

"Stay parked here, just in case Liam comes out," I said. "You don't want to be right in front of him."

I hopped out of the SUV and headed back for the office. The clerk looked up and sighed as I walked in.

"What now?" he asked.

I handed him the room key and he looked relieved.

"I saw a guest leaving when I walked out of my room," I said. "She's a suspect in a murder investigation."

His relief turned to dismay. "Of course she is."

"Since she lives in Sinful, I can't see any reason for her to be here unless she was meeting someone."

"Maybe she moonlights at a glitter job like you."

"I'd like to show you some pictures and see if you recognize these people."

"Do it. And hurry up about it. You know, I'm certain that all your questions are going to get me killed one day."

"Maybe if you weren't always renting to criminals, that wouldn't be the case."

"Then the place would go broke. Do you think the most upstanding citizens stay here?"

I flipped my phone around with a picture of Tiffany on it.

He leaned forward and shook his head. "No. I'd remember her if I'd seen her. She's totally my type. Shame about the murderer thing. Let me know if she's not guilty. Maybe I can get her number. Who is she suspected of killing?"

"Her husband."

He swallowed. "Okay, maybe skip the number. I don't need a date that bad."

I pulled up Liam's picture and showed him. He studied it for a few seconds, then shook his head again.

"I don't think so," he said. "But he's a really normal-looking dude. I mean, I don't give dudes a big look, you know. Unless they have something out of the ordinary going on, most of them don't register."

"How full is the motel right now?"

"About eighty percent booked."

"Really? I thought the parking lot looked fuller than usual."

He nodded. "Fishing rodeo over in Mudbug. We get the overflow."

"Okay. Thanks."

I headed back out to the SUV and filled Ida Belle and Gertie in.

"Do you want to stay here longer?" Ida Belle asked.

"No," I said. "Like you said, he could have left before Tiffany. And if she wasn't meeting Liam, there's no way we'd know who she *was* meeting—not with a bunch of fishermen staying here. He'd just be another guy in the crowd."

"We could do a drive-by of the butcher shop and Liam's house and see if the moped and truck are there," Gertie said.

"It wouldn't matter," I said. "If he left before Tiffany, he's had plenty of time to get home."

"You know," Gertie said, "we've been assuming Tiffany was talking to a guy, but what if it was a girl?"

I groaned. "Let's not add more questions to this already convoluted mess."

"I agree," Ida Belle said. "Until we know differently, we'll assume she was talking to another man. So, NOLA?"

I nodded. "Might as well, but can you get one of the Sinful Ladies to do a little reconnaissance for us?"

"Sure," Ida Belle said. "What do you need?"

"In about twenty minutes, I'd like someone to see if Tiffany is at home," I said. "At least that way we'd know that she was meeting that person here and there wasn't another assignment."

The last thing we needed was more people in the mix.

———

BECAUSE WE HAD SOME HOURS TO KILL AND ALSO BECAUSE WE were starving, we had lunch when we arrived in New Orleans, then set out to look at some hot tubs. I had zeroed in on the one that I thought I wanted but figured since we had the time, I might as well check out the competition. We made it to the place that I figured I would buy about 4:00 p.m. and I located the salesman I'd talked to on the phone. The hot tub was everything I hoped it would be and even better, they had it in stock and could deliver it as soon as I had the proper base and electrical wiring for it. Ida Belle assured me that was all a simple matter and could happen in a couple days, so I scheduled delivery for the following Monday.

The way this week was going, I figured the sooner, the better.

When we finished at the hot tub place, I called Carter to set up the whole 'we're sticking around for the salesman' alibi and was relieved when he didn't answer. I left the message and we headed off to do a short review of the buildings surrounding the parking lot where Gil was killed. We had an hour to kill before the actors showed up for rehearsal, and I was hoping rehearsal hadn't been canceled because of what had happened to Gil.

We talked to several people exiting the buildings surrounding the parking lot, but none of them were at work past five or six, so wouldn't have seen anything. One building had a night security guard, but the day guard told me he mostly slept, which corresponded to what the police report said. By the time we'd walked the block, talking to everyone we could get a hold of, the parking lots had emptied, but a couple cars were parked in the theater lot.

"Looks like we're on," I said.

"How are we going to play this?" Ida Belle asked. "I mean, we're not cops, and now that this is a murder investigation, Casey will probably be back over here going over their statements again."

"We'll tell them we're friends of the family and trying to get some closure for Gil's son," I said.

Gertie rolled her eyes. "You hate words like 'closure' and I doubt Liam would like it much better than you."

"None of them know that," I said. "And it's not like we have to worry about Liam coming to talk to these people or them to him."

Ida Belle nodded. "I think it's a good ploy. It will be hard to say no to helping when they think it's for the victim's child, even if he's grown."

As we headed across the parking lot for the back door, a man parked next to the entrance opened the back of his SUV, and began to struggle with removing a door from the vehicle. I hurried over and grabbed one end and he looked up in surprise.

*Midfifties. Six foot even. Two hundred ten pounds. Couldn't lift a fifty-pound door without help. Zero threat.*

I indicated he should walk and, apparently, he was so surprised that he simply did as I instructed.

"Are you one of the acting troupe that rehearses here?" I asked as we walked.

He nodded. "I'm Paul Easton. This door is for the play. A neighbor has been making it for us. Are you three here to audition? Because I'm afraid we've had all the actors in place for months now."

"Nothing like that," I said. "My name is Fortune Redding. I'm a private investigator and these two ladies are my assistants. I'm looking into what happened to Gil Forrest for his son. He's having a hard time with all this and thought I might be able to bring him some closure if he just had a better understanding of his father's last day."

He glanced back at me and frowned. "I can't imagine how

hard that must be. But I didn't think Gil and his son were close."

"They weren't," I said. "Which sort of makes it worse rather than better."

"Ah." He nodded his head in understanding. "No more chances to right old wrongs."

"Something like that," I said.

Ida Belle ran ahead and opened the door so that Paul and I could go in with the door we were carrying.

"I was hoping you guys wouldn't mind talking to me about Gil," I said as we stepped inside and started down a hallway. "Maybe there's nothing to be learned, but maybe there's something that would help the situation."

"I don't mind speaking with you," he said. "The others, of course, have their own opinions, but you can ask. We won't all be here tonight though. Just the ones that run things, so to speak. We have to figure out what to do about Gil's part."

"You don't have an understudy?" I asked.

He shook his head. "It wasn't a major role. We have a couple people in mind who could fill in, but we have to see if they can match up their availability to our travel schedule. We were due to start touring in two weeks."

"What happens if no one can cover?" I asked. "Do you have to cancel?"

"No. We can't do that, or we risk never getting to book those venues again. If the guys we have in mind can't cover, then we will rewrite the role to make the character a woman. That way, our director can fill in."

"It's good that you have options," I said.

I heard women's voices carrying down the hallway and stopped talking so that I could listen in.

"Are we going to use the Driscoll emeralds for the play?

Since they haven't been on display in years, I'm sure they'd generate a lot of buzz."

"I'm not sure yet. I have to check with my insurance agent first. There was some concern."

"We can hire some off-duty policemen for extra security. It's not too expensive. I think the door take will be a lot higher if we can have them be part of the show. And you know Prescott being a former jeweler absolutely loves when he can get close to fine pieces with historical significance. He'll advertise to everyone he knows."

"As I said, I have to clear it with my insurance agent, but I'll find out."

We stepped into an auditorium and three women on the stage stared down at me, clearly curious.

*First woman fortyish. Five foot seven. One hundred thirty pounds. One of those thin bodies with very little muscle. It belonged on a runway or a stage. Zero threat as she probably couldn't lift more than her purse or sprint more than five feet.*

*Second woman, midthirties. Five foot five. One hundred fifty pounds and not enough muscle. Didn't exercise regularly and was either shy or guilty because she wouldn't look me in the eye. No threat to anyone, ever.*

*Third woman, midsixties. Five foot six. One hundred ten pounds. An unhealthy state of thin, unlike the first woman who had the genetics to pull it off. Little muscle tone. Zero threat.*

We went up a set of side steps onto the stage with the door and I helped Paul set it upright. The three women walked over and the model-looking one nodded as she inspected the door, looking pleased.

"This is perfect, Paul," she said, and I recognized her voice as the owner of the emeralds that might or might not be on display. "Please give your neighbor my thanks again. I wish we had the budget to pay him something."

"It's no big deal," Paul said. "He's a contractor and the materials were just scraps he would have thrown away. He was happy to help."

She looked over at me, Ida Belle, and Gertie and then back at Paul, obviously assuming we were with him and he needed to take care of introductions.

"Sorry," he said, realizing his faux pas. "I met these ladies in the parking lot, and they helped me with the door. I'll let them explain why they're here."

I introduced myself, Ida Belle, and Gertie and gave them the same pitch that I'd given Paul. The younger woman kept biting her lip, and her eyes started to mist up. The model frowned as I talked and nodded a lot. The older one shook her head the entire time, looking troubled. When I finished, the model sighed.

"I can't imagine what that young man is going through," she said. "My name is Brigette Driscoll. I run the theater and this is my assistant, Gwyn Simmons. Lil Davis is a volunteer who helps on set. We're happy to assist any way we can, but I have to admit that I'm not sure how to."

I studied her for a moment. She was all about being refined and reserved, and it appeared that she belonged in a museum or a palace rather than on a stage. So I decided to see if I could shake her demeanor.

"Have you spoken to Detective Casey recently?" I asked.

"Not since the day after the...incident," she said.

"Oh," I said. "Then you haven't heard."

"Heard what?" she asked.

"They found Gil's car in a bayou in Sinful," I said. "Murder is now the primary crime. The stolen car was simply to hide the fact that killing him was intentional."

Her eyes widened, and the assistant, Gwyn, gasped. Lil went paler than she was before. Paul looked stunned.

"That can't be," he said. "Who would want to kill Gil?"

"That's one of the things his son would like to know, which is why we're here," I said. "Obviously Gil did something to make someone angry enough to kill him. And since this acting troupe was such a big part of his life, I figured you might know some things that Sinful locals didn't know about him."

"You're looking for motive," Paul said. "How ironic."

"What do you mean?" I asked.

Brigette cleared her throat. "He means that the play we're currently doing is a murder mystery. Gil played the part of the detective."

"Ah, I see," I said. "Anyway, what I wanted to know is more about Gil's personal life. You spent a lot of hours rehearsing and on the road. Did he ever discuss his son, his marriage, or any other issues with you?"

Brigette glanced at Gwyn, then frowned. "Not with me. I'm displeased with people who complain about their spouse or children to others, so I tend to avoid putting myself in situations where that might occur."

"Can I ask why you avoid those situations?" I asked.

"First, I believe it's tacky and disrespectful," Brigette said. "Second, I think it's unfair to present only one side of an issue concerning another person when they're not able to give their own take. When complaining about family dynamics, people have a tendency to portray things in their own best light, not necessarily the correct light."

I smiled. "Very true. And I imagine not being a sounding board saves you a lot of hassle, especially since you run things. What about you, Paul? You travel to perform...did you and Gil ever throw back some beers and shoot the bull?"

Paul looked a bit flustered but finally nodded. "A little. I mean, not the beer part. I don't drink, but Gil liked to have a couple when we were done for the night. I get wound up after performances and can't go straight to bed. I need to stir around a bit to wind down."

"So you'd sit in the hotel bar with Gil to wind down sometimes?" I asked.

"Yes, I mean sometimes," Paul said, then looked a bit guilty. "To be honest, I usually tried to sneak away. Gil was a nice guy but he could be overwhelming. He never really got off the stage, if that makes sense."

"Not exactly what you're looking for to wind down," I said.

"No," Paul agreed.

"So did he ever talk about his wife or his son, Liam?" I asked. "Or maybe problems he had with his business or a customer?"

"Gil told me that his son didn't speak to him over a falling-out some years ago," Paul said. "He said he'd made some attempts to start communication, but he didn't hold out much hope."

"Did he ever tell you why they had a falling-out?" I asked.

"No," Paul said. "And I never asked."

"Would it surprise you if I told you Gil married his son's girlfriend?" I asked.

Paul's eyes widened and a flush crept up his face. Gwyn looked positively ill. Lil blanched and then looked away. Brigette cringed as if she'd smelled something incredibly foul. Which wasn't exactly incorrect.

"I, uh...I had no idea," Paul said. "That's horrible. We've all met Tiffany of course, and no one could miss the age difference, but I never knew... No wonder Gil didn't think his son would ever speak to him again. I don't think I would either."

"That's really true?" Gwyn asked, and I realized it was the first time she'd spoken. She was the woman who'd been asking if Brigette was going to use the emeralds in the play.

I gestured to Ida Belle and Gertie and they both nodded.

"We've known the family since before Gil was even born," Ida Belle said. "It's all very unfortunate, but very true."

"Oh," Gwyn said and stared down at the floor.

"Well, ladies," Brigette said, "it sounds like you have your motive already."

"Except we don't think Liam did it," I said. "Why wait years to get revenge? He doesn't inherit and I doubt he'd want Tiffany back even if she made a move in that direction. He's got a good job with a bright future. It simply doesn't fit. And we don't want to see him railroaded from his career by the police focusing on the wrong person."

"So does Tiffany inherit everything?" Gwyn asked.

"According to what we've heard, yes," I lied.

"And that's why you want to know if he ever talked about his wife," Paul said.

"Did he?" I asked.

"Some," Paul said. "At first, he complained that she didn't want to travel when we went out of town to do the shows. He'd told me she had that thing—you know—where you don't want to leave the house?"

"Agoraphobia?" I suggested, even though I already knew that was just a lie Gil had fed them.

He nodded. "He said it wasn't really bad but that he basically had to force her to come with him to rehearsal or to see a play. I assumed he finally gave up trying because he stopped mentioning it about a year ago."

"Anything else you guys can tell me about Tiffany?" I asked.

They all shook their heads.

"Really, we barely knew the woman," Brigette said. "She seemed polite enough but clearly not interested in acting. The couple times she came with Gil, it was obvious she'd rather be somewhere else. If I had to guess, it's been two years or better since she's been here."

"Lil?" I questioned the one person who hadn't volunteered anything.

"Me?" she asked. "I'm not really part of the troupe. I work for the theater during the day—simple maintenance and janitorial. I volunteered to help some with the props because I'm good with a hammer and screwdriver and well, I found it all interesting. But I don't travel with them and only come to rehearsal if I'm needed for prop stuff. Usually, I work on things during the day when I have the spare time to tinker."

"What about the other members of the troupe?" I asked. "Were any of them friendly with Gil after rehearsal or performances?"

They all shook their heads.

"I can't think of anyone that he talked to outside of rehearsal," Paul said. "The people here tonight are what you'd call the regulars. A lot of the other actors drift in and out, taking the best gigs they can get, and that's not always with us. The others that are most consistently with us on tours are mainly married couples, and they tend to stick together."

"And what about the security cameras?" I asked. "I understand they're not working."

"That's correct," Brigette said. "The system is an old one to begin with, and the owner of the building simply doesn't see the point in upgrading. It's always been spotty with recording and even when it works, the feed is grainy."

"So it's not completely broken," I said. "Just unreliable."

"Yes," Brigette said. "But according to the owner, it stopped functioning the week before and he hadn't noticed. Nothing has ever happened here, so he said he's not in the habit of checking it. I'm sorry, but we really need to get on with our business for the night. Gil's...absence requires some changes, and we don't have long to get them implemented."

"No problem," I said. "I appreciate your time. Let me give

you guys my card. If you think of anything important, please give me a call."

We headed off the stage and I paused at a wall with several pictures hanging on it. I assumed they were inventory since the wall itself didn't look like a prop, but the painting at the bottom looked just like the one Gil had in his hallway.

"I guess this is where he got the idea for that tacky painting," I said and shook my head.

We headed down the hallway and Gertie snorted.

"I'm surprised that uptight Brigette even allows something that crass in her production," Gertie said.

"She's definitely got the snooty thing down," Ida Belle said. "So are we heading home?"

"Not just yet," I said. "I'd like to park across the street and watch when they leave. If possible, I want to catch Gwyn on her own."

"You think she knows something?" Gertie asked.

"Did you see the look Brigette threw at her when I asked if Gil ever discussed his personal business with any of them?" I asked.

They both shook their heads.

"You think Gil confided in her," Ida Belle said.

"Yeah, and I think she had a thing for Gil," I said.

Ida Belle whistled. "You might have found your other woman."

# CHAPTER SIXTEEN

I HAD NO IDEA HOW LONG THE MEETING WOULD TAKE BUT figured it would be lengthy, so I was surprised to see them exit the theater thirty minutes later. Brigette had that controlled look on her face but I could tell it was masking anger. Paul looked as if he'd been whipped but I had a feeling that was probably his default expression. He didn't seem to be a person who stood up for himself on a regular basis. Lil just hurried to her car, her head down, and pulled away, Paul close behind her.

Gwyn looked worried and stopped to talk to Brigette at her car. I couldn't see their lips, so no way of getting anything from the conversation, but by the shaking of heads and body language, I could tell the talk wasn't pleasant. After arguing with Gwyn, Brigette jumped into her car and pulled out of the parking lot at a fast clip. Gwyn stood there several seconds, staring after her, her expression one of utter confusion.

"Make your move," I said to Ida Belle.

She fired up the SUV, glanced to make sure she had the clear, then crossed the street and came to a stop next to Gwyn, who was unlocking her car. She stared at the SUV, clearly startled, and I realized since she couldn't see through the tinted windows, we'd probably just given her a slight heart attack. Ida Belle must have realized it as well and rolled down her window. Gwyn's shoulders slumped and she let out a huge breath of relief.

"Sorry," Ida Belle said. "We didn't mean to startle you, but I can understand why you would be."

"Yeah," Gwyn said and I could tell she was still a little flustered. "I guess I'm kinda on edge after what happened."

I leaned across the center console.

"We'd like to talk to you alone, if that's okay," I said.

"Here?" she asked.

"That's certainly not required," I said. "Is there a coffee shop nearby that you like?"

She nodded and pointed. "Just around the corner to the right. It's two shops down. This time of day, there's usually parking in front. This area tends to clear out fairly early."

"Okay," I said. "We'll meet you there."

Ida Belle pulled away and I watched to make sure Gwyn was coming behind us. There was plenty of available spaces, so Ida Belle pulled in right in front and Gwyn parked next to her, then we all went inside. The place was empty except for one other occupied table, so we headed for the other side and sat in a corner. A waitress came by to take our order and we all put in for coffee and I asked for a plate of beignets for the table.

"Thanks for talking with us," I said after the coffee was served.

Gwyn nodded and fiddled with her napkin. "I'm not sure what I can do to help, though."

"I think you might know something about Gil that's important," I said.

"Like what?" she asked.

"Like your relationship with him," I said.

Her eyes widened. "We didn't have a relationship. I mean, we were friends, but that's it."

I sighed. "Gwyn, I'm going to share with you a little bit about my past. I'm a former CIA agent. Do you know what one of the first things we're taught is?"

She shook her head.

"How to tell when someone is lying," I said. "Now, either you can tell me, or I'll shame it out of Brigette, citing propriety, because I think she knows as well and she's unhappy about it."

Gwyn stared down at the table for a bit and when she looked back up, I could see tears in her eyes.

"Gil and I were sorta seeing each other," she said.

"Just sorta?" I asked.

"I guess that's not really accurate," she said, clearly miserable. "The truth is, I loved him and he loved me."

"Is that what he said?" Gertie asked.

She nodded.

"What about Tiffany?" Ida Belle asked.

"I ignored his flirting for a long time because he was married," Gwyn said. "But he kept telling me how he should have never married her and that she didn't love him and never had."

"That's what they all say, honey," Gertie said.

"I know," Gwyn said and started to cry. "I shouldn't have done it. It was wrong. But I can't change that now. At least, knowing that she was his son's girlfriend first makes me understand things a little better."

"How is that?" I asked.

She shrugged. "I didn't have the best childhood. My parents weren't abusive but they were neglectful. I married the first guy I dated to get out of their house, and it ended in disaster a couple months later. He was a lot older than me as well. I guess I figure Tiffany saw a lifestyle with Gil that she couldn't have with his son—at least not right away given their ages—so she took it. Which means Gil was probably right and she didn't love him."

I sighed as she made an attempt to excuse bad behavior. If everyone called out bad behavior, then people like Gil couldn't keep getting away with it.

"But Tiffany has been married to Gil for seven years," Gertie said gently. "If she regretted her decision, she would have left already."

"You're right," Gwyn said and sniffed. "I know I shouldn't have gotten involved. It was wrong of me and I swore I'd never be that kind of woman. But I know Gil loved me. He said he was going to divorce Tiffany. That they just didn't work anymore."

"Did he talk to a lawyer?" I asked.

"He said he did," Gwyn said.

"I don't suppose you know who it was?" I asked.

"Not for sure," she said. "I gave him the number of the guy I used. He's in New Orleans, so I thought that would be better for Gil than using someone from Sinful. I know lawyers aren't supposed to talk but I figured just to be safe..."

"Will you give me that name, please?" I asked.

She nodded and pulled out her phone. When she found the contact information, I had her text it to me.

"Is it true that the police don't think it was a carjacking now?" she asked.

"Yes. They've changed the scope of the investigation," I said. "I imagine Detective Casey is going to talk to all of you again. You should tell her the truth. *All* the truth."

"I will," Gwyn said. "I didn't say anything before because it didn't seem relevant. We all thought it was one of those horrible, random things."

"I understand," I said. "Did Gil ever talk about Liam?"

"Yeah," Gwyn said. "He was real torn up about their relationship being bad. And before you ask, he never told me about Tiffany dating Liam. Tonight was the first I heard that. He just said they'd had a rift years ago and he was in the wrong. But he didn't think Liam was ever going to forgive him unless certain things happened."

"What things?" I asked.

She shook her head. "He never would say. But now I wonder if he meant divorcing Tiffany. I mean, it would be hard for Liam to forgive Gil if he was still married to her, right?"

"Would have been hard even if he divorced her," Gertie said. "But it might have shifted Liam's mind some. It's hard to say."

"Did you notice Gil acting different lately?" I asked.

"In what way?" Gwyn asked.

"Nervous? Edgy?" I asked.

She frowned. "He was a little strange the last time we met. The night he...anyway, I got a bad headache and had to leave early. He expressed concern, but I could tell his mind wasn't on me. And the week before, he'd insisted that we walk out together and leave at the same time. Normally, some of us would chat after rehearsal or I would stay to finish up some prop work. But he asked me to leave without finishing up a design I was working on since everyone else was cutting out then."

"And that was odd?" I asked.

She nodded. "I've stayed by myself after rehearsal plenty of times to finish up some work. And besides, Lil was still there that night, but he wouldn't let it go. I would have liked to finish up, but he was so insistent I figured it was just easier to go along although I knew I'd pay for it the next day. Brigette is a very talented woman but not the easiest to work for. I have to make sure everything is perfect if I want to keep my job and I really enjoy it most of the time, so I usually go above and beyond."

"So you're an employee and not a volunteer?" I asked.

"Right," she said. "Brigette is the artistic director for the theater and I'm her assistant. We're both on the theater's payroll. Us and Lil. The actors are paid a percentage of door take based on their contracts. And then there's some local volunteers, like Lil. She's paid for her day job but not for working on the plays. Well, except the volunteers get free tickets for family and friends."

"Did any of the other members of the troupe spend any time with Gil? Someone else he might have confided in?" I asked.

"I don't think so," Gwyn said. "I knew he'd talked to Paul some, but Gil was a bit much for him. Paul's a great actor—really comes alive on stage—but in real life, he's a total introvert. It's rather interesting really. And then like Paul said, most of the others aren't regulars or they're married couples."

"And how long have you and Gil been involved?" I asked.

"I don't really know how to answer that," she said. "I mean, we started talking more personally a little over a year ago. You know, sometimes just a chat after rehearsal and then that turned into going for coffee after rehearsal..."

"And that turned into a relationship," I finished.

She nodded. "I feel guilty and sad about the whole thing but now I'm also angry. Angry that Gil didn't tell me the truth about his marriage to Tiffany. Angry that we don't ever get the chance of a future together. And most of all, angry that no one can ever know how much I loved him because I had no right to."

She started to cry again and Gertie patted her hand.

"It's difficult, keeping all that in," Gertie said. "But you're doing the right thing. The fewer people who know about your relationship with Gil, the better. Other than the police, of course. It only serves to hurt everyone else and doesn't change anything."

She wiped her eyes with the napkin and nodded. "I keep telling myself not to be jealous of Tiffany but it's so hard. She had him for seven years and she had him all to herself. I never had that and I never will."

"You'll get past this," Gertie said. "And maybe when you're ready to try again, you pick someone who's completely unencumbered. I've rarely seen a case where a start with a married man ended well. And you deserve better than a man with split obligations."

Gwyn gave her a small smile. "Thank you. I need to keep reminding myself of that. Is that all you need from me? Because I'd really like a long shower and an even longer cry. Maybe a pint of chocolate mint ice cream."

"That's all," I said.

"And we're really sorry for your loss," Gertie said.

Gwyn gathered her purse and left, still sniffling. Ida Belle gave me an appreciative nod.

"You nailed that one," she said. "The hunch that there was another woman, where to find her, and then the woman herself. You're batting a thousand."

"It just made sense," I said. "We know Tiffany never really cared for Gil and I'm sure he knew that too. Pair him up with someone who loves acting but is another much younger woman, who is an easy target and will worship him because she's got her own issues that need addressing, and you've got Gil's next move. Honestly, given what I know about him, I'm surprised it took him this long."

"Maybe it didn't," Ida Belle said. "He could have had others before her but never made a move to change his current situation."

"But why wouldn't he?" I asked. Romantic relationships were still somewhat of a mystery to me.

"Didn't want anything serious with the other women, most likely," Gertie said. "Being married is the best way to avoid having to *get* married."

"Ah," I said. "So do we think Gil was serious this time? Or was Gwyn just another passing fancy?"

They both shook their heads.

"It's impossible to say," Ida Belle said. "Unless he actually talked to that attorney about a divorce."

I frowned. "And that attorney is not going to talk to us, even though Gil is dead."

"No," Ida Belle said. "But he'd have to talk to Detective Casey. I just don't know that it's smart to feed her information. Puts her in a bad position with her captain if he's keeping a close watch, and he doesn't sound like a picnic."

"Yeah, I'm keeping my mouth shut on everything for the time being," I said. "If I thought there was any risk to others, I would say something, but it looks like Gil was the only target. And I have no doubt Casey will make it back around to the troupe soon, following the same line of inquiry that we did."

"So I guess we head home now?" Gertie asked.

I tapped my fingers on the table and stared out the window.

"Maybe we should drive by that attorney's office," I said. "You know, just to see."

Ida Belle laughed. "You mean to see what kind of security system he has?"

"I never said that."

"You didn't have to."

The office of Randoll P. Maxwell, Attorney at Law, was just

outside the French Quarter in the business district. It was very quiet there given the hour, as most of the businesses closed in the evening. Randoll's office building was one of the newer ones, with five stories and glass sides. A quick check online listed Randoll's office on the second floor. There were staircases that led to the second-floor walkway on each end of the lobby. In the middle of the lobby was a desk with a security guard.

"A live guard," Ida Belle said and frowned.

"Harder to bypass, but not impossible," I said. "And guarded means the individual offices probably don't have alarms or cameras."

"Even if you could get by," Gertie said, "there's still lobby cameras and I don't have any masks since they exploded in my purse."

"This is New Orleans," Ida Belle said. "Masks are the least of our worries."

I nodded. "Let's go get some masks. I have a plan."

————

THIRTY MINUTES LATER, WE WERE PARKED AROUND THE corner from the building and getting ready to put my plan into action. The plan was, Gertie was going to wander down the sidewalk, looking muddled, and attempt entry into the building until she summoned the security guard. Once she got inside, she was going to pretend dementia and a need for something that would send him away from the lobby. At that point, Gertie would unlock the door and let me in. I would bolt up the stairs to the second floor, break into the attorney's office, go through his records, then text Ida Belle to come 'rescue' Gertie and distract the guard again while I made my escape.

"Why do I always have to be the crazy old lady?" Gertie complained.

"Because we're typecasting," Ida Belle said.

Gertie gave her the finger.

"She's right," I said. "Ida Belle is better for the other role, and I'm definitely the one who should be running upstairs and breaking into offices."

"Fine, whatever," Gertie said. "But if I have to play some batty old woman, then I'm going to do it up big. I have to have some fun somewhere."

"The crazier you are, the better," I said. "As long as the security guard is confused, he'll break protocol. Just don't scare him so much he calls the cops."

She nodded. "Hand me the bags from the dollar store."

I had no idea where she was going with this, but the next thing I knew, she'd stripped off her pants, revealing lime green biking shorts, and pulled on the cheap robe she'd bought. Then she grabbed the shampoo and a back scrubber and looked at Ida Belle and me.

"Ready," she said.

"Works for me," I said and hopped out of the SUV. I donned a pair of gloves from Ida Belle's SUV stash, then pulled on the hoodie and Mardi Gras mask I'd picked up just before. Ida Belle was ready to go as is and was going to hang back until it was closer to her time to appear.

I followed close behind Gertie and when she reached the building, I ducked behind a trash can right at the edge of the building and waited for the show. Gertie went up to the glass doors and pulled on them, but they were, of course, locked. Then she started banging on the doors, cursing at someone named Billy for taking too long in the bathroom. I peered around the edge of the trash can and spotted the security guard as he jumped up from his chair and stared at Gertie, clearly uncertain what to do.

Gertie locked in on him and started waving. "Yoohoo, Martin! Help me out with this door. I have an emergency."

The guard shifted from uncertain to stricken and hurried to unlock the door. "Ma'am, are you injured?" he asked as he directed her inside.

He led her over to a bench and she sat and started waving the shampoo bottle around. Then she lifted it up and took a drink, then spit it out on the floor. If the security guard could have been swallowed up by the floor, I was certain he would have. I saw Gertie gesturing and the guard nodded, then ran off down a hallway.

I bolted from behind the trash can and Gertie unlocked the door just as I arrived. I dashed up the stairs and barely made it before the guard came rushing back with a cup of water. I waited long enough to watch Gertie dump the water over her head and start rubbing the shampoo in, then hurried off to find the office before I couldn't hold in my laughter any longer.

I made quick work of the door and located Maxwell's desk. There was a stack of files on top, so I sorted through those first. Nothing. I headed for the file cabinet next and was glad to see they were filed alphabetically. I flipped through the $F$s.

Bingo!

I pulled out the file and found a set of notes but no legal documents. I took pictures of the pages for reading later, then put the file up and hurried back out, leaving everything as it had been before I came in. The office door could only be locked from the outside, so I just left it unlocked, figuring the last person out would assume they forgot to do it or that it hadn't latched properly. Then I crept down the hall to the balcony to peer over.

Gertie had discarded the robe and was now standing in the water feature below me, dipping her brush into the water and scrubbing her back. She was singing something about rub-a-dub-dub. The security guard was attempting to entice her out. I sent a text to Ida Belle, letting her know I was ready to escape so she could make her move. It was a good thing I found what I was looking for quickly because the guard kept swapping glances between Gertie and his cell phone.

"Ma'am, I'm going to have to call the police," the guard said.

Crap! If the police showed up, I was cornered and Gertie was off for a twenty-four-hour psych hold. The guard lifted his phone to dial when Ida Belle started banging on the doors and yelling.

"Margaret!" Ida Belle exclaimed as the guard let her inside. She hurried over to the fountain. "Thank goodness I found you."

The guard clearly wanted to be relieved but was still apprehensive, his arm still hovering up with the phone.

"Do you know this woman?" he asked Ida Belle.

"She's my sister," Ida Belle said. "She's gotten a bit confused lately. An age thing. She's my *older* sister."

"I'm not old," Gertie protested, and shook her head, flinging shampoo everywhere. "If Billy didn't take so long in the bathroom, I would have been ready on time. And where is Martin? I keep asking for him but this man won't call his office. We're going to be late for our lunch reservation."

"I don't know a Martin," the guard explained. "And no one is here right now. I've tried to tell her that."

Ida Belle nodded. "Her son used to work in this building and they did lunch once a week. He passed a year ago. Things have been downhill from there."

"Okay, look," the guard said. "I'm sorry about her son and

her issues and all of that, but you can't be in here. I'm going to call for an ambulance. She needs a doctor."

"She's fine," Ida Belle said.

"No, she's not," the guard insisted. "And if you won't do a better job keeping sight of her, then she needs to be somewhere that she can be watched. My grandma went this direction. Your sister could have walked into traffic because you're not taking proper care of her."

"Yeah!" Gertie said. "See. I told you Billy would have a problem if you didn't put whipped cream on my pancakes."

"She's got a doctor's appointment tomorrow," Ida Belle assured the man, but I could tell he was itching to call, if for no other reason than to cover his butt if anything came up later on.

"I don't care," the guard said and dialed. "Hello? I have an elderly woman who needs medical attention. I think she has dementia and is lost." The guard gave the address.

Double crap!

Gertie looked up toward the balcony and I waved from the plant I was crouched behind. There was no way I could get away. One glance up or at the opposite staircase and the guard would see me. I needed him out of the lobby or focused on something so hard that he didn't notice me getting away.

Suddenly, Gertie threw the scrub brush across the lobby, climbed out of the fountain, and took off running for the staircase on the opposite side of the room.

"Look!" she yelled as she ran. "It's the Cinderella staircase! I love Disney World!"

"She'll break a hip!" Ida Belle yelled and took off after her, the panicked guard close behind.

# CHAPTER SEVENTEEN

As soon as the guard turned his back to me to sprint after Gertie, I hopped on the railing and slid silently down, then fled the building. Then I crept over to the edge so I could peek in and watch the rest of the show and since everyone was yelling, I could still hear what was going on as well.

Ida Belle managed to partially block the guard going up the stairs, so he was unable to catch Gertie before she reached the balcony. When she got to the top, she yanked off her top, revealing a lime green sports bra that matched her shorts, and threw it off the balcony. Then she went running for the staircase on the opposite side.

"It's the waterslide!" Gertie yelled as she threw a leg over the stair railing as I had done.

Good. God.

I watched in horror as Gertie, slicked up from all the shampoo, went flying down the railing at double the speed I'd managed, then flew off the end and crashed into a plant, splitting the vase in two. Ida Belle and the guard ran down to help her up while Gertie kept trying to wave them away. The guard looked at the broken vase, and I thought for a moment that he was going to cry. Ida Belle grabbed his shoulders and shook him, and I could see her giving him a stern talking-to, but since her back was to me, I couldn't make out what she was saying.

Finally the guard nodded and hurried over to the desk where I saw him access a computer. I could hear sirens in the distance and silently urged them to hurry.

"You got it?" Ida Belle yelled.

"Yes," he said. "Just go!"

Ida Belle grabbed Gertie's shirt and the robe, and they hurried out. Then we all took off at a dead run until we rounded the corner and jumped into the SUV. Ida Belle fired it right up and pulled away without turning on her headlights. When we were several blocks away, she looked back at Gertie.

"Do you know how close you were to being arrested?" she asked. "They would have put you on a twenty-four-hour hold."

Gertie shrugged. "So?"

"So I'm not so sure they would have released you after," Ida Belle said.

"Fortune needed a distraction. The cops were coming. I did what I had to do. And I didn't even blow anything up this time."

"That's because you blew up everything in your purse earlier today," Ida Belle said.

"Technicalities," Gertie said.

"What did you say to the guard?" I asked Ida Belle.

"I told him that we were both in big trouble when the cops showed up because he'd let Gertie in to begin with and hadn't called for help right away. I said he could probably glue the vase back together and gave him the name of the glue. Then I suggested he delete the last hour or so of security footage and if anyone asked, claim no knowledge of a problem and deny that he ever let the crazy woman in the building."

"See," Gertie said. "No evidence of our existence there. Things went perfectly."

"You're a wet, slimy mess, dripping in my SUV," Ida Belle said. "That cover is only water-resistant, not waterproof."

"It's shampoo," Gertie said. "I'm just giving it a wash."

She started shifting her butt back and forth across the seat and for a minute, I wondered if Ida Belle was going to pull over and take action.

Ida Belle looked over at me. "Please tell me you got something so that I don't have to shoot her."

"I did," I said. "He had a file for Gil but no documents yet, only notes. I took pics so I could get out quickly. Let me pull them up."

I accessed the images and started scanning the notes, reading the relevant parts out loud. The bottom line was that Gwyn had been telling the truth—Gil had been filing for divorce. And as part of that filing, he wanted to change his will, yet again, this time leaving everything to Liam, which brought into question his plans for a future with Gwyn but that wasn't exactly surprising. Per the prenuptial agreement, Tiffany would leave the marriage with what she brought into it and earned during the marriage. So basically, nothing.

"Hello motive," Gertie said when I finished.

"Is it?" I asked. "If Tiffany was already planning to leave Gil, she wasn't going to get anything on the way out. She had to know the contents of the prenuptial."

"True," Ida Belle said. "But what if she started making plans to leave, then realized her very limited skill set wouldn't pay for much of a living? Tiffany appears to be driven by an overwhelming need for security. If she could be rid of Gil but still have the security of the money, that would be the ultimate solution."

I nodded. "I could see that. She starts looking at apartments and comparing that to what she can make as unskilled labor and realizes that her days of comfort are over. She'll be struggling just to keep a roof overhead and food on the table."

"I wonder if Tiffany knew he was filing," Gertie said.

"No way to know unless she admits it," I said.

"It was incredibly bad timing for her to kill him now if she didn't," Gertie said. "Because the cops will never believe she didn't know. Then on the other hand, we're assuming she's the lead suspect because she has the most to gain and lose, but what if she didn't do it?"

"When Detective Casey finds this out, it's definitely not going to look good for her," I agreed. "Especially if Casey also finds out she's been plotting to leave. The assumption will be that her plans were for after his death, not before."

"But that's not what she said," Gertie said. "When she had that phone conversation with whoever she went and met, it sounded like she was planning to leave before he died."

"If you were Detective Casey, would you believe that?" Ida Belle asked.

Gertie frowned. "No. I guess I wouldn't."

"Besides," I said, "we have no way of knowing if she was telling that other person the truth either. The reality is, we have a lot of moving parts, a lot of secrets, a lot of lies, and more than one person with motive."

"Two, right?" Gertie asked.

"Maybe three," I said. "Maybe more that we don't know about."

Gertie looked confused. "Tiffany and Liam...but who else?"

"Gwyn," I said. "We only have her word that he was leaving Tiffany for her. But what if his plan was to leave Tiffany but that's where it ended. He was changing his will to leave everything to Liam. That doesn't sound like he was making moves to settle down with another woman. Maybe

Gwyn found out that Gil's plans didn't include her like she'd thought."

Ida Belle nodded. "And even though she claimed she didn't know about Tiffany and Liam's relationship prior to Tiffany marrying Gil, that might not be true. If she knew the truth then she had reason to distrust anything Gil said. Working with the troupe, she could have snooped in his belongings when he was on stage or overheard a conversation with his attorney."

"Or with another woman," Gertie said. "If he had one extra and it looked like he wasn't settling down with her then who's to say he doesn't have another?"

"Or was at least on the lookout for one," I said. "And then there's a fourth prospect."

"Who?" Gertie asked.

"Judith," I said.

"Why Judith?" Gertie asked.

"Well, Gil told Judith about his first will change," I said. "What if he told her about the divorce and Judith took that opportunity to tell him how she really felt? What if he told her about Gwyn? Even if he had no plans for a future with Gwyn, she would be a good excuse for not telling Judith the truth—that he didn't want to be with her."

Ida Belle nodded. "And maybe Judith didn't want to watch the love of her life set up house with another young woman. After all these years, if she finally thought she was going to get her opening, only to find out that slot was already filled or that she was never going to get a chance, it would have been a huge blow."

"But enough of a blow to kill him?" Gertie asked. "Judith seems so settled and normal. I just can't picture it."

I shrugged. "She's still a woman who's been in love with the same man most of her life. She's not getting any younger, and my guess is it gets lonely out on the farm with no other family around, and it's hard to maintain friendships with all the hours she has to put in every day. Judith may not be an extrovert but she's no River, either."

Gertie sighed. "I know you're right. Jeez, I'm usually the one who leaps to the crime of passion. I guess I just don't want it to be Judith."

"I don't think any of us do," Ida Belle said. "Or Liam."

Nobody said they didn't want it to be Tiffany. Which wasn't quite the same thing as wanting her to be the perp. It was more like, if it was one of the three, then Tiffany was the one they were most willing to sacrifice. Given what she'd done to Liam, I got it.

"There's something else that's bothering me," I said. "Gwyn said Gil had been edgy lately and didn't want her staying after rehearsal. But why? Was he trying to protect Gwyn because he thought someone was after him? And if that's the case, then why was he the last to leave the night he was killed? Shouldn't he have been out there pulling away with everyone else?"

"All good questions," Ida Belle said. "Maybe he forgot something and went back for it."

"Maybe," I said. And it was certainly possible, but it still didn't feel right.

I stared out the windshield as we sped down the highway, mulling over everything I'd learned. There was something bothering me but I couldn't figure out what. Something hovering right at the edge of my field of vision. Something off, but I couldn't put my finger on it.

And for some reason, I knew it was important.

---

WE MADE IT BACK TO SINFUL ABOUT THE TIME THE FESTIVAL was closing for the night. Ida Belle dropped me off at home and I practically sprinted for the shower so I could take one last pass at the glitter, figuring Carter would be on my front porch as soon as he wrapped up his festival duties. I knew he was suspicious about all my trips to New Orleans, especially when we hadn't attended the festivities that Ida Belle and Gertie never missed. I also figured he'd want to complain about being cut out of the investigation by Detective Casey. So far, he hadn't mentioned it, but I knew it had been festering there all day, just ready to boil over once he was off duty and clutching a beer.

I managed to get showered, dressed, and in the kitchen heating up a piece of pie by the time I heard my front door open.

"Kitchen," I yelled.

He trudged in and slumped into a chair before giving me the eye. "Did you get your spa business in NOLA taken care of?" he asked, his tone one of complete disbelief.

"Yep," I said.

I put a beer and the piece of pie in front of him, then popped another piece in the microwave. Then I grabbed the folder from the hot tub company and slid it in front of him. He opened it up, pulled the brochure out, and eyeballed it, then saw the receipt and his eyes widened.

"You bought it?" he asked.

"I told you I was going to," I said. "One of these days, you're going to give me the benefit of the doubt on things."

He grunted and put the folder back on the table.

"A little more enthusiasm is in order here," I said. "That hot tub is going to be awesome to decompress in and quite frankly, you look like you need it. Problems at the festival?"

"No. It's actually been quiet for Sinful. Probably because you three weren't there."

"Hey, we didn't have anything to do with that skunk-in-the-maze thing. We barely got out of there without the stink on us. And we definitely didn't cut off Gil's head and put him on that horse."

"I notice you didn't mention the glitter skunk explosion."

"We weren't even in town. So what's eating you, then? The investigation not going well?"

He scowled and I knew it was coming.

"I wouldn't know," he said. "I'm no longer in charge of the investigation."

"What? Why not?" I asked, putting on my best surprised look.

"Because a detective from New Orleans contacted me this morning and informed me that since Gil was killed there, it's already their case."

"Oh. I guess that makes sense."

He gave me a dirty look.

"What? You're the one always preaching to me about jurisdiction and rights and all."

"That's not the point," he grumbled.

"Why? Because it's *you* who's getting cut out this time? Is the NOLA detective an idiot?"

"She seems very competent, but again, not the point."

"She? Good for her. Can't be easy making rank in the city. Not with the good ole boy thing and all."

"I'm sure it's not," he said, rather begrudgingly.

"So since it's no longer your investigation, that means you can talk about it, right?"

He raised one eyebrow and stared.

"What? It's not your case. So all bets are off on the confidentiality thing."

"So you think this is an opportunity for you to load up on information and get in the middle of a NOLA police department investigation? That doesn't sound like a very good plan, even in theory. And since I know the guy who runs that department, I'm going to warn you that poking your nose in would be a very, *very* bad idea."

"Doesn't like civilians?"

"He doesn't like PIs. His wife left him for one."

I winced. Okay, so that doubled down on the risks of getting caught.

"So I guess that means you won't be sharing the gossip with me?" I asked.

"I don't deal in gossip. I deal in facts."

I waved a hand in dismissal. "Are you still working the case or not? I don't want to waste time trying to get something out of you if it's pointless. I have better things to do and much to your dismay, there are easier ways to get information if I wanted it."

"Don't pretend that all this doesn't interest you."

"Of course it interests me. A dead man rode through the park and lost his head right in front of me. Movies aren't that engrossing, and they're fiction. People in Sinful who died ten years ago want to know what happened. You're not breaking new ground here."

He sighed. "You're right. I don't suppose there's a single person in town who isn't looking for the inside scoop or making their own predictions."

"Maybe not Nora. Depending on what she's smoked."

He gave me a pained expression and I couldn't help but feel a tiny bit sorry for him. It sucked when you were told you weren't allowed to do your job. I didn't like it either, but I also didn't let it stop me. Since Carter was official, he didn't have that luxury.

"Look, I'm sorry you got kicked off the investigation," I said. "But if this detective is smart, then she'll ask you to help. It's a small town and you know all the players. She could spend weeks drumming up background that you have at your fingertips."

He sighed. "And that's pretty much what she said when we talked. She got the rundown on the major players before she headed out to interview them herself and said she'd check with me tomorrow to update me on anything I needed to know."

"It could be worse. Do you want some dinner to go with your dessert? I still have tons of the food you brought over."

"I thought you'd never ask. I don't suppose I could borrow your shower too, and then maybe crash here after."

"What about Tiny?"

"He's staying with my mom until the festival is over. My hours are too odd."

"Works for me."

And then I said a quick prayer that there was no pink glitter in my shower.

---

I WAS IN THE MIDDLE OF A VERY ODD DREAM WHERE I WAS playing the lead role in a play about a crime-solving librarian when a beeping noise jolted me awake. I bolted up—almost levitating out of bed—landed with my feet planted on the ground, pistol in hand, and spun around, ready to fire. Carter looked at me and smiled, holding up his cell phone. Merlin, who'd played this game more than once, glared at me and set off down the hall.

"No matter how many times I see it," he said, "it never ceases to impress me."

"You wouldn't be so impressed if I actually fired."

"Why do you think I haven't gotten out of bed yet? At least the shot would go over me."

"So you think," I said. "Well, are you going to answer that? It's 2:00 a.m. Nothing good happens in this town at 2:00 a.m."

He frowned and answered. His expression shifted to worried as he listened.

"Are the paramedics on the way?" he asked. "Good. I'll be there in five minutes. Tell her to sit tight and don't touch anything."

"What's wrong?" I asked. "Is someone hurt?"

"Someone broke into Tiffany's house and cracked her over the head."

# CHAPTER EIGHTEEN

"WHAT?!" I YELLED, STILL TRYING TO PROCESS WHAT HE'D said. "Do you need me to come with you?"

I had no idea what I could do as I wasn't a medical professional or a cop and not friends with Tiffany, but this was Sinful, and it was my town too now, and that was the sort of thing you offered when there was a crisis.

"No," he said as he pulled on his clothes. "I've got to secure the scene and get a statement, and I suppose I have to call Detective Casey and fill her in as soon as possible."

"You think this is related to Gil's death?"

He shrugged. "No idea, but I don't like the timing, and anything that might be related is something she needs to know about."

"Okay. Let me know if there's anything I can do. Or Ida Belle's ladies. If Tiffany needs someone to sit with her or go to the hospital or whatever."

I followed him downstairs and let him out.

"Remember to reset the alarm," he said as he hurried for his truck.

I frowned as he drove away, then ducked back inside and

set the alarm. Something was up. Figuring I would catch hell if I didn't inform all interested parties right away, I sent a quick text to Ida Belle and Gertie. That way, I'd gotten in timely notification even if they didn't read it until morning.

*Break-in at Tiffany's. She sustained head injury. Carter on his way. That's all I know.*

A couple seconds later, I got a text back from both of them.

*On my way.*

*Be there in a sec.*

I turned off the alarm, unlocked the door, and headed to the kitchen to put on a pot of coffee, wondering if anyone in Sinful had regular sleeping hours. By the time the coffee was done, Ida Belle was already in her usual chair and we were just waiting on Gertie. She rolled in a couple minutes later, and one glance at her had me wishing she'd taken a few minutes more.

She was wearing neon-orange booty shorts with *Hot to Trot* stamped across the butt. Paired with that was a hot-pink tank but with weird straps under and on the sides of her boobs— like she was wrangling them like a calf at a rodeo. She hadn't even bothered with shoes. Half the rollers were coming out of her hair and the remnants of whatever face mask she was trying this time was spotted across her face. Pink glitter twinkled on her scalp.

"Good God, give her a robe," Ida Belle said.

"Fortune doesn't own a robe," Gertie said. "She's too young for robes. And too fit. If I was built like her, I'd walk around naked all the time."

"You're already half naked and you've never been built like Fortune," Ida Belle said.

I went into the laundry room and grabbed one of Carter's T-shirts. "This will have to do," I said, mentally adding robes to my list of things to buy since I was about to install a hot tub. I didn't need the drama that might come with Gertie, the tub, and the lack of a fenced yard. Plus, the point of the tub was decompressing, and seeing Gertie dressed like an MTV reality show wasn't going to do it. Ida Belle's shooting her wouldn't be very relaxing either, except maybe for Ida Belle.

Gertie pulled on the T-shirt, which helped matters since it was fairly long on her, and then we all sat with our coffee.

"So, a break-in at Tiffany's," Ida Belle said. "That's unexpected."

I nodded. "And makes no sense."

"Doesn't seem like much about this case makes sense," Gertie said. "Do you have any ideas?"

"Not without more information," I said. "I mean, the usual reasons for a home invasion are to attack someone or steal. We don't know if anything's missing, but it sounds like they popped Tiffany hard enough that the paramedics were on their way."

Ida Belle shook her head. "If they were there to hurt Tiffany, they'd be calling for the coroner, not paramedics. If they were there to steal, then what?"

"Maybe Gil had a collection of something valuable," Gertie said. "Coins, stamps, art?"

"You saw his taste," Ida Belle said. "And I can't imagine him collecting anything else that a thief would zero in on. Besides, if Gil collected anything of value, he would have driven everyone crazy talking about it."

"True," Gertie agreed. "Maybe it was an opportunity thing. Someone figured Gil wasn't there anymore and Tiffany would be easy to work around. Maybe he figured out he could pick up loose cash, jewelry, and electronics."

"But Gil was out of town a lot with the acting troupe," I said. "Someone could have tried that stunt before now with a lot less risk since all eyes are on Tiffany now due to the murder investigation."

Ida Belle nodded. "It does seem foolish. I don't suppose we think this one is faked like the chicken might have been, do we?"

"For what purpose?" Gertie asked.

"Well, it probably gives her a valid reason to leave town," I said. "Carter wouldn't insist she remain in the house, and I can't imagine Casey wants that liability, either. No law enforcement would. And even if there was an officer to leave with her, they still can't force her to remain in an environment where she feels unsafe. If it turns out she's innocent, there could be hell to pay."

Ida Belle slowly nodded. "It's rather extreme, assuming that crack on the head was hard enough to need medical attention, but it still wouldn't be the craziest thing I've seen."

"No," Gertie said. "The craziest is chopping off a dead man's head and sending him off through the park on a horse. Instead of figuring out reasons for the crazy, we're just adding to the list of things we have no good explanation for."

I sighed. "And the worst part is you know Carter's not going to play ball on this. We'll have to get information third- or fourth-hand once the paramedics talk."

"You know, it really does seem unfair that you can't get a shred of information out of the man who got out of your bed to go to work," Gertie said.

"You know Carter," I said. "All that honor and respecting the rules and crap."

Gertie nodded. "The military ruins a lot of people that way."

My cell phone rang and I lifted an eyebrow in surprise. Carter.

"Hello?" I answered.

"Listen, I have a situation here," he said. "I have to keep the scene secured until forensics can get here and since this is probably related to Detective Casey's investigation, I can't turn it over to Deputy Breaux. Unfortunately, the good deputy is still putting off enough fumes to make your eyes bleed so I can't send him to the hospital with Tiffany either. So would you guys mind getting over there so that she has someone with her and has a way to get back home?"

"Sure," I said. "Ida Belle and Gertie are already here."

"Of course they are."

"Is Tiffany hurt badly?" I asked.

"She got a good crack on the head and the paramedics think she should have it checked. She didn't argue, so I have to assume it hurts bad enough that she agrees. They left a couple minutes ago. How quickly can you get going?"

"We just have to find Gertie some clothes, then we'll be good."

There was a long silence.

"Is she sitting in your kitchen naked?"

"No. She's wearing your T-shirt but I'm not telling you which one."

"Call if you need anything," he said and disconnected.

I looked at Ida Belle and Gertie, unable to contain my excitement.

"We're up."

———

SINCE GERTIE AND I WEREN'T EXACTLY THE SAME SIZE AND Carter's shirt looked more like a really short dress, we made a quick stop by Gertie's house for her to run in and change and grab a wet washrag to try to get the rest of that mask off her face as we drove. She yanked the curlers out on the way as well and ran a brush through her hair, which resulted in a confused mess of straight, curly, and frizzy. Finally, she pulled a hat out of her new purse and called it done.

"I can't believe Carter is sending us to the hospital," Gertie said. "Maybe spending the night with you *is* influencing him."

Ida Belle snorted. "Not even close. Not to disparage any of Fortune's, um...skills, but this one is so obvious to me."

"Really?" I asked. "Then fess up, because I'll admit to being a little floored myself."

Ida Belle grinned. "Think about it—what are we going to do when we get to the hospital?"

"Try to get information out of Tiffany before Detective Casey shows up," I said. "Ooooohhhhhh..."

"Exactly," Ida Belle said. "He knows good and well we won't be able to resist getting the story and he's using us to keep himself in the loop since it's no longer his case."

"Sneaky," I said. "I can appreciate that."

"Seems a bit one-sided," Gertie said. "Him expecting us to feed him information when he never helps us out."

"That is where that honor and rules thing comes in again," Ida Belle said. "Carter can't talk to us or he's breaking the rules, but we can talk all we want because we don't have those limitations."

"True," I said, "but the problem comes in where Carter has to give Casey anything he finds out. So how does he explain that? Carter and Casey have both warned us about getting in the middle of things."

"Well then, I guess if we don't tell Carter anything, then we can't get into trouble, can we?" Gertie said.

Ida Belle laughed. "I can't wait to see the look on his face when Fortune lays that one on him. He thinks he's being sly but he hasn't thought it all the way through."

"That's what happens when you have to jump up in the

middle of the night and work," Gertie said. "It's hard to think when your rollers are pulling on your scalp."

"I don't think Carter has that particular problem," Ida Belle said. "But lack of sleep is a good enough deterrent against long-term thinking ability. It's been a long week for him, and then add the disappointment of having his case yanked from beneath him, and I imagine he's got a good round of mad piled on the disappointment, especially after that whole thing with Emmaline and St. Ives."

"I definitely think he's having flashbacks to that," I said.

The last big crime that we'd gotten involved in solving had Carter's mother, Emmaline, as one of the victims. That had meant Carter couldn't work the case and it had been handled by the state police. Or mishandled, as the case was. Ida Belle, Gertie, and I had solved it and caught the bad guys. And now it looked as if we might have to go that route again. This attack on Tiffany worried me. Gil was murdered for a reason, but whatever that reason, it obviously wasn't resolved with his death. We needed to figure out what was going on before more victims stacked up, even if they were just victims of a police investigation, as Liam could potentially be, assuming he wasn't involved.

Ida Belle parked and we headed inside. Thankfully, the niece of one of the Sinful Ladies was working the front desk in the ER. Ida Belle explained why we were there and she nodded.

"She's in a room now," she said. "They're waiting for MRI to clear so they can take her for testing."

"Is she okay?" Gertie asked.

The nurse glanced around and leaned forward. "She wasn't sexually assaulted. Thank God."

I felt some of the tension leave my shoulders. I had hoped

it wasn't that kind of attack, but we hadn't really known, so it was a relief to hear it now.

"She seems a little out of it," the nurse said as she waved us down the hallway. "And very edgy. But then, I can't blame her. I got my own apartment a couple months ago and this is the kind of thing that had me installing an alarm and dead bolts."

I nodded. "Women living alone can't be too careful."

She knocked on a door and pushed it open. "Mrs. Forrest? Deputy LeBlanc sent some people to see to you while you're here."

Tiffany looked up as we entered the room, looking so relieved when she saw us that I briefly wondered who she'd thought was going to walk in the door.

"Thank you for coming," she said. "I'm a bit of a mess. It's so nerve-racking sitting here alone waiting, but I was afraid for a moment that someone from the church might have offered to come. The Catholic church, I mean."

"Carter would never send Celia to check on anyone," Gertie said. "Unless maybe he really didn't like them."

Tiffany smiled, then grimaced and put her hand on her forehead.

"How bad does it hurt?" I asked.

"Not bad if I don't move," she said. "Or smile. I sneezed earlier and asked for morphine."

I went over to get a better look at the injury. There was a fairly large gash on the side of her head, right around her temple. Blood was caked in her hair, but I could tell it had stopped bleeding some time before.

"Ouch," I said. "Couldn't be a worse location. Every movement of your face is going to aggravate it, and don't be surprised if you have a black eye before too long. Do you remember what happened? It looks like this is hours old."

"I remember," she said. "For what it's worth, anyway. I

went to bed around eleven. I think I dozed off about thirty minutes later. I sleep with the TV on and the show I had on was a repeat and close to the end, so that's how I know. Anyway, a noise woke me and when I sat up, something cold and hard hit me right in the side of the face."

She shook her head, then grimaced again. "You know that expression about seeing stars? Well, I get it now. It was like my head exploded into balls of pain and light and then I was gone. When I came to, I was still in bed and there was blood everywhere. I grabbed my cell phone and called 911 while I dug the shotgun out of the closet."

"So you were out for over two hours," I said. "Did you get a look at the person who struck you?"

"Not really," she said. "My eyes weren't focused yet and even though there was light from the television, he seemed really dark. At least, that's the impression that I have, but who knows if it's right."

"He might have been wearing all black," Gertie said.

"That would make sense," Tiffany said.

"No impression as to size, height?" I asked.

"None at all," she said. "It all happened so quickly."

I nodded. "Was anything taken or did you even have a chance to look?"

"The cash we kept in a kitchen drawer was still there and my wedding ring was on the dresser along with a couple other good pieces. My purse was on the kitchen counter and all the cash and credit cards were intact. Carter said the stereo equipment and my laptop were in the living room...I don't get it."

"Me either," I said.

A tech popped in the room. "I'm going to take Mrs. Forrest for an MRI. She'll be back in about an hour. You can wait in the lobby if you'd like."

"Will you please stay?" Tiffany asked, sounding more like a little girl than a young woman.

"Of course," Gertie said. "We're going to drive you home when you're released."

Her expression clouded a bit as they rolled her away.

"Well, looks like we're hanging in the lobby for a while," I said. "Want to flip a coin to see who goes for coffee and Danish?"

"I'll go," Gertie said. "You two never buy enough Danish."

"I bought six last time," I said.

"And ate three," Gertie said.

"I was hungry," I said. "I ran ten miles that morning."

"Be that as it may," Gertie said.

I pushed the door to enter the lobby and it almost smacked Detective Casey right in the face. Her eyes widened as she caught sight of us, then narrowed.

"What are you doing here?" she asked.

"Seeing to Tiffany," I said. "And when she's done here, driving her home. Ida Belle and Gertie sorta run the support end of things in town."

"She doesn't have any family to do that?" Casey asked.

"No," Ida Belle said. "And she doesn't exactly have friends in Sinful given how her marriage came about."

Casey sighed. "Yeah, I guess she wouldn't. I keep forgetting that whole small-town dynamics thing. Did you see her?"

I nodded. "She's got a hell of a good crack on the head. Knocked her out for two hours or better, best I can figure. That's the only injury though."

Casey looked relieved. "That's good. Can she identify her attacker?"

"No," I said. "She was asleep, heard something and woke up, got cracked on the head before she ever saw the guy. And there's nothing stolen that she could tell either. Wallet, cash, jewelry all intact."

Casey frowned. "That doesn't make sense."

"I know," I agreed. "But she only had time for a cursory review before the ambulance came, so you can't be sure nothing's missing."

"All right," Casey said, and she straightened. "Well, I best get to the crime scene then. I thought I'd stop and talk to Tiffany on the way there, but it doesn't sound like she's going to be able to shed any light on this. You ladies stay out of trouble."

We all nodded, knowing exactly what she was implying.

"So what do you make of this?" Ida Belle asked as we slumped into chairs in the corner of the lobby.

"Nothing good," I said. "If nothing was stolen, what was the point? He had hours to take whatever he wanted out of the house. And if the goal was to kill Tiffany, she was out cold and an easy target. So if it isn't about assault or theft or murder, what the heck do we have left?"

"Maybe something was stolen that she isn't aware of," Ida Belle said.

"It's possible," I agreed. "But Carter won't know if anything is missing and Tiffany seemed to cover everything of reasonable value."

"I guess we'll have to wait until Tiffany's up to taking a harder look at everything," Ida Belle said.

I nodded. Somehow, a robbery didn't feel right. But then, nothing else did either.

# CHAPTER NINETEEN

IT WAS ANOTHER THREE HOURS BEFORE THE DOCTOR reviewed the MRI and cleared Tiffany to leave. Even then, he hesitated when she asked about release, but since the MRI was clear and even her headache was going away, there wasn't much he could keep her on. And given the reason she was there in the first place, I figured he knew there was no way she was staying put as long as she was able to walk out on her own.

So we collected the records for the cops, and the three of us drove Tiffany home. Carter was standing on the front porch when we pulled up, looking aggravated, but he tried to hold it in as he asked Tiffany how she was feeling.

"The MRI was clear," Tiffany said. "So fine, I guess. Are they done in there yet?"

"No," Carter said and his jaw flexed. "Detective Casey wants her forensic team from New Orleans to do the job, and they haven't arrived yet. I should let you know she has a warrant so it will be a complete search, not just coverage of the break-in."

Ah. The source of his aggravation. Carter and his team had been pushed out.

Tiffany just nodded, still pale and looking like a child more than an adult.

Casey must have heard her name because she stepped outside and gave Tiffany the once-over. "If you're up to it, I'd like for you to do a walk-around and let me know if anything is missing."

She looked back at me and asked, "Is it okay if she comes with me?"

I was a little surprised, but Casey gave her a nod and motioned us inside. I followed Tiffany, and we stopped in the living room as she checked a couple drawers and inside a television cabinet.

"I don't see anything gone," she said. "But then, there was nothing really valuable in here."

Casey walked over to a table, removed a putty knife from a stack of books, and picked one up. I glanced at the titles and realized they were books on art.

"What about that painting?" Casey asked and pointed to the heinous Jesus playing poker mess. "Is it worth anything?"

"Good Lord, no," Tiffany said. "That thing is horrible. Gil got all interested in art some months back and started reading up on things. Apparently, they're using a painting like that on the set of the play. He took pictures and had an artist paint him one. I told him it was beyond offensive and tacky, but he said that the artist's style had merit—whatever that was supposed to mean—and he was using the painting to get into character. I didn't bother to argue after that. It's not like anyone came to visit us anyway."

"Was that a common thing for him to do?" Casey asked. "That getting into character thing?"

"Oh yeah," Tiffany said. "Ask me about the time he was playing a scuba diver and almost drowned in our garden tub because he forgot to turn his tank on."

Casey stared for a couple seconds, then nodded. "Then let's check the kitchen."

We went through all the rooms, with Tiffany looking in drawers, cabinets, and other storage spots, but she couldn't think of a single thing that was missing. And several reasonably valuable items were right out on display.

"I don't understand," Tiffany said. "Why aren't things missing? They even left the cash."

Casey frowned, glancing around Gil's office, the last room we'd checked. "Did Gil have anything sensitive that someone might want?"

"Sensitive how?" Tiffany asked. "I mean, I guess he has information on a lot of people that he's sold insurance to."

"I meant the kind of information that wouldn't be on a form," Casey said.

Tiffany stared at her, confused for a moment, then her eyes widened. "You think Gil had dirt on someone doing something bad? Is that what you're saying?"

Casey shrugged. "I've seen it before. Your husband knew a lot of people from his business and the acting. Could be he ran across things people didn't want him to know and really didn't want him to tell."

"And you think—what—that he had pictures or video?" Tiffany asked.

"Anything is possible," Casey said. "I'll have the team take his laptop in to search it. Do you have a computer?"

Tiffany shook her head. "I just used Gil's if I needed one, but most things I can do on my iPad. Do you need that?"

Casey nodded. "I'll need all electronics, including your phone. I have a spare I can issue you until tech has had a chance to check yours out. But since robbery wasn't the motive and you appear to be a casualty of the break-in and not the target of it, I have to assume the perp was looking for something else."

"I just don't know what to say," Tiffany said. "Except that I'm not staying here and none of you can make me. Not anymore."

"I understand," Casey said. "You're free to leave. Just remain in the state and let me know where you'll be staying when you land."

"I need to pack some things," Tiffany said.

"I'll send an officer in to make a log of the things you remove and to get you that phone," Casey said and strode out of the room.

"They're going to inventory my toothbrush and deodorant?" Tiffany asked.

"It's standard procedure," I said. And it wasn't exactly untrue. If you felt someone was hiding things, it was absolutely standard procedure to make sure they didn't leave the house with evidence. I just wasn't telling Tiffany that. Mainly because I already knew she was hiding things. I just didn't know if she was hiding anything to do with the break-in.

I waited as Tiffany packed some clothes and toiletries and then I carried her bag outside and put it in the trunk of her car, which had already been searched. Carter's truck was no longer parked in front of the house, so I assumed he'd gone off to tackle other things. We stood in the driveway and I made a split decision...a test, of sorts.

"You're welcome to stay with me," I said to Tiffany. "I have plenty of room and an excellent security system."

"Not to mention she's former CIA and the best shot in the state," Ida Belle said.

Tiffany bit her lip, then shook her head. "I can't put you out. I'll just find somewhere in the city. You know, where I can get lost in the crowd. I'm tired of being under a microscope. I always have been here, but now it's worse. I think... I think I just need to be away from it all."

"We understand," Gertie said. "But if you need anything, you call us."

I handed her a business card since Casey had taken her phone.

"Thank you," Tiffany said. "I really appreciate everything you ladies have done for me. No one else has even called or come by or anything since Gil died. I knew everyone was mad over our marriage, but I guess I never realized just how much damage we'd caused."

Her entire expression and body language was full of regret, but it was too late to rethink things already done that couldn't be undone.

"Please be safe," Gertie said.

I nodded. "Just because the cops think this all centers on Gil doesn't mean they're correct. You should still watch your back as if you are a target. I'm not saying that's the case but being extra careful is not wasted action."

Tiffany swallowed and nodded. "I will. Thank you again."

She practically ran to her car and jumped inside. We watched as she backed out of the driveway and quickly pulled away.

"She could hardly wait to get out of here," Gertie said.

"But she's not as scared as she pretends to be," Ida Belle said. "Or she would have taken Fortune up on her offer. I can't imagine a safer place to be."

"So either she doesn't think this has anything to do with her, or she's in it up to her neck and doesn't want any witnesses when the house comes crashing down," I said.

"We need to find out which one," Gertie said. "Are we going to follow her?"

I shook my head. "I slipped a tracker in her trunk when I put her bag in."

Gertie grinned. "Have I told you lately how smart you are?"

Ida Belle nodded. "So what's on the agenda now?"

"My house," I said. "There's something that was bothering me about the interview with the acting people last night. I want to check on a couple things and maybe give Mannie a call. I think we might need another background check."

———

IDA BELLE WENT FOR THE REFRIGERATOR AND SOME OF Molly's dip as soon as she hit my kitchen. I just grinned and patted myself on the back for remembering to put another batch in the fridge to thaw the night before.

"We're having dip for breakfast?" Gertie asked.

"We had Danish at the hospital," Ida Belle said. "So technically, this is lunch or snack before lunch. I could put it back…"

"That won't be necessary," Gertie said and went into the pantry for chips.

I grinned and headed off to grab my laptop out of my office. Gertie and Ida Belle had the table ready to go when I got back. I plopped down in my chair and accessed the internet.

"What's up?" Gertie said. "You have that look you get when something clicks."

I nodded. "I think something did. I had this nagging feeling that I was missing something with the drama crowd interview. I think I know what it was. Look."

I flipped my laptop around and pointed to the woman in a newspaper photo at a charity bake event.

"That's Emilia Davis, Tiffany's mother," Gertie said.

I nodded. "Now give her thirty years of hard living or maybe a long illness and who does she remind you of?"

They both leaned toward the laptop, frowning. Then Ida Belle's eyes widened.

"The maintenance lady from the theater," she said.

"Yeah," I said. "Lil was her name."

"Short for Emilia," Gertie said. "Good Lord, I still don't think I would have seen it if you hadn't pointed it out. She doesn't look anything like that photo, and it wasn't that far back."

"She's definitely aged in a bad way," I said. "But the big question is, how did she come to work at the theater? Was she there before Gil showed up with the acting troupe or after? I can't imagine that he didn't know who she was."

"I don't know," Ida Belle said. "If we've learned anything the past couple days it's that Gil was even more self-absorbed than we originally thought. And she does look remarkably different. But there's zero doubt that she knew who Gil was."

"I agree with the self-absorption thing, but I think he knew," I said. "Remember that Gwyn told us Gil didn't want her working late one night, and her argument was that Lil was still there but it didn't matter to him."

"You think he didn't want her working alone with Lil because he was afraid Lil would spill the beans on his marriage to Tiffany," Gertie said.

"It makes sense," I said.

"Do you think that's why Gil wanted the gun?" Ida Belle asked. "Could Lil have threatened him in some way?"

"I don't know," I said. "Which is why I want to get some background information."

I grabbed my cell phone and called Mannie, then quickly explained what I needed and gave him everything I had on

Tiffany's mother. He promised to get on it right away. Then I pulled my laptop back over and started typing again.

"Now let's see what we can drum up on the others," I said. "First up, Paul Easton, because I'm betting we can rule him out straightaway."

Ida Belle nodded. "Struck me as a bit of a wet fish. Can't imagine him having the fortitude to kill someone or chop off a head."

"I can't even imagine him walking up to that horse, much less getting it in a trailer," Gertie said.

"Well, I'm still operating under the theory that the murder and the Headless Horseman stunt might be two different people," I said. "But the Horseman stunt had to require two to make it work. I just don't see how a single person could have pulled it off unless they were Iron Man and the Lone Ranger combined."

"Agreed," Ida Belle said.

"So let's see," I said as I cruised the sites that mentioned Paul Easton. "Nothing much of note. Easton is a retired high school math teacher who still substitutes and does private tutoring. He must really turn on the personality to act."

"Gwyn said he did," Ida Belle said. "The math teacher thing fits him perfectly, though."

"Well, I don't see a part time as a rodeo clown," I said. "And I can't come up with a decent motive, so I'm going to push him to the bottom of the list."

"Maybe he really didn't like those chats in the bar after plays," Gertie said. "Remember the hot tub and Nora?"

"Which is a great reason to avoid her but not kill her," I said. "Next up is the other woman, Gwyn. And it looks like the only mention is as her being the assistant to Brigette Driscoll in an article about Brigette bringing class and history into the productions."

"I wonder if they're talking about those emeralds Gwyn wanted her to bring to the performance," Gertie said.

"Let's look up those emeralds," I said. "Here we go. Family heirloom passed down for over a hundred years. Originally made for a great-great-great-whatever in Europe and brought to America. Family held on to them through lean years even though they could have sold for survival, and blah, blah...looks like Brigette is the current owner."

"And what about Brigette?" Ida Belle asked. "She gives off the air of money."

I nodded. "Her father was an attorney and state senator."

"So money and connections," Gertie said.

"So no motives for any of them that we can see except for Lil," Ida Belle said. "Well, and maybe Gwyn if we think she had any idea Gil was lying to her about leaving Tiffany for her."

I leaned back in my seat, trying to process all the pieces. "We have too many connected people here. That can't be coincidence."

Gertie nodded. "But with everyone hiding things and several of them with motive, how do we narrow it down? I mean, if we ask where everyone was the night Gil's body was stolen, they will say in bed. If we ask about the night he was killed, they'll say at home and the acting troupe will say on their way home. And I'm sure everyone will have similar unprovable things to say about the night of the Headless Horseman ride."

"I agree," I said. "Opportunity is not going to help us because, as far as we know, everyone had it. So the question is motive, which still doesn't narrow things down a lot. Obviously, Tiffany had the strongest one, especially if she knew about the divorce, but people kill over feelings too, so that doesn't leave out the ones who don't financially benefit."

I grabbed my phone and called Mannie again and gave him the names of everyone in the acting troupe, Liam, Judith, Tiffany, and River. I asked him to do a basic sweep and let me know if anything popped.

"No problem," he said. "I got something back on Emilia Davis. After her second husband was arrested, she was hospitalized for a nervous breakdown."

"The rumor mill mentioned something to that effect," I said.

"Did the rumor mill also mention that she spent two years in a mental health facility?"

"No. They did not. Interesting. I don't suppose you have more details on that?"

"Only a few. There's an orderly who used to work there and owes us money. Orderlies don't have access to patient files, but he said he was told her stay wasn't voluntary and that she was considered dangerous to herself and others, so she was on his watch list. Apparently, they have patients they keep more of an eye on. Anyway, that's it for now. I'll let you know when I have more."

I thanked him, then filled Ida Belle and Gertie in.

"I think Emilia just moved up the list," Ida Belle said.

"I think it's time we have another chat with her," I said. "A private one."

"And we can check out where Tiffany went while we're there," Gertie said.

I nodded. It was all about to break wide open.

I could feel it.

# CHAPTER TWENTY

WE WERE JUST GETTING READY TO LEAVE FOR NEW ORLEANS when my doorbell rang. Carter wouldn't bother to ring the doorbell when it was daylight, so it definitely wasn't him. I headed for the door and was surprised to find a very agitated Judith Trahan standing there.

"I need your help," she said.

I waved her inside. "Ida Belle and Gertie are here—back in the kitchen."

"Good," she said and followed me back.

I offered her something to drink, which she refused, so we all sat and waited for her to tell us what was wrong.

"Liam's being railroaded," she said. "The local cops have searched his house and the butcher shop already, and then he called and told me some New Orleans detective showed up this morning, asking him for an alibi for last night and the night Gil was murdered. How the hell does someone who lives alone provide an alibi for the middle of the night?"

"Most people can't," I agreed.

"He said the detective told him Tiffany was attacked last

night." Judith looked at the three of us, clearly not wanting to believe it.

"That's right," I said. "Someone broke in last night and hit her so hard they knocked her out. We brought her home from the hospital this morning."

"I thought he'd heard wrong, maybe," Judith said. "Was it a robbery?"

I shrugged. "We don't know. The cops are still working the house, far as I know."

"That woman detective isn't," Judith said. "She's the one asking Liam for an alibi. There was...hell, Gil changed his will a while back and split the money between Tiffany and Liam. That detective told him she knew all about it and that meant if something happened to Tiffany, it would all go to him. I guess she talked to Gil's attorney."

"That doesn't look good," Gertie said.

"No," I agreed. "But it also doesn't apply as Tiffany didn't die. And whoever hit her had plenty of time to make that happen."

Judith nodded. "Liam pointed out that since she wasn't dead, he didn't see how that pointed the finger at him, but that detective wasn't having any of it."

"It's possible for people to panic," Ida Belle said. "Especially if this isn't normal behavior, and it's not for the majority of people. But if they get worked up to that level of desperation, they might think someone was dead or realize what they did and then flee the scene before they get caught. The detective has to consider that possibility."

Judith slumped in her chair. "That boy wouldn't hurt anyone, not even that useless cheater."

"That statement could refer to Tiffany or Gil," I said and gave her a pointed look.

Judith stared at me for a moment, then lowered her eyes to the table.

"She's right," Ida Belle said. "Gil owed Liam more than Tiffany did. If you're going to cast any blame over what happened back then, it all starts with Gil. You have to stop defending him, Judith. Gil had no reason to take up with Tiffany except selfishness, unless you honestly believe he ever really cared for her."

Judith sighed. "No. I guess I don't. I think he just cared about how he looked—the old guy with the young, hot girl."

"It's not a good look when the young, hot girl was your son's girlfriend," Gertie said. "And Tiffany had far better reasons for what she did than Gil."

"What reasons?" Judith asked.

"Her stepfather is in prison for assaulting multiple young women," Gertie said. "Tiffany showed all the signs of living in an abusive situation. Gil had the money and assets to get her out, so she took advantage of it."

Judith's face paled. "I didn't know. I swear."

"No one did, and only a few suspected," Gertie said. "Tiffany has never confirmed it, but with all my years of teaching, I'd bet on it."

"Gil never said anything," Judith said. "Or Liam."

"I doubt Gil knew," Ida Belle said. "He just thought a young, pretty girl wanted him and that's all Tiffany wanted him to know. And I'd bet money Liam didn't know or he would have tried to help. And since he took off right after they married and wasn't really friends with anyone in Mudbug, then he wouldn't have had access to any talk about her stepfather after his arrest."

Judith shook her head. "That changes things for sure. At least as far as my opinion of her, but Gil knew what he was doing to Liam. And now the man's dead and still messing with

Liam's life. I tell you, that boy did not hurt Tiffany and he didn't kill his father."

"I guess you heard it's a murder investigation now," I said.

She nodded. "The boy who delivered some fencing material told me about the car. Then that woman detective from New Orleans came by and had a chat with me. A chat, she called it, seeing as how I was friends with Gil and would know better than anyone if he'd gotten mixed up in something that got him killed. I told her straight-out that the only thing I knew of that Gil had gotten mixed up in was his marriage."

"Did you tell her about him asking you about a gun?" I asked.

"Yeah, but like I told you guys, I couldn't tell her why," Judith said. "Just that I found it odd. But none of that matters. What matters is that I think this detective has Liam in her sights because of the will. Liam's boss is making noise about all the negative attention. He's going to lose his future if that detective doesn't back off, and she mentioned a search warrant when Liam wouldn't agree to let her search his house again. If she comes back with one for his house and the butcher shop, the future Liam had is as good as over."

"It's definitely a bad situation for Liam," I said, "but I don't know what I can do about it."

"Carter is your man," Judith said. "Surely you can talk to him. Have him call off that detective."

"It doesn't work like that," I said. "Carter has been more or less removed from the case. The murder happened in New Orleans, so it's theirs. Detective Casey uses him to answer questions, but she doesn't have to loop him in on anything, much less involve him in the investigation."

Judith looked so sad that I felt sorry for her. And I felt sorry for Liam and wished there were something I could do, but my hands were tied. Carter's hands were tied. At this point, the only thing that would help Liam was finding the murderer, assuming it wasn't him. I studied Judith as she stared out my back window, slowly shaking her head, and decided to see what kind of reaction I got from her since she appeared to be in a vulnerable position.

"Did you know Gil had found a new girlfriend?" I asked.

Judith's eyes widened. "What? No. That's not possible. He would have told me."

"Would he?" I asked and studied her.

She stared at me for a couple seconds, then dropped her gaze down, shifting to a look of defeat.

"Maybe not," she said. "Who is she?"

"Someone involved in the acting troupe," I said.

"I guess it would be," she said. "How old is this one?"

"Older than Tiffany, but not nearly as old as Gil," I said.

Judith sighed. "It shouldn't surprise me. I knew Gil and Tiffany never had a real marriage. I don't think he ever really cared about her as a person. More as a collectible, you know? Someone that made him look successful and hip and made the other guys jealous. Mind you, that's what I think *he* thought, not what I think other people thought."

"Good," Gertie said. "Because other people thought he was a fool. At best."

Judith pushed herself up from the chair and gave me a forlorn nod. "I appreciate you talking with me. I'm going to call my lawyer and set up an appointment with Liam. I've got to do something to protect him. He doesn't deserve this. Any of this."

"Let us know if there's anything else we can do," Ida Belle said. "And if Liam needs anything that we can help with. "

Judith gave us a nod and headed out. I waited until I heard the door close behind her, then asked, "Do we believe she didn't know about Gwyn?"

Ida Belle and Gertie both shook their heads.

I sighed. Exactly what I'd thought.

We weren't sure.

---

I CHECKED THE TRACKER I'D PUT IN TIFFANY'S CAR BEFORE we left my house and it showed her location in New Orleans, so we headed out. When we got to the city limits, I pulled it up again so that we could home in on her exact location. Ida Belle snaked around the city streets until we arrived at a boutique hotel just outside the French Quarter. There was a lot across the street and I spotted Tiffany's car in an end slot.

"This is definitely the place," I said and pointed.

Ida Belle entered the parking lot and backed into a space on the row farthest from Tiffany's car and next to a van. I hopped out and ran to shove some bills in the collection box and then hurried back to the SUV.

"Only one hotel here, so that has to be the place, right?" Gertie said.

"Unless she's staying somewhere farther down and this is the closest lot," Ida Belle said. "Or the closest one with available parking. And that's assuming she got a room right away and isn't just meeting her mystery friend from the motel."

Gertie sighed. "Why do you have to make everything so difficult?"

Ida Belle shrugged. "Just pointing out all the options. We can't assume anything until we lay eyes on her."

"Well, start assuming," Gertie said and pointed.

I looked up and saw Tiffany exiting the hotel with a young man.

"Does he look familiar to you guys?" I asked.

Ida Belle lifted binoculars and nodded. "I think it's one of the boys from that photo. One of the rodeo kids Tiffany used to hang out with."

Gertie grabbed the binoculars. "Kip Ranger."

We both looked at her.

"What?" she said. "I read the names. His stood out. How many Kips do you know around these parts, and last name Ranger, like the Lone Ranger? It stuck with me."

"So it wasn't Liam that Tiffany had reconnected with," I said. "It was this guy."

"Who knows how to handle horses," Gertie said.

"Still doesn't mean she killed Gil," Ida Belle said. "But it sure looks suspicious."

"Looks better for Liam, though," Gertie said.

"But also brings up the question of what she wanted from Liam that day at the butcher shop," Ida Belle said.

I took a couple pictures with my phone and then we waited while the two of them got into Tiffany's car and pulled away.

"Do you want to follow them?" Ida Belle asked.

"No. The tracker will let us know where they're going, but I'm guessing it's just for something to eat," I said. "Let's go tackle the Emilia situation."

The theater wasn't open, but a young woman wearing a college insignia T-shirt and a bored expression answered the door when we knocked. I explained that we needed to speak to Lil, and she waved us inside without so much as a raised eyebrow and pointed to a set of double doors.

"She was in the theater working on some prop or something last time I was out of the office," she said. "You don't mind finding her yourself, do you? I've got a chemistry test tomorrow that I'm cramming for. I keep telling my dad I can't sit in his building all day because I have things to do but he doesn't listen."

"No problem at all," I said and we headed off.

"Good thing we're not serial killers," Gertie said, "since she lets anyone have the run of the place."

"I don't think she'd care as long as we weren't here for her," Ida Belle said.

We located Emilia near the stage, painting a prop. She looked up as we approached and immediately stiffened. *Oh yeah, lady. You're so caught.*

"Hi, Lil," I said. "Or do you still go by Emilia?"

# CHAPTER TWENTY-ONE

Lil's expression was so panicked that I wondered for a moment if she was going to attempt to leap over the prop and run for it. But she must have decided that would be futile because her shoulders slumped and she sighed.

"That was a different part of my life," she said. "I'm Lil now. Emilia has been gone for a long time."

"But Gil knew who you were, right?" I asked.

She slumped down on a stool she'd had there for the painting and motioned for us to sit in the front row of seats.

"He knew after I told him," she said.

"He didn't recognize you?" Ida Belle asked.

She shook her head, the resigned expression replaced by one of slight disgust. "Gil didn't notice anything about anyone else."

"Not even Tiffany?" Gertie asked.

"Gil's only interest was Gil," she said. "Tiffany was a trophy to him. Something pretty to sit on the mantel and brag about. I doubt he knew much about her at all."

"Including why she was so quick to marry a man old enough to be her father?" I asked.

Lil looked down at the ground, a flush creeping up her neck. "That was on me. I should have known, but I was a weak person back then. I thought I had to have a man to get through every day. When Tiffany's dad died, I lost my husband and my best friend, but I also realized that I'd been taken care of for so long that I didn't know how to be alone."

"Was sleeping alone so bad that you'd offer up your daughter in exchange for company?" I asked.

"No!" she said. "It wasn't like that. I really didn't know." She shook her head. "Didn't want to know, I guess. I know now that I didn't process things correctly. That I should have never taken up with that creep, but at the time, no one could have told me different."

"But you still hate Gil for marrying Tiffany," I said.

She shrugged. "He was a predator. Just a different sort. She might not have told him what was going on, but he knew how to target people and she was ripe for the picking. I know because I've been there myself. Predators know how to spot the weak one in the crowd."

"Sounds like you've had a lot of therapy to understand the dynamic," Ida Belle said. "Was that while you were in the mental facility?"

She averted her gaze again. "I guess I should have figured you'd know about that too. I sold the house and left right after all that stuff went down. Didn't keep in touch with anyone from Mudbug, but I guess things still get around."

She let out a big sigh. "Look, I had a breakdown, all right? And then I made some really bad decisions and needed that stay. It took a while for me to realize all the mistakes I made, and I wish to God I could take them back, but that's not an option. The only thing I can do is try to move forward."

"And did moving forward include trying to renew your relationship with your daughter?" I asked.

"It was the number one thing on my mind," Lil said. "When I got out, I found an apartment here and started cleaning at one of the hotels. Then I saw a billboard a couple years ago for the theater and there was Gil with that insincere smile of his. In the window was a sign saying they were looking for maintenance help, so I figured if I applied and was hired, that was my sign that it was time to approach Tiffany."

"But you wanted to scout out the situation first, by watching her husband," I said.

She nodded. "Do you blame me? It had been years since I'd heard anything about Tiffany. She never did social media and all Gil posted were pictures of himself. I don't know people in Sinful and wasn't about to ask people in Mudbug for favors. Not when I'm the reason a monster was living there."

"I can see where that would have been difficult," I said. "So you did reconnaissance first."

"I tried, but I didn't learn anything about Tiffany," she said. "That man was completely incapable of thinking about anyone but himself. I spent a couple months lurking around during rehearsal and never once saw her or heard her name. I was starting to think they were no longer married when Brigette asked the others who would be bringing their spouses on the next tour so that she could arrange the hotel rooms properly and he said Tiffany wouldn't be joining him."

"Wasn't he wearing a wedding ring?" I asked. The Headless Horseman hadn't been wearing one, but it might have been removed at the funeral home while prepping the body.

"Yes, but all that told me was he was married but not to whom," she said then shook her head, clearly disgusted. "When I overheard Brigette complaining about funds to get the props done, I saw it as an opportunity to spend more time hanging around without it looking suspect. And I saw right away that the ring didn't count for nothing."

"What do you mean?" I asked.

"He was putting the moves on Gwyn," Lil said. "I could see him coming a mile away, but then, I know what to look for now. But Gwyn bought every word he told her, hook, line, and sinker. Like I said, predators know how to pick their prey. Gwyn wears neediness like a scarf, just like I used to. It's right there for a man like Gil to see and take advantage of."

"And that made you mad?" I asked.

"Of course it made me mad," she said. "The man used my daughter and now that he was done, he was moving on to the next victim."

"Some might also argue that your daughter took advantage of Gil," I said.

"She was a child," Lil said. "And she had reasons for what she did—good reasons. Not that I'm saying that excuses it, but what was Gil's excuse? What were his reasons? Certainly not as important as Tiffany's."

"So did you ever approach Gil?" I asked.

She nodded. "He was the last to leave one night—fiddling around with props for the play. He was always fiddling with those props."

"What do you mean—like painting or something?" I asked.

"Good Lord no," Lil said. "Gil wasn't that useful. He'd gotten on some bender about the art. Probably took an online class or something and thought he was an expert. That would be his speed. He was always complaining about the vases and paintings and dishes and pillows—the decorative stuff. Always questioning Brigette on her choices and pushing for something different."

Remembering the painting in his house, I frowned. "I've been inside his house and he has horrible taste."

Lil nodded. "I know. Don't get me wrong, some of the things here I wouldn't display in a garage, but that's Brigette's department and the things she picks suit the story, I guess. I have to admit, I don't really care for plays, so I don't pay a lot of attention, but I understand Brigette comes from money, so I assume she knows art way better than Gil did."

"So you told Gil who you were one night when he stayed after rehearsal to critique the artwork?" I asked.

"Yes."

"What was his reaction?" Ida Belle asked.

"Less than stellar," she said. "He accused me of stalking him, trying to break up his marriage, trying to upset Tiffany. It took me several minutes just to convince him that I hadn't even tried to make contact with her. I told him I didn't know anything about their marriage because I'd moved away from Mudbug and hadn't been back. But when I realized who he was, I couldn't help asking about my daughter. I hedged a little on that last part, but I wasn't about to tell him that his stalker comment was closer to the truth."

"And what did he have to say?" Gertie asked.

"He said Tiffany was fine and that she had no desire to speak to me," she said. "He claimed she'd made it clear from the beginning that she had no family except him and that was how she intended to keep things. He warned me to stay away from her or he'd slap a restraining order on me. And then he said to stay away from him as well."

"So did you contact Tiffany anyway?" I asked.

She nodded. "I dug through Brigette's files one night and got her cell phone number. All the actors have an emergency contact. I tried calling but she made it clear that she didn't ever want to hear from me. That there was no making up for the choices I'd made. That she had Gil now and he was taking care of her like I never had."

"I'm sure that hurt to hear," Ida Belle said.

"It did," she said. "I know and accept the truth of what I

did, but hearing her talk about Gil like some white knight when I knew what he was up to with Gwyn...well, it just didn't sit right with me."

"Did Tiffany tell Gil you'd called?" Ida Belle asked.

"I don't think so," Lil said. "At least, he never said anything to me about it, so that's the assumption I made. I can't imagine him letting it go."

"Probably not," Ida Belle agreed.

"Did you ever confront Gil about Gwyn?" I asked.

"No," she said. "Couldn't see the point. He was going to do what he wanted just like he always has, and it wouldn't do any good to tell Tiffany because even if she took my call, she wouldn't believe me. And even if she did, she wouldn't have left him. It would take him setting her out like a stray cat before she let go of the security."

She frowned. "I do wonder if Gil didn't mention something to Gwyn though."

"Why do you say that?" I asked.

"She got strange at rehearsal," Lil said. "I mean, the girl's not overly normal, but she seemed nervous—on edge. Even Brigette got onto her lately to focus better. I wondered if Gil had said something to her and she guessed that I had figured out they had something going on."

"He might have," I said, remembering Gwyn saying that Gil insisted she leave rehearsal one night rather than stay late when Lil was the only person left in the building.

Lil stared off at the wall, her jaw flexing. Then she slowly shook her head.

"This entire thing is a tragedy," she said. "And the one who got the worst of it is Liam. He's the only truly innocent party in all of it and I hope you find a way to help him." She sighed. "If you don't have anything else, I'd like to finish this up. I have a doctor's appointment this afternoon. Breast cancer."

"I'm sorry to hear that," Gertie said. "Are you going through treatment?"

"Doubt it," she said. "I was too far gone by the time I got it looked at. If I did treatments, they would wipe me out and there's only a small chance that they'd work. I don't have the money to sit in bed all day and no one to help look after me even if I did. The best thing to do is let it run its course."

Her expression was a mixture of sadness, anger, and regret that was so overwhelming, it felt as if a huge blanket of despair had been draped over all of us.

"I'm really sorry," I said.

She nodded. "If you don't have anything else, I really have to get back to this. All these props go onto a truck early tomorrow morning to ship out to the opening location and it has to be dry before it goes on the truck."

"They're not opening the show here?" I asked.

"They're closing it here," she said. "Brigette likes to do it that way. Says then they've worked out any kinks and bring the absolute best performance back to their home theater."

I gave her my card. "If you can think of anything that would help, please let me know. You're right—Liam is the only innocent one in all of this, and I have to make sure that's proven because right now, a detective has him in her sights."

"I wish I could help," she said. "That boy deserves better. Always did."

She went back to her painting and we headed out. No one said a word until we climbed into the SUV.

"Well, that was a depressing conversation," Gertie said. "All the stuff about Gil was bad enough but then she had to throw dying into the mix."

"That and all the mental strain explains her aging so quickly," I said.

Ida Belle nodded. "I have to wonder how much of her own life she's projecting onto Tiffany's."

"Good question," I said. "I don't figure Gil cared much about Tiffany one way or another except for how he thought she made him look, but we never heard anything about abuse and Gil certainly wasn't a violent felon."

"But if Lil saw him as just another predator," Ida Belle said, "and she's lumping them all in one box..."

"And she's dying," Gertie said.

"Yeah," I agreed. "She could have justified killing him. Especially if she thought he was cheating on Tiffany and would abandon her after preying on her. Lil already has a history of being mentally unsound, so her thinking might not be the same as regular people."

"Motive and opportunity," Ida Belle said.

Gertie sighed. "Just what we needed—another suspect."

———

AFTER OUR CHAT WITH LIL, WE GRABBED A LATE LUNCH IN New Orleans, then headed back to Sinful. I'd already checked Tiffany's car location and it was back in the parking lot across from the hotel we'd seen her leaving earlier. She was supposed to check in with Casey and give her the location she was staying at, so unless someone said otherwise, I was going to assume she'd done so.

"So do we tell Casey any of this?" Gertie asked.

"Tell her what?" Ida Belle asked. "That there's a ton of suspects, all with motive and opportunity, and we have no proof against any of them?"

"It might send her in the right direction," Gertie said.

"Or send her boss looking for her source," Ida Belle said. "And we don't know what the right direction is anyway. I like

Casey well enough, but I'm not interested in spending time in a NOLA jail cell because her boss has a problem with PIs. If we were just dealing with Carter, things would be different."

"I agree," I said. "Casey herself warned us to stay low and said she wouldn't be talking to us. If we had concrete evidence against anyone, that would be different. But all we have is speculation and the same information she'll get herself as soon as she has time to question everyone again. I don't think any of the suspects are a flight risk, so if it takes her a couple days to catch up, that's really not a big deal. And if it keeps us off the hot plate, I'm all for it."

"You're right," Gertie said. "I guess I'm just wanting this one solved and over so that we can get back to enjoying Halloween like we usually do."

"Who's saying we can't?" I asked. "We're going to be home in plenty of time to go to the festival tonight. And honestly, after the last few days, I think that's exactly what we should do. Not like we have anything else to look into at the moment."

Gertie perked up. "That would be great!"

———

MANNIE CALLED WHILE WE WERE ON OUR WAY BACK TO Sinful with background updates on the list of people I'd given him. I put him on speaker.

"What do you have?" I asked.

"Well, for starters, Lil is actually Emilia Davis and she's Tiffany Forrest's mother," Mannie said. "You didn't say why you needed these, but given that incident at the Halloween festival and the subsequent finding of Gil's car, I assume this is now a murder investigation and you're in the middle of it."

"Something like that, and yeah, we figured out the Emilia connection and just talked to her," I said.

"Did she fess up about her mental health stay?" he asked.

"She did," I said.

"Did she also include that she was arrested twice for assaulting two different men? One was hitting on a much younger server in a bar in New Orleans and the other was a coworker who was cheating on his wife. She got the cheater good—broke his wrist before he managed to get away."

"Interesting," I said. "Was this before or after her mental health stay?"

"Before. Apparently, the stay was required by the court as mental health was cited for the reason she shouldn't be charged."

"I wonder if it did any good or if she just managed to fool the doctors enough to get released," I said. "She definitely didn't mention any of those things."

"I don't suppose she would," he said. "Moving on, Brigette Driscoll is the daughter of a fairly prominent politician and attorney. Family money and all that, but for some reason, he suddenly stepped away from his position with the senate and retired from his firm about five years ago, died not long after. I'm assuming some undisclosed illness, but still trying to run down some information on that. Unfortunately, my contacts don't lend themselves to higher social circles, so I'm limited unless it was big enough to hit the newspapers."

"Makes sense," I said.

"I'll let you know if I get more," he said. "As for Brigette herself, nothing interesting really. She works for the theater and has a condo in the business district—got a mortgage rate on it that makes me envious as I'm looking to buy right now and rates are high, but that's the only thing I could find on her except for all the publicity about the plays and some inherited emeralds, which apparently have historical significance."

"Yeah, I did a bit of research on those jewels myself," I said. "And it's interesting, but I can't work them into why Gil was killed. What about Paul Easton?"

"Nothing on Easton, who might be the most boring person on earth," he said. "I'm kinda surprised he's an actor."

"Yeah, he really doesn't come across that way," I said. "But we've been told that he comes alive on stage. Last up is Gwyn Simmons. I don't expect you found anything of interest on her either."

There was a slight pause and then he began. "I saved her for last. She had a bit of a problem with an ex-husband. Sounds like an abusive situation where she finally managed to get loose. Nothing interesting since then about her life...except her death."

"What?!"

We all yelled at once.

"Gwyn Simmons committed suicide," he said.

# CHAPTER TWENTY-TWO

I took a deep breath and let it slowly out, still reeling from what Mannie had just told us.

"When did it happen?" I asked.

"Sometime last night," Mannie said. "I don't have much information but apparently, she took a handful of painkillers, drank a lot of wine, went to sleep, and didn't wake up. I'll update you if I hear more, but it seems kinda open and shut. No sign of forced entry and she left a note. I don't know what it included."

"I bet I can guess," I said.

"What?" Mannie asked.

"She was having an affair with Gil," I said.

Mannie whistled. "This Gil really left a wake of destruction wherever he went, didn't he?"

"Seems like it," I said. "He also seems to be collecting as many victims in death as he did in life."

I told Mannie about suspicion falling on Liam and putting his future in a precarious position and the attack on Tiffany the night before.

"There's a lot going on with that man at the center," Mannie said. "*Too* much going on."

"I know," I agreed. "I wish I could clear out the things that don't matter so that I could focus on the things that do."

"Maybe it all matters," Mannie said. "Anyway, let me know if you need anything else. I'll call back if I get more."

He disconnected and I looked over at Ida Belle and Gertie.

"What the hell?" I said. "Please tell me we did not cause Gwyn to take her own life."

Gertie shook her head, her expression sad. "All we did was tell her something she would have found out anyway when Casey got a hold of her."

Ida Belle nodded. "And quite frankly, something she probably already knew but just didn't want to admit to herself."

I blew out a breath. "Yeah, I guess so, but man, I feel horrible. Gwyn obviously had some things she needed to work out, but this wasn't the solution. And God knows Gil wasn't worth it."

"This wasn't about Gil," Gertie said. "Not really. He was just one piece in the bad decisions Gwyn was making. Maybe if she'd been honest with herself and gotten help, things could have been different. But please don't blame yourself. She knew he was married when she got involved with him."

"And if it hadn't been Gil, it probably would have been another guy who sent her over the edge," Ida Belle said. "Remember what Lil said about predators. I happen to agree with her. Men like Gil can spot women like Gwyn a mile away."

"Yeah, but most of them don't get murdered," I said.

"It's an unfortunate set of events," Ida Belle said. "But we didn't do anything to put them into motion."

I shook my head. "How in the world does a person cause more trouble after dying than he did while he was alive? And

I'm talking someone who caused a serious amount of trouble while he was alive."

"He definitely outplayed himself on this one," Gertie said.

"And wasn't even here to see the dramatic fallout," Ida Belle said. "Typical of Gil—create a mess, then skip away and pretend it had nothing to do with him."

I stared out the windshield and frowned. "Do we think Gwyn could have been the one who killed Gil? I mean, she had opportunity. What if she knew the truth about Gil's marriage? Or what if even though he was divorcing Tiffany, he told Gwyn he wasn't going to settle down with her? We only have her word that they were an item. Maybe that was in the recent past. Maybe Gwyn was just as tired of men taking advantage of her as Lil was of seeing it."

"And we see how Lil flipped out over two men doing people wrong that she didn't even know," Gertie said. "There's nothing saying Gwyn couldn't have flipped the same way."

"Anything is possible," Ida Belle said. "But could Gwyn have pulled it off? She didn't strike me as the sharpest of people. Disposing of the car in Sinful, changing the plates... Those are all things that require some planning and a cool head."

"True," I said. "But she's also on-site for his rehearsal and would have known about the faulty security cameras, just like Lil."

Gertie sighed. "Can you please stop adding suspects to the list? I'm going to have to write them all down."

"Just pull out the phone book for southern Louisiana and you might have it under control," Ida Belle said. "At this point, I'm convinced Gil had more enemies than friends."

"Well, since it appears he had no friends except Judith, I'd agree," I said.

"Who is also a suspect," Gertie said. "It's like the man was an anger and disappointment pandemic."

I nodded. It was a totally accurate description.

But it didn't mean I wasn't going to figure out who killed him.

---

IDA BELLE DROPPED ME OFF AND HEADED OUT, SAYING SHE'D be back to pick me up at 6:00 p.m. for the festival that night. We decided to skip costumes because the makeup took so much effort and we were all feeling rather tired. I hoped fat snacks from the festival vendors would perk us up some. We were really counting on the night being normal. No dead people—except those in costume—and no skunks. If we were really lucky, no seeing Celia's underwear. We couldn't hope to avoid the woman herself as she always seemed to be there trying to ruin fun, but we could pray for limited contact with no fleshy displays.

I headed straight for the kitchen and grabbed my laptop to make some notes on our conversation with Lil and on the background information that Mannie had given me. When I was making the notes on Brigette, I remembered that Mannie had said her father stepped away from everything suddenly, so I did some googling. He'd passed away a year after his retreat from society, but no cause of death was given. Just the ole standard 'had been suffering from illness,' which would explain his disappearance from the public and his firm.

There was a photo of him, his wife, and Brigette included with the obituary. Brigette had definitely taken after her mother in the looks department. She also had that refined structure to her face. I did a quick search on the mother and found that she'd passed from heart issues less than a year after

Brigette's father had. Brigette was an only child, according to the article, so I felt a moment of sadness for her. It was hard losing both parents, even though Brigette hadn't been a child when it happened. Well, and technically, I hadn't necessarily lost my dad to death. At least, not that I was aware of. But since he wasn't exactly around, I figure it counted as death.

I heard Carter call out from the front door and directed him back to the kitchen. He had abandoned his trudge, which had been his elected walking method of late, and this time strode purposely into the kitchen, looking both aggravated and flustered.

"Whatever it is, I didn't do it," I said.

He grabbed a bottle of water from my refrigerator and plopped into a chair across from me. "I know you didn't do it. Tiffany did."

"What?" I sat up straight. "Do you mean..."

He nodded. "Casey's forensics team found the murder weapon in the attic under some insulation. The only prints on it are hers."

I stared. "You've got to be kidding me."

"I wish to hell I was." He threw his hands up. "Do you know how this makes me look—that my team missed that gun? Things like this are the reason small-town cops get a bad rap."

"Ah," I said, understanding now why he was so upset. His team had dropped the ball.

"Don't get me wrong," he said. "Detective Casey was cool about it all—at least to my face—but I know what she was thinking because I would have thought the same thing."

"But your team searched the house after the Headless Horseman incident, right?" I asked. "Wasn't the scope completely different since Gil's death was still classified as a carjacking?"

"Yeah. We were looking for a reason that someone might have a score to settle with Gil. Nasty letters or email, diaries, notes he might have made about people, that sort of thing. But still, when you get a search warrant, you usually check everything you can. I asked the team and apparently, they only did a cursory search of the attic just to make sure there was no paperwork up there."

"Is cursory standard in that case? Meaning, I assume they could have done more, right?"

He sighed. "Their team leader is on leave. His wife just had a baby. The guy they moved up for the duration is a good tech, but I don't know that he has the experience to direct yet. At least, I wasn't certain at the time, but I guess I know for sure now. I should have stayed and made sure they did things right, but I was executing a search of Liam's house and getting an order for the butcher shop at the same time."

"You can't be everywhere and do everything," I said. "You have to depend on your coworkers and your team to do their job. But honestly, even though the old team leader might have pushed for more, it doesn't sound like the new one did anything wrong given the scope of the investigation at the time."

He grunted but didn't say anything for several seconds. Finally, he shook his head. "Anyway, I guess it doesn't matter at this point. Casey has it all wrapped up."

"I assume she's going to arrest Tiffany?"

"She headed to New Orleans right after the ballistics and fingerprint reports came back. Tiffany had reported in and gave a hotel in the city as her address."

I slumped back in my seat, feeling somewhat let down. I mean, it made sense. Of all the people on our list, Tiffany had the most to lose if Gil had remained alive and definitely the most to gain if he was gone. But still, it was singularly unsatisfying that the solution was back to the old, boring standard of killing a spouse for money.

Then I remembered the other side of the equation.

"Does Detective Casey have a fix on her accomplice?" I asked. "Because there's no way Tiffany hauled Gil's body up on that horse by herself. And honestly, while I can buy into her shooting him, I can't see her getting the car into the bayou and definitely can't see her cutting off his head."

"There's no accomplice that I've been informed of," Carter said, his voice slightly bitter, "but if I had to guess, I'd say she's going to pick up Liam after she has Tiffany in custody."

"No!" I sat up straight. "Why Liam?"

"Because they're the two who get the financial benefit from Gil's death."

"So you know about the will change."

He raised an eyebrow. "How do *you* know about the will change?"

"Judith told us."

"And you didn't think that was something worth mentioning?"

"Since I didn't want suspicion to fall on Liam, no."

He shook his head. "You can't change the facts. Liam stood to gain a lot. Enough money to buy out the owner of that butcher shop now. And if he wanted, maybe another shot with Tiffany."

I bit my lip, trying to decide how to approach what I had to say, but also trying to figure out how to do it in a way that didn't put me in the hot seat. Finally deciding a scorched tush wasn't as important as making sure a man I still thought was innocent didn't get railroaded, I blew out a breath and let it all out.

"Tiffany had another man on the side," I said.

He narrowed his eyes at me. "How do you know that?"

"Because we saw her coming out of the shady motel up the highway the other day and since people don't usually check in there for alone time, I figure she was meeting someone."

"Maybe she was meeting a friend—a *girl* friend. Plenty of people in town for the fishing rodeo in Mudbug."

"Yeah, we might have also seen her today, coming out of that hotel in New Orleans with a guy."

He looked confused. "Tiffany told you where she was staying?"

"Not exactly."

He stared at me for several seconds, then closed his eyes and blew out a breath. "You put a tracker on her car when she left her house this morning, didn't you?"

"I'm sure I don't know anything about that. We just happened to be in New Orleans and saw her coming out of a hotel with another guy."

"You've happened to be in New Orleans a lot lately."

"Hey, I have a receipt for a hot tub, at least two extra pounds from all the food, and Gertie has sexy undergarments to prove what we were doing."

"So today you were...?"

"Not buying underwear or a hot tub?"

"You know what, forget it. Did you know the guy?"

"Not personally, but I recognized him from a photo. He was part of the rodeo crowd Tiffany hung out with when she was in high school."

He stared at me for a second, then ran a hand through his hair. "Rodeo crowd?"

I nodded, knowing he was processing the pieces as they fell into place.

"You don't think Liam was her accomplice," he said.

"Do you? Really? What does your gut tell you?"

He blew out a breath. "That Liam is going to get the short

end of the stick all over again because of his dad unless I figure out how to get that information to Casey without her asking questions."

"May I make a suggestion?"

He held out his hands. "Why not. You seem to be full of ideas lately."

"Only lately? Never mind. Anyway, call Detective Casey and tell her that your girlfriend and a couple friends from town were shopping in New Orleans today and saw Tiffany come out of a hotel with this guy."

"Do you have the guy's name?"

I nodded and gave him the information.

"She knows who you are, you know?" he said. "She insinuated as much when she reminded me how much her captain hates PIs. Probably did a background on me before she headed this way."

"There's no law against shopping in New Orleans. People do it every day."

"People don't accidentally run into murder suspects while they're shopping. What happens if Casey decides to sweep her car?"

"For all we know, Gil could have put that tracker on there because he suspected Tiffany was about to make a break with another guy."

He sighed. "Anything else you think I need to know?"

"Not that I could find a viable explanation for knowing myself," I said.

"Why am I not surprised?"

I shrugged. "Detective Casey is going to have to do her job. The information isn't that difficult to find. But where does all of this leave you with the Headless Horseman case?"

"Waiting on her. But honestly, I don't think it matters. If she has a solid case for murder one against Tiffany—and it's looking that way—I don't see the point of adding the Headless Horseman ride to it. Tiffany will be lucky to avoid the death penalty as it is, and I don't have any evidence for that stunt. So unless one of them flips on the other..."

I nodded. "You know, I'm glad that Liam is probably going to be left out of this as soon as Detective Casey tracks down Tiffany and her real side man. But I have to say, I'm a little disappointed with the outcome."

"You wanted it to be someone else?"

"Not necessarily. I guess I just wanted something other than the trite crap I see on the news every night. Or on every other episode of those forensic shows. Doesn't anyone kill any more for something other than money or to get out of their marriage?"

"There's a reason the spouse is the first suspect."

I studied him for a moment, frowning. "Those stats don't make marriage out to be that good a deal, do they?"

He leaned forward and took my hand. "It's not for a lot of people. But then there are people like my parents. Their marriage was the kind that makes me think it's worthwhile."

"I didn't know your father, but I guess I can see that knowing Emmaline."

He rose from his chair and I stood with him. He pulled me into a hug and gave me a soft, sweet kiss.

"Now that all this is behind us, do you have anything on your schedule for tonight?" he asked.

"As a matter of fact, I do. We're going to the festival. This whole mess has us kind of tired and a little down, especially being worried about Liam being caught up in it all. I guess now we can enjoy the downtime since we won't have this hanging over our heads anymore. Or maybe 'head' isn't a good choice of words here."

He smiled. "Then I guess I'll see you there."

"And that thing with Tiffany's side man?"

"I'll get it passed along to Casey, but I can't see any way around telling her where I got the information as the three of you will probably have to testify."

"That's fine," I said, but a slight feeling of unease and sadness passed over me.

After everything I'd learned about Tiffany, I'd started to feel sorry for her. She hadn't asked for the horrible changes in her life that had been thrust on her at such a young age. And she certainly hadn't asked for her mother to abdicate her duties as parent and protector. She had some culpability in marrying Gil, but I couldn't necessarily blame her for the choice. I just wished all the fallout hadn't landed squarely on Liam, who was probably still completely in the dark on everything.

Maybe when all of this was wrapped up and Liam was completely off police radar, Ida Belle, Gertie, and I would pay him a visit and explain some things to him. He deserved answers, and maybe he'd be able to find it in his heart to forgive one of the people who'd betrayed him.

For his own good.

# CHAPTER TWENTY-THREE

IT WAS AN ABNORMALLY QUIET AND SOMEWHAT MOROSE drive to the festival. I'd called Ida Belle and Gertie and filled them in as soon as Carter had left. Neither was overly surprised at the outcome, but they didn't sound happy about it, either. Which is where I currently sat on things. I'd let them know what Carter would be passing along to Casey and how I'd presented it to avoid explaining the tracker in Tiffany's car, so when Casey got around to talking to us individually, we all had the same story up for grabs.

"You know what's bugging me?" Ida Belle finally said as she pulled up to the curb to park.

"The elastic in your underwear is loose?" Gertie asked.

We both stared at her.

"Well, that's what's bugging me," Gertie said. "And since Ida Belle never replaces anything, I figured her underwear are older than mine."

"What's bugging me," Ida Belle continued, "is why Tiffany hid the gun in her house. Why not throw it in the bayou along with the car? Or into a ditch on the drive from New Orleans? Heck, at least clean your prints off of it."

I shook my head. "Yeah, it's a huge lapse. But even hardened criminals make mistakes. Maybe she panicked. For all we know, she might have suspected Gil was cheating and driven up there, seen him with Gwyn, and confronted him afterward. Things might have gotten out of hand and then she rushed to cover her tracks."

"And since she's not a hardened criminal, she messed up," Ida Belle concluded.

"Stranger things have happened," I said. "For all we know, she might have thought she'd keep the gun in case she needed it in the future."

"Then why not bring it to her buddy when they met at the motel?" Gertie asked.

"Because she was afraid of being followed, maybe?" I said. "Remember, she said something about maybe she was being watched on that phone call. She probably figured her house had already been searched and they didn't find it, so she was good."

"So the break-in at her house last night," Ida Belle said. "Do you think she staged it?"

I shrugged. "I can't see any other explanation, can you? And she could have struck herself in the front. If it had been a blow to the back of the head, I would have said probably not."

"But why crack yourself on the head and not remove some items from your house to make it look like a robbery?"

"Because a robbery isn't personal?" Gertie suggested. "I'll bet that the cops wouldn't have allowed her to leave town if it had been perceived as something mundane."

"That's a good point," I said. "And she seemed really desperate to get out of here."

"It's also easier to disappear in New Orleans," Ida Belle said. "She probably thought the carjacking would stick and she'd just pack up the gun when she moved from Sinful, but once the car was found, maybe she figured she better position herself to fade into the sunset."

"But if she thought the carjacking was going to stick, why pull the Headless Horseman stunt and stir everything up?" Gertie asked. "Seems counterintuitive."

I sighed. "I wish I knew. The only thing I can think of is that maybe she didn't do the Headless Horseman stunt. Maybe that was Liam—figuring he wouldn't have another opportunity to take a shot at his father. He might have viewed the entire thing as embarrassing. And cutting off the head as cathartic."

"Slaying the enemy and all that," Gertie said. "It's rather old-school, but I guess the sentiment still stands."

Ida Belle shook her head. "The whole thing has been a convoluted mess from the beginning. I honestly don't think we're ever going to know all the whys unless Tiffany starts talking. And I have my doubts that will happen."

"I hate not knowing why," I said. "It's like finishing a puzzle and you're missing ten percent of the pieces. It's just going to nag at me."

"Well, you best get used to it," Ida Belle said. "There's a lot of things that happen around here that defy any logical explanation."

"At this point, I'd take an illogical one," I said.

"Well, let's get out and enjoy the festival," Gertie said. "I bet a corn dog and some caramel corn will make you feel better."

I considered this for a moment. "You might be right about that."

Gertie nodded. "I have it from a higher authority."

"That would sound better if you were in costume," I said.

"Then I'll say it again tomorrow," she said. "Looks like we've got some days off coming."

We headed for the corn dog stand first and snagged a

couple of dogs. Gertie was right. As soon as I took my first bite of the juicy goodness, I felt better.

"What is it about food that's bad for you that makes you feel so good?" I asked. "And why can't I feel this way about lettuce?"

"If you can solve that mystery, you'll be a billionaire," Gertie said.

"I hate to agree with you two over your bad food debauchery, but if you could make it so Molly's cream cheese dip had no calories, I might divorce Walter and marry you. You could also have all of my money."

"I don't need any money or another person to date," I said.

"I'll throw in half my freezer," Ida Belle said.

Gertie whistled. "She's going hard-core now. Walter only got a tiny corner."

We all laughed.

"Caramel corn or candied apples?" Gertie asked.

"Let's go with caramel corn," I said. "I'm going to take the apple home with me so I can cut it up before I eat it. Last time I bit into one, I thought I was going to chip a tooth, and you know how I hate the dentist."

"You just hate sitting still while a strange man hovers over you with weapons," Ida Belle said.

"True," I agreed. "So what's the event tonight?"

"Arts and crafts," Gertie said. "So no big attraction for us except for the food."

"And pissing Celia off," I said. "Don't look now, but here she comes."

The pioneer dress had been retired—probably due to the overwhelming smell of fish and skunk—so Celia had returned to her usual Rose Kennedy look. Her hat had more flowers on it than I'd had in my beds this year. The entire outfit was a bright glowing purple. Except for Celia's face. It wasn't glowing at all. It wore the permanent frown it always did. And the smell still lingered.

"I know you had something to do with that skunk incident," Celia said to Gertie as she stomped up.

"Not unless I've developed the ability to be in two places at one time," Gertie said. "If you remember correctly, we were *behind* you in the maze. You practically ran us over trying to get out. So how did I throw a skunk at you at the exit?"

"Then you had an accomplice," Celia said.

"My two accomplices were with me," Gertie said.

Ida Belle and I both nodded.

Celia's face turned red. "The three of you are insufferable."

"At least we don't stink," I said. "If you're going to keep ranting can you at least do it downwind?"

Celia sputtered a little and I smiled.

"Are you trying to warm your mouth up so that something logical comes out of it?" I asked.

She gave me a look that could kill—if it had been anyone other than Celia—then whirled around and stomped off. Gertie, Ida Belle, and I were rolling laughing before she even made it all the way around.

"Still making friends and influencing people, I see." Carter's voice sounded behind us.

We turned around, still laughing.

"It's Celia," I said.

"Yeah, that pretty much covers everything I need to know in so many cases," he said.

He was smiling but I could tell he was strained. And tired. And even though Carter would never feel defeated, he had just the tiniest thread of it in his expression. He was definitely taking not recovering the murder weapon hard.

"Did you talk to Detective Casey about Tiffany's guy?" I asked.

He nodded. "She wasn't thrilled with my source, but she put the information to good use. She called about an hour ago and told me they've booked Tiffany and are holding the boyfriend for questioning. And after I talked to you, I did some walking around the woods and found a set of horse tracks that led from a road a little ways behind Tiffany's property to the park. You know the one—there was pink glitter everywhere."

"I don't know where you keep getting these ideas," I said.

"I can't imagine," Carter said.

"I don't suppose Tiffany has offered up a confession and an explanation for all of this, has she?" Ida Belle asked. "Because we'd love to have the blanks filled in."

"So would I," he said. "But Tiffany is insisting she didn't do it and asked for a lawyer."

"What does Detective Casey think?" I asked.

"She thinks her case is a wrap," he said.

"What do *you* think?" I asked.

"I think Casey has a darn good motive, opportunity, and a murder weapon with only one person's prints on it," he said. "It's a solid case. More solid than a lot that go to trial."

"But do you think she did it?" I asked.

"I guess I have to," he said. "Understand, I don't know Tiffany any better than anyone else in this town, so I can't speak to her character or her sanity. But Casey said one of those actor guys told her Gil said he was thinking about divorcing Tiffany. According to their prenuptial, she would have been out with the clothes on her back."

"Sounds like our work is done," I said, feeling a bit miffed that Paul Easton had held out on us about the divorce thing, because I was sure he was Casey's source.

"You were never supposed to be working it to begin with,"

he said. "And I'm not even going to ask why you didn't so much as raise an eyebrow over the divorce revelation."

"Over half the marriages in the US end in divorce," I said. "If I was playing the odds, I'd go with divorce every time."

"Uh-huh," he said. "I'm going to leave you guys to it and go make my rounds. Try not to cause any trouble."

"He says that like we're always the ones causing trouble," Gertie said.

"I'd say our record weighs more heavily in being in the midst of trouble rather than being the catalyst," I said.

"I don't think Carter wants to differentiate," Ida Belle said. "That's why I don't tell Walter anything and he doesn't ask. What little he knows has him shooting back a dose of whiskey every night."

"Marrying you was probably the worst thing he's done for his health in his entire life," Gertie said.

"Probably," Ida Belle said. "But he had a lot of decades to see that. His choice. Do you think the actors told Casey that we questioned them?"

I shrugged. "Hard to say. And even if they did, since they weren't suspects, technically, we weren't interfering in her investigation."

"Do you think technically will matter to her captain?" Ida Belle asked.

"Only if he finds out," I said. "Hopefully Casey will keep that to herself if someone tattles."

Ida Belle nodded.

"Hey, there's Emmaline over at the arts and crafts booths," Gertie said. "Do you guys want to go say hello?"

"Sure," I said. I hadn't seen Emmaline in a while as she'd been busy getting her paintings ready for her upcoming show.

She looked up and gave us a big smile as we approached

and directed the kids she was leaning over to start with the glue, then add glitter to their paintings.

"How are you ladies tonight?" she asked. "I loved your costumes the other night but didn't get a chance to see you before all that trouble happened. Did you see Celia while you were wearing them?"

"Saw and offended her," Gertie said.

Emmaline laughed. "That woman is so predictable. *And* gullible."

"Are you ready for your show?" I asked.

"Almost," she said. "I have to tell you, it's been nerve-racking, trying to pick the right paintings for this. And then second-guessing what I picked and the framing and just doing the show altogether, really."

"You've waited a long time for this and you deserve it," I said. "I don't pretend to know anything about art, but your stuff looks great."

She gave me a huge smile and I could tell she was pleased. "Thank you so much. I hope you ladies will be able to make the show."

"We wouldn't miss it," Gertie said and Ida Belle nodded.

I picked up a putty knife from a table, remembering I'd seen one with Gil's art books.

"What do you use a putty knife for?" I asked.

"That's actually a palette knife," she said. "They look similar. Artists use them for mixing paints, scraping off paint, and some paint with them."

"I've seen those paintings," Gertie said. "They look like they have lines in them."

"Some do," Emmaline said. "It's a different style and a way to add a different texture to your work."

"Interesting," I said. "Have you painted any that way?"

She shook her head and gave me a curious look. "It

doesn't suit the work I'm doing right now but I suppose I might try it someday. I didn't know you were interested in art, Fortune."

"I'm not really," I said. "We were sort of poking around into that business with Gil and apparently, he'd gotten into art and was bumping heads with the creative director at the theater who is in charge of all the artwork."

"You're talking about Brigette Driscoll," Emmaline said.

"Yes," I said. "How did you know?"

"The art gallery that is presenting me carries fliers for the theater, and the theater carries fliers for the art gallery," she said. "A lot of the art businesses in the quarter advertise for each other."

"That's cool. Do you know her?" I asked.

"Not really," she said. "We met a time or two years ago, but I can't say I know her personally. Sad what happened with her family though."

"You mean her father dying?" I asked. "Sounds like he'd been sick for a while. Sad that her mother went so quickly after."

Emmaline frowned. "Not just his passing... There was talk."

I perked up. "What kind of talk?"

"That her father had a gambling problem," she said. "The rumor is he stepped down from the senate and his firm because he was afraid it would go public."

"I guess we're not talking about losing a couple thousand down at the casino," I said.

She shook her head. "The rumor was illegal gambling and that he'd lost everything. If you ask me, that's what caused his wife's heart problems."

"So he bowed out before he could be made a spectacle," I said.

"It was the least he could do for his wife and daughter," Emmaline. "The *very* least."

I shook my head. "That's unfortunate all the way around."

"Let me help you with that." Gertie's voice sounded behind me.

A second later, a shower of pink glitter rained down on me, Emmaline, and Ida Belle. We all turned to look at Gertie, who was guiltily clutching a plastic bag with a few remnants of pink glitter in it.

"Oops?" Gertie said.

"What the heck are you doing?" Ida Belle ranted and started brushing the glitter off her clothes.

"I was trying to help this girl get the bag open," Gertie said.

The little girl, who was staring up at us, started to giggle.

"Well, mission accomplished," I said. I leaned over and brushed what I could off my clothes and out of my hair and onto the little girl's picture.

"Thanks!" she said and went back to her drawing.

"I think I better find a mirror," Emmaline said and hurried over to a storage box to retrieve her purse.

Ida Belle glared at Gertie.

"Like this wasn't hard enough to get off the first time and now you have us up for round two of the glitter wars," she said.

"Hey, it has an advantage," Gertie said.

"I'd love to hear it," Ida Belle said.

"We all still had glitter in our scalps," Gertie said. "I see some shining in Fortune's when we're in sunlight. I assume Carter hasn't noticed because he hasn't been around much and he's been preoccupied."

"What the heck does that have to do with anything?" Ida Belle asked.

"Now we all have a reason to have glitter in our scalps," Gertie said triumphantly. "And his mother is a witness."

"And a victim," I said.

Gertie waved a hand in dismissal. "Anyway, now Carter can't prove it was us that caused the explosion behind Tiffany's house."

"You mean he can't prove that *you* caused the explosion," Ida Belle corrected.

"I have news for you," I said. "Carter absolutely knows it was us and nothing would convince him otherwise. Not even video of us in another country at the same time."

"But he can't prove it," Gertie said. "And that's all that matters."

Her words struck me for some reason and I frowned, trying to figure out why...'all that matters.'

*Maybe it all matters.*

Mannie had said that earlier. I stared at a painting a young boy was doing of ghosts playing cards.

*He never really got off the stage.*

*The problem with people like Gil is he spent so much time in character that I think he forgot who he really was.*

*Gil played the part of the detective.*

It couldn't be. Could it? But it made sense. At least most of it did.

"What's wrong?" Ida Belle said.

"I think Detective Casey arrested the wrong person," I said. "We have to get to New Orleans now."

"For what?" Gertie asked.

"To make sure I'm right."

# CHAPTER TWENTY-FOUR

I filled Ida Belle and Gertie in on my theory on the drive to New Orleans, and will be the first to admit that I delivered my entire monologue while clutching the armrest due to the speed at which Ida Belle was driving. It seemed that with every point I put together, she found more horsepower to squeeze out of the SUV. The fact that she hadn't even once mentioned all the pink glitter falling in her beloved vehicle told me I was onto something.

Well, that and the fact that they were both on board with helping me break into the theater.

We made the drive in record time and the parking lot to the theater was empty. It was well past dark, and the entire area was mostly devoid of human traffic except for the very occasional car passing by. I instructed Ida Belle to park in the garage across the street, just in case one of the actors drove by, saw the vehicle, and went to check and see if someone was inside.

We donned our gloves and headed across the street. I made quick work of the back door lock and eased the door open, having already spotted the lack of alarm system when we were there before. We slipped inside and hurried down the hall and to the front of the stage where all the props for the play were collected, ready to be loaded on the truck the following morning.

"We need to find that ugly painting with Jesus playing poker," I said.

We spread out and started going through the wrapped items, cutting through the Bubble Wrap on anything that might contain paintings. It was going to be a mess to clean up, but if I was right, the play was about to close before it even opened.

"I found something!" Gertie said.

Ida Belle and I rushed over to the large cardboard box she'd opened and peered inside. Several paintings were wrapped and inserted into dividers. We all grabbed paintings and began unwrapping them.

"Here!" Ida Belle said and held up the painting we were looking for.

I pulled the palette knife that I'd swiped from the arts and crafts booth out of my pocket and told Ida Belle to lay the painting across the box.

"Are you sure about this?" Gertie asked.

"No," I said. "But that's why we're here."

I inspected the painting and found one corner where the paint appeared to be fresher than the others. I scraped a tiny bit of paint off. Underneath was more paint, but a different color and with a shiny coat on top. I kept scraping until I had a two-inch section exposed.

Gertie's eyes widened. "You were right."

Ida Belle shook her head. "Ingenious."

"Yes. It is."

A woman's voice sounded behind us and we whirled around to find Brigette standing in the doorway, clutching a pistol that was leveled at me.

"It's a shame you were too smart for your own good," she said. "Just like your friend Gil. If only he would have minded his own business, but he had to play detective. I should have never given him that role."

I made a split-second assessment of my options, but they weren't good. I could dive behind some of the furniture, risking that Brigette wasn't a great shot, and probably come out okay. But that left Ida Belle and Gertie in the line of fire. My weapon was at my waist, but I couldn't pull it before Brigette got off a shot of her own.

My only option was to buy time to think of another option.

"You're the one who broke into Gil's house and attacked Tiffany," I said. "He had a painting like this commissioned and swapped them out because he suspected you were smuggling something much more valuable underneath. You realized he was onto you and killed him, but you had to recover the painting."

She smiled. "I couldn't very well wait around until that trashy wife of his had a garage sale, now could I? Besides, the buyer is expecting his merchandise this week."

"You dumped the car in a Sinful bayou, figuring if it was found, that would throw suspicion on Tiffany," I said. "But when his death was labeled a carjacking, you thought, even better. Until they found the car."

"My one miscalculation," she said. "If I'd known his death would have been so easily labeled as ancillary to another crime, I would have disposed of the car differently and it would have never been found."

"But since it turned into a murder investigation, you planted the gun in the attic after you knocked Tiffany out, figuring the police had already done a search of the house but might have missed something in the attic that they might find on a second sweep," I said.

"Clever girl," she said. "It's a shame you couldn't find something else to do with all that talent."

"What I can't understand is why you killed Gwyn," I said.

Gertie and Ida Belle both gasped.

She raised her eyebrows. "Can't you? As soon as she heard that the investigation had gone from carjacking to murder, she could barely string a sentence together. Maybe it was just because she had no backbone and was worried about something happening to her, or maybe she was upset that her white knight had been intentionally killed. But maybe it was because Gil had told her his suspicions about me, and that was something I couldn't risk."

"Gwyn didn't know anything," I said. "You killed an innocent woman for no reason."

"Let's not pretend that Gwyn was an innocent," she said. "She was up to her neck in an affair with Gil. If she'd had morals, she wouldn't have been in that position and then she'd still be alive."

"So it's her fault you killed her?" I asked. "That's some interesting logic. I wonder how it will stand up in court."

"Fortunately for me, it doesn't have to," she said. "Now drop that palette knife and move away from the painting. I can't afford to get blood on all those props, especially as you've removed the plastic wrapping from so many."

A faint click sounded from somewhere on stage and we all jerked our heads in that direction just in time to see a giant bird on a rope swing out from the ceiling on stage and straight toward the auditorium.

Brigette jumped back as the bird flew past and I yelled at Gertie and Ida Belle to dive. Brigette's finger tightened on the trigger and she squeezed off a round. I flung the palette knife at her, then dived behind the box of paintings. A round of bullets sprayed around me and I covered my head and face as glass burst everywhere.

Then there was silence.

I pulled out my weapon and prayed that Ida Belle and Gertie were tucked safely away behind boxes, then inched forward and peered around the corner of the tattered box I was hiding behind. I blinked once in disbelief, then rose.

The palette knife had lodged in Brigette's cheek and her hands were locked around it, but she wasn't moving. I rushed over to check her pulse but it was strong. She'd either passed out from pain or fear or cracked her head when she fell. I grabbed some rope I'd removed from a crate and tied her wrists together, then kicked the gun across the room after I frisked her to make sure she didn't have another weapon hidden somewhere.

No more activity had come from the stage area, which was eerily silent, but I knew someone lurked in the shadows. I shifted my attention to the stage and aimed my weapon. Someone had let that bird loose and I couldn't be certain they were friendly, even though it had helped me.

"Come out!" I yelled. "If I have to pursue you, it's not going to end well."

The curtains moved at the back of the stage and Lil stepped out, all color drained from her face, and her hands above her head.

"Don't shoot," she said. "I heard everything. I called the police but I was afraid they wouldn't get here in time. I thought if I distracted Brigette, you could get away."

I lowered my weapon and Ida Belle and Gertie popped up from their hiding places.

"You did a hell of a job with that distraction," I said. "Don't worry, I'm not going to shoot you."

"We might hug you though," Gertie said.

Lil let out a huge breath and her shoulders relaxed.

"I've never been so scared in all my life," she said as she made her way off the stage. "When I heard her admit to killing Gil, I was shocked, but when she admitted to killing Gwyn, I was just mad. I couldn't let her get away with it."

Gertie pulled Lil into a hug and squeezed her so tightly, Lil winced.

"Of course you couldn't let her get away," Gertie said. "Especially with your daughter sitting in a jail cell awaiting trial for a murder she didn't commit. Or did you even know Tiffany had been arrested?"

Lil nodded and started to cry. "A boy she knew in high school called me. He said she'd been arrested, and he was afraid he was going to be as well. He knew I'd been trying to get in touch with Tiffany, and he wanted me to know that she didn't kill anyone. I told him I never thought she had."

"Well, lucky for us you were working late," I said.

"Oh, I wasn't," Lil said. "I left hours ago, but when I drove by earlier, I saw Brigette's car in the parking lot. I was afraid something might be wrong with the props that were set up for shipping, so I let myself in. That's when I heard you talking."

"You're a hero, Lil," I said.

She blushed and stared at the ground. "No. I'm definitely no hero."

"You were tonight," Ida Belle said. "Fortune is the best at what she does, but even she can't outrun a bullet. And Gertie and I wouldn't have stood a chance at all."

I nodded. "Brigette might have gotten away with killing

five people and sending two more to the death chamber if you hadn't stopped tonight. You could have called the police and just waited silently for them to show."

Lil shook her head. "I stuck my head in the sand in ignorance once before and it cost me my daughter. I will never make that mistake again."

Sirens sounded outside and we all put up our hands as cops rushed into the auditorium, guns drawn. Detective Casey was the last one in and she took one look at us and groaned.

I grinned. "How do you like me now?"

———

DETECTIVE CASEY HADN'T BEEN LYING ABOUT HER CAPTAIN'S hatred for PIs. He wouldn't believe a word Carter said, so I had to roust Morrow from bed to verify my credentials. I made an emergency call to my former federal prosecutor friend, aka the Grim Reaper, and while that had the captain lowering his voice while he chewed me out, it still hadn't gotten me out of a jail cell visit. Finally, I pulled my Louisiana trump card and mouthed 'Mannie' to Ida Belle. She managed a text and a couple minutes later, the captain's personal cell phone rang.

He stiffened as he looked at the display, then stepped out of the room and into the hallway. We watched through the window as he complained, then shut up, then his shoulders slumped, and he sighed.

Gotcha.

He walked back into the room with a completely different attitude. "You have an interesting set of allies, Ms. Redding," he said.

"That's because I'm fighting for the good guys," I said. "You just need to believe that."

"Well, considering your service to this country, I suppose I can allow that your focus is different from the majority of these pissant PIs I have roaming my city like rabid dogs. But that still doesn't excuse breaking and entering, regardless of your reasons."

"It was only entering," I said. "The door was open. Someone must have forgotten to lock it. So you could book us on trespassing. What's that—a fine? A couple hours community service?"

Gertie snorted. "You just did a couple hours of community service. You caught a murderer, exposed an art smuggling ring, and kept an innocent woman from the death chamber. I'd say your debt to society is more than paid."

The captain's jaw flexed, and I knew he was mad but he couldn't really argue. His department would have worked with the DA to get a murder conviction on Tiffany, and given the evidence, it would have stuck. But what if the truth surfaced years later? It was the biggest black mark in the world for law enforcement to put an innocent person in prison, especially for something like murder. Heads rolled everywhere when that happened. So I'd saved the captain and his department from the potential of career-ending trouble.

He knew it but he definitely didn't like it, and no way he was admitting it.

"Just get out," he said finally. "I expect all of you back here tomorrow morning to give your statements."

As we left the station, Carter said, "Do you have any idea how lucky you are?"

"Not as lucky as Tiffany, Kip, and Liam," I said. "Far luckier than Gil and Gwyn."

He slung his arm around my shoulder and pulled me close.

"Why couldn't I fall in love with a real librarian?" he asked.

"Because you'd be bored in a day."

"Yeah. I'd miss out on all those pink glitter explosion skunk adventures. I see it in your scalp. Totally busted."

"I probably have it everywhere," I said. "Gertie flung a bag of it over all of us at the craft booth. She even got your mother."

His look of dismay was comical. "Of course she did."

# CHAPTER TWENTY-FIVE

WEDNESDAY WAS A WHIRLWIND OF ACTIVITY. IDA BELLE, Gertie, and I made yet another trip to New Orleans—this time to give our official statements. Detective Casey had seemed a little miffed over being upstaged, but finally thawed as I laid out the evidence we'd collected and how it had finally all come together because of some random statements by other people and a kid's drawing at an arts and crafts booth.

Brigette wasn't talking but there was so much evidence against her, she didn't really have to. Casey told us the painting had been confiscated and my suspicions were correct. The original painting had a layer of special varnish over it and then had been painted over to disguise the valuable—and stolen— item underneath. She had a replacement for the prop shipped to the buyer and just swapped them out when they came to collect. After collection, the buyer had an artist delicately strip the fake painting from the top, revealing the perfectly intact painting below. Brigette had been smuggling art in plain sight and the cops suspected it wasn't just limited to paintings. Vases and other high-end items could easily be camouflaged with removable coatings and moved as props for the play.

My theory about Brigette's finances had been correct as well. Emmaline's comments about the real reason her father had stepped away from his public life combined with Mannie's comment about the good interest rate Brigette had on her condo mortgage, her constant complaints about the lack of budget for the play, and her diverting conversation about displaying the family emeralds all added up to Brigette being broke, the emeralds being long gone, and Brigette not the least bit happy about any of it. She'd been raised with a certain lifestyle and had figured out a way to get back to it.

Unfortunately, Gil had decided to step into his role of a detective in real life and had gone up against someone who had no problem killing to hide her side business. Getting into character had been a deadly choice. His curtain drop, you might say. And poor Gwyn was the real tragedy in all of it. She'd gotten caught up in something she knew absolutely nothing about and had died because of it.

Tiffany had been released and had apparently been filled in on the reason why because I had five phone messages thanking me before I finished up at the police department. The captain sat in when I gave my statement and I saw a tiny hint of grudging respect as I laid out my case. Casey worked to hold in a smile at his occasional grunting and when I was done, he gave me a nod, then left.

"That's high praise," Casey said. "I think he likes you. Not other PIs, mind you. Just you. You know, you're an excellent investigator. I know that wasn't really what you were trained for but your instincts and your ability to put things together is stellar. Have you ever considered law enforcement?"

I shook my head. "I don't like rules."

She laughed.

It was after lunch before we finished with the New Orleans police, but none of us felt like stopping to eat before heading home. We were all exhausted and, quite frankly, were done with visiting the city for a while. Ida Belle had left ground beef out to thaw, predicting that we might want to collapse at home once we were done, so we all headed to our respective homes and pulled together the odds and ends from our pantries. By midafternoon, we were sitting in my backyard, drinking beer, with burgers on the grill. I'd let Merlin out of jail since we were all outside and he was perched on a wide limb on the oak tree, looking overly pleased with himself.

"You know what's still outstanding, right?" Gertie said.

"The Headless Horseman," Ida Belle said. "That wasn't Brigette. She was thrilled when Gil's death was considered a carjacking. No way she was drawing more attention to it. She'd almost committed the perfect crime."

"She should have been smart enough to take a couple items from Gil's house when she broke in to make it look like a robbery," Gertie said.

"I thought about that too," I said. "I assume she was hurrying to get out as fast as possible before she was seen, and maybe Tiffany started to stir and she panicked and left before finishing up what she'd planned."

"We'll probably never know as she's not talking," Ida Belle said.

"So the Horseman thing... What do you think?" Gertie asked.

I shrugged. "I don't know what to think. Tiffany and Kip probably had the ability to handle the horse, and those tracks were behind her house. But I can't lock onto a reason why."

"Maybe it wasn't just that she didn't love him," Gertie said. "Maybe she'd realized that she was nothing more than an object to Gil. Maybe it was like you said when we thought it might be Liam and the entire thing was meant as an insult to Gil and his only caring about acting."

"It wouldn't be the oddest thing that's happened here," Ida Belle said. "What is Carter saying?"

"Ultimately, I think he's going to stick the whole mess in a box and file it under unsolved," I said. "Everything about the Headless Horseman case is wrapped up in the case against Brigette, and the captain is not going to play nice. Besides, what would the perp get out of it anyway—a charge of tampering with a corpse? Assuming it's a first-time offender and they play it off as a practical joke because of the festival, they're not likely to get jail time over it."

"True," Ida Belle said. "I think that's probably the best route for Carter to take for sanity's sake. Chances of him proving who did it were slim anyway even if he has a good idea."

"So it just goes down as one of those Halloween legend stories?" Gertie asked. "I guess I could deal with that. It makes a good tale for around a campfire."

"That it does," Ida Belle agreed, and looked at me. "Did Judith call you?"

I nodded. "Thanking me for everything I'd done to help Liam and promising me free-range eggs and milk for a year."

"That's a really good deal," Gertie said. "And I guess now that Tiffany and Liam are in the clear, Gil's estate will be settled and they'll have the money to move forward with their lives. Tiffany can get that apartment in New Orleans, and Liam might have enough to buy that butcher out early."

"Judith said he probably would," I said.

"I wonder what Tiffany went to see Liam for that day you spied on them," Gertie said.

"You mean the day you almost got killed for stealing a moped and boudin?" Ida Belle said.

I laughed. "Liam told Judith that Tiffany had contacted him several times in the past few months to apologize."

"I guess while she was planning to get away, that was still the one thing hanging over her head," Gertie said.

I nodded. "But the best call I got was while I was waiting on you guys to show up with the food."

"From who?" Gertie asked.

"Lil," I said. "Tiffany called her, and they got together and had a long talk. The cops told Tiffany what her mother had done—how she'd saved us and by doing so, had saved Tiffany as well. Things are still shaky, but Lil said Tiffany wants to try to repair their relationship."

"Did Lil tell her about the cancer?" Ida Belle asked.

"No," I said. "She said she didn't want Tiffany to have a relationship with her because she felt guilty about her health. She wanted an honest relationship and she'd tell her when the time was right. But the best part is, Lil's doctor thinks she might be a candidate for a new treatment."

"I'm really glad to hear that," Gertie said. "It's nice to have some silver lining in this sea of despair."

"Both of them deserve some happiness," Ida Belle said.

"So do we," Gertie said and held up her beer can. "To solving another case, catching the bad guy, and setting the innocent free."

We clinked cans and I smiled. Life was perfect.

―――――

THE DAYS FOLLOWING BRIGETTE'S ARREST WERE SUCH A whirlwind of activity, phone calls, and people 'dropping by to catch up' that it wasn't until Friday after lunch that I found the time to myself to sneak off on a solo mission. I made the drive to River's home and parked some distance past her driveway, then worked my way through the woods toward her barn. She did have an excellent camera system in place, but it had a hole in it, and I intended to make use of it.

I made it to the spot where the cameras didn't reach and put my head against the barn. I could hear talking inside, so I hurried down the side of the barn, figuring River wouldn't be watching the cameras. I knew she'd have her sidearm though, so I had to announce my presence before she caught wind of me on the premises.

The barn door was cracked open, so I slipped inside and made my way down a corridor of stables and to an indoor arena. River was in the middle of the arena, working Shadow. The horse was performing those complicated show maneuvers that looked like dancing. And he was doing it all based on hand signals and whistling. I heard a laugh off to the side and saw Judith start to clap. I smiled. I couldn't have picked a more perfect time.

I strode out from my hiding spot and let myself into the arena. River's eyes widened and she shot a nervous look at Judith, who made her way to the center of the arena to stand next to River. Shadow stopped prancing and relaxed in place. I stepped up and gave both of them long stares.

"Anything the two of you want to tell me?" I asked.

They glanced at each other, neither knowing what to say, then Judith looked at me for a long time, and finally, her shoulders slumped.

"She knows," Judith said.

"That the two of you pulled the Headless Horseman stunt?" I asked. "Yeah. I knew but seeing this horse work clinched it. There was a zombie at the festival that night who had what I thought was a perfected limp, but turns out it was the real deal."

River shot a dirty look at Judith. "I told you it was a horrible idea."

Judith looked completely contrite. "I know. I should have never gotten you involved. Is Carter on his way to arrest us?"

I shook my head. "I haven't told him. I haven't told anyone."

They looked at each other, then back at me, clearly confused.

"Why not?" Judith asked.

"Because I think I have a good idea why you did it, but I wanted to know for sure," I said.

"Might as well tell her," River said.

"I cooked it up after Gil's murder," Judith said. "I never thought it was a carjacking. All his acting weird and asking me about a gun... I was afraid he'd stepped in it again and this time it was serious business."

"You thought he was afraid of Tiffany," I said. "Which means you had an idea he was running around on her."

"Maybe," Judith said. "I didn't know for sure, but he'd said some things that made me think in that direction—the girl-friend thing, I mean. I just assumed that Tiffany was who he was worried about getting crossways with because if he divorced her, she wouldn't get a dime."

"So you assumed Tiffany found out about his affair and killed him," I said.

She nodded. "But the NOLA police weren't treating it that way. They were convinced it was a carjacking, and I was afraid it was going to be shoved into a file and pushed into a back cabinet and forgotten. Then I remembered that incident at the Halloween festival last year—where the guy was already dead but creating a scene had everyone taking a closer look at his death. Especially you. I know everyone tries to play down the things you do but people talk, and I have an idea you're right at the center of everything. I figured if anyone wouldn't be able to resist looking into Gil's death, it would be you."

"So you staged the entire thing to get me to investigate," I said. "You know, I actually do that for a living. You could have given me a call and hired me. Made all the things I did legitimate. Well, most of them."

She stared at the ground, shuffling her foot around in the dirt. "I would have, but I don't have the money for that sort of thing. Farms barely pay the bills most of the time, especially small ones like mine. Any time I get a little extra, it goes right back into repairs or new equipment."

"Like the new tractor?" I asked.

"Yeah, that's where this year's crops went," she said. "But there wouldn't have been a next year without it. Look, I'm sorry for what I did. Even sorrier for dragging River into it. She didn't want to. Thought I was crazy."

"Were you really that certain that Tiffany killed Gil?" I asked.

Her eyes widened. "Why wouldn't I be? I mean, all that other stuff about the art and all—who could have imagined that? I just figured it was your old standard husband, wife, other woman, and money thing."

"You made a serious miscalculation when suspicion fell on Liam," I said. "You had to know that change of will would have the cops looking right at him if they thought Gil's death was suspicious."

"Liam wasn't supposed to be in town that week," she said. "He was scheduled for a workshop for butchers in Nebraska or something. He told me about it the week before when I picked up steaks. If I'd known he was still in town when Gil was murdered, I wouldn't have done it, even if it meant Tiffany got away with it. I screwed up. I should have checked. I almost ruined that boy's life and that is something I'll carry around guilt about for the rest of my own."

"At least it ended well," River said and squeezed Judith's

shoulder. "For Liam anyway. He's off the hook for the murder and he'll get inheritance. He'll be able to move forward with owning the shop sooner rather than later, and he doesn't know what you did."

"Yet," Judith said.

"He doesn't have to know," I said.

"But when Carter arrests us, he'll find out," Judith said.

"I'm not going to say anything to Carter," I said. "I don't agree with what you did but I understand your reasons. And I'm guessing you've paid in stress and guilt these past few days."

"Probably not enough," Judith said.

"You think that because you're a good person," I said. "And your instincts were right about Gil's death. But your focus has just always been so narrow when it comes to him that you couldn't see the possibility of anything else."

She nodded. "I feel bad about that too—the things I said and thought about Tiffany. I mean, I get that she's not exactly an angel but she was a kid in a horrible situation. And if I'm being honest, Gil took advantage of that."

"I believe he did," I said. "I know you cared about him—a lot—but he wasn't a good person to waste your heart on. I hope in the future, you can find someone worthy of the kind of loyalty you have to give."

Judith sniffed and then clutched me in a bear hug. "Thank you for figuring it all out. I'm so happy you weren't hurt. And I'm sorry about the way I did things. In the future, I'll talk to you and see what can be worked out before I go on with some crazy ideas."

She released me and I smiled. "And no more trying to scare widows with dead chickens either. That was childish and beneath you."

"I know," she said. "I just wanted her to leave town so I

never had to see her again. If I had things to do over... Well, none of this would have happened."

"And Brigette would have gotten away with murder," I said. "I'm not saying you shouldn't feel bad about the way you went about things, but remember that the end result was best for everyone."

She nodded and gave River's shoulder a quick squeeze before she headed off. River watched her walk away and sighed.

I looked at her. "I hope in the future, *you* find someone worthy of the loyalty you have to give as well."

River looked at me, surprised, then let out a single laugh. "How did you know?"

"You would have never risked Shadow for anyone unless you cared about them just as much as you do that horse."

She gave me a sad smile. "I guess we can't control where the heart wants to go."

"Does she know?"

River nodded. "It's never affected our friendship, but I've always known that's where things end."

"You're a good friend, River," I said. "I have a couple of friends just like you and they're worth their weight in gold. But there are plenty of good people out there. You just have to get out sometimes and find them. Trust me, my existence was similar to yours as far as people went until I came here. And my life is a thousand times better for it."

"Maybe you're right. Maybe I should get off the ranch sometime...see if there's someone else out there like me."

"Trust me. There's no one out there like you. But I bet there's someone who'd love to get to know someone like you."

She extended her hand and I shook it.

"You're all right, lady spook."

I laughed. "You know that's how I knew you and Judith were friends, right? You both refer to me the same way."

"You don't miss anything, do you?"

"I wouldn't still be alive if I did. Hey, I have a question."

"Another one?"

"Yeah, if I wanted to learn how to ride a horse...I mean I know the general stuff, but if I wanted to learn how to really ride, is that something you could teach me?"

"You want to take riding lessons? Can I ask why?"

"Because you never know what you might need to use to evade the enemy...or Carter. He really doesn't like it when I get in the middle of police business."

Her lips trembled, then she broke into a grin. "You're telling me you have man problems?"

I sighed. "Men can be difficult."

"Honey, I could have told you that." She slung one arm around my shoulders and pulled me toward the stables. "Let's go find you a horse to ride. I'm thinking a mare."

"Perfect."


For notification on new releases and to see other works by Jana, visit her website at janadeleon.com.